MW00534730

# NOW OR NEVER

## BY JANET EVANOVICH

### THE STEPHANIE PLUM NOVELS

*One for the Money*
*Two for the Dough*
*Three to Get Deadly*
*Four to Score*
*High Five*
*Hot Six*
*Seven Up*
*Hard Eight*
*To the Nines*
*Ten Big Ones*
*Eleven on Top*
*Twelve Sharp*
*Lean Mean Thirteen*
*Fearless Fourteen*
*Finger Lickin' Fifteen*
*Sizzling Sixteen*
*Smokin' Seventeen*
*Explosive Eighteen*
*Notorious Nineteen*
*Takedown Twenty*
*Top Secret Twenty-One*
*Tricky Twenty-Two*
*Turbo Twenty-Three*
*Hardcore Twenty-Four*
*Look Alive Twenty-Five*
*Twisted Twenty-Six*
*Fortune and Glory* (Tantalizing Twenty-Seven)
*Game On* (Tempting Twenty-Eight)
*Going Rogue* (Rise and Shine Twenty-Nine)
*Dirty Thirty*

THE GABRIELA ROSE NOVELS

*The Recovery Agent*

THE FOX AND O'HARE NOVELS

(with Lee Goldberg)

*The Heist*

*The Chase*

*The Job*

*The Scam*

*The Pursuit*

(with Peter Evanovich)

*The Big Kahuna*

(with Steve Hamilton)

*The Bounty*

KNIGHT AND MOON

*Curious Minds* (with Phoef Sutton)

*Dangerous Minds*

THE LIZZY AND DIESEL NOVELS

*Wicked Appetite*

*Wicked Business*

*Wicked Charms* (with Phoef Sutton)

THE BETWEEN THE NUMBERS STORIES

*Visions of Sugar Plums*

*Plum Lovin'*

*Plum Lucky*

*Plum Spooky*

THE ALEXANDRA BARNABY NOVELS

*Metro Girl*

*Motor Mouth*

(with Alex Evanovich)

*Troublemaker* (graphic novel)

# NOW OR NEVER

## THIRTY-ONE ON THE RUN

A STEPHANIE PLUM NOVEL

JANET EVANOVICH

ATRIA BOOKS

New York London Toronto Sydney New Delhi

ATRIA
BOOKS

An Imprint of Simon & Schuster, LLC
1230 Avenue of the Americas
New York, NY 10020

This book is a work of fiction. Any references to historical events, real people, or real places are used fictitiously. Other names, characters, places, and events are products of the author's imagination, and any resemblance to actual events or places or persons, living or dead, is entirely coincidental.



First Atria Books hardcover edition November 2024

**ATRIA** BOOKS and colophon are trademarks of Simon & Schuster, LLC

Simon & Schuster: Celebrating 100 Years of Publishing in 2024



Manufactured in the United States of America

1 3 5 7 9 10 8 6 4 2

Library of Congress Control Number: 2024946666

ISBN 978-1-6680-0313-8
ISBN 978-1-6680-0316-9 (ebook)

# CHAPTER ONE

I parked my blue Chevy Trailblazer in front of the bail bonds office and sat for a long moment. My name is Stephanie Plum and I'm a fugitive-apprehension agent working for my cousin Vinnie's bail bonds business in Trenton, New Jersey. I have my BA from Rutgers University and an advanced degree in doing dumb things, destroying cars, and finding love in too many places. It's the last specialty that's keeping me in my car right now. I've very recently gotten engaged to two men. Okay, so this would also fall under my first specialty of doing dumb things. In my defense, I would like to say that it wasn't entirely my fault. It was circumstances. Still, here I was in this dilemma. And I was going to have to explain the dilemma to my two coworkers who were sitting in the office, looking at me through the large plate glass window.

I gave up a sigh and grabbed the messenger bag that was on the seat next to me. Might as well go in and get it all out there. Just spew out the whole hot mess. Now or never, right? The phrase was cringe. It was the line of thinking that had pushed me into the two engagements.

Connie Rosolli, the office manager, held up a sheet of paper with a big question mark on it. The question mark had been written with a thick black marker. And it had an exclamation point after it. I did an internal eye-roll, wrenched the car door open, and went into the office.

"We're dying here," Lula said. "Last we saw, you were engaged to Mr. Dark and Dangerous. And then Mr. Hot and Handsome showed up. That was two days ago. We gotta know details."

Lula is a former ho who is now the office file clerk. Since almost all the files are digital and don't need filing, Lula just does whatever she wants. She's a little shorter and a little younger than me. She's also several skin shades darker than me, has a lot more boob and booty than me, and has a much more extensive and exotic wardrobe.

"Where's the ring?" Lula asked. "I gotta see the ring."

"I don't have a ring," I said. "I didn't think there was a big rush to get a ring."

"Uh-oh," Lula said. "We thought you might even be married by now, but no ring don't sound good."

"Ranger had to go out of town for a couple days."

Ranger is Mr. Dark and Dangerous. Former Special Forces, former bounty hunter. Currently owns a high-tech security company in a stealth building in downtown Trenton.

"Well, when's he coming back?" Lula asked. "Is he back?"

"Not yet," I said.

"And what about Mr. Hot and Handsome? How's he taking the news?"

Mr. Hot and Handsome is Joe Morelli. Former bad boy, now a

Trenton PD detective working crimes against persons. Has a nice little house and a big orange dog.

"He doesn't exactly know," I said. "There's a bit of a hitch."

"A hitch?" Lula asked. "What kind of hitch?"

The door to Vinnie's inner office burst open and Vinnie stormed out. "What's going on out here? What is this, a ladies' tea party? I don't pay you to sit around on your fat asses eating doughnuts all day."

Vinnie is a forty-something barely human version of a weasel in skinny pants. His father-in-law, Harry the Hammer, owns the agency and owns Vinnie.

"I have two big-ticket bonds in the wind," Vinnie said. "Harry's got me by the nuts and he's squeezing."

"I hear that's your second-favorite thing after getting spanked with a spatula," Lula said.

Vinnie narrowed his eyes and retreated into his office. He slammed the door shut and threw the bolt.

I hiked my messenger bag higher onto my shoulder. "I'm on the move. Gotta catch some bad guys."

"What about the hitch?" Lula asked.

"Later," I said. "Are you coming with me?"

"Might as well," Lula said. "There's only one doughnut left in the box and it's one of them plain cake ones. I'm the kind of girl that needs chocolate and extra sugar in the form of attached granules or creamy frosting."

When Vinnie writes a bond, he guarantees that the bondee is going to show up for his court appearance. If the bondee doesn't show, Vinnie is out the bond money. So, Vinnie sends me out to find the miscreant and drag their sorry body back to jail. Lula is on salary, but I only get paid when I make a capture. This ensures that I have incentive to go to work every day.

We got into my SUV, and I pulled two files out of my messenger bag and handed them to Lula. "Eugene Fleck and Bruno Jug. Which one do you want to go after first?"

Lula paged through Bruno Jug. "It says here he's charged with tax evasion. That's what the feds use when they can't prove anything else on account of people involved keep getting dead. Previous charges were racketeering. That includes narcotics trafficking, extortion, and here's my favorite . . . murder for hire. He don't sound like a lot of fun. Let's see what's in file number two." She opened the second file and read down. "This is a good one. Eugene Fleck, AKA Robin Hoodie on account of he always wears a hoodie, and he robs from the rich and gives the shit to the poor. The guy is a porch pirate first class. Looks like nobody was complaining too much until he got carried away with himself and hijacked a UPS truck."

"He made the six o'clock news for that," I said. "He drove the UPS truck to a homeless tent city under one of the bridges and emptied it out. It was like Christmas in October with everyone ripping packages apart."

"I'm all about this guy," Lula said.

"Where do we find him?"

"He's twenty-six and lives with Mommy and Daddy," Lula said. "I'll plug the address into the GPS. Doesn't look like he's got a job. He lists his occupation as 'gamer.' Guess when he's not stealing stuff, he's on the computer." Lula looked over at me. "Are you sure you don't want to tell me about the hitch?"

"It's complicated."

"I bet."

I pulled out into traffic. "I'm working on it."

Twenty minutes later we were in front of the Fleck house on Elm Street. It was a medium-size colonial. Painted white. Black shutters and red front door. Two-car attached garage. No car in the driveway. Nice middle-class neighborhood.

"Who are we going to be today?" Lula asked. "Good cop, bad cop? Pizza delivery? Church ladies come to say hello?"

Lula's hair was fluffed out into a big puffball, and the hair color of the day was fuchsia. She was wearing a navy spandex dress that would have been tasteful on a much smaller woman. On Lula, it was a traffic stopper. There was a lot of cleavage and excess breast struggling to be set free from the plunging scoop neck of the dress, and the skirt was stretched to its limit across her butt. The hem was inches below what should never be seen in public. Her feet were happy in six-inch-high stiletto heels. I was in stark contrast in sneakers, jeans, a girly T-shirt, and a gray hoodie. My brown hair was pulled up into a ponytail and I'd gnawed my lip gloss off worrying about my engagement dilemma. I learned early in our friendship that it was hopeless to try to compete with Lula. She was a birthday cake with sparklers, and I was a bran muffin. Okay, maybe that's too harsh. If I swiped on some mascara and lip gloss, I could bring myself up to an almond croissant. Maybe even a cupcake. No sprinkles. Bottom line is that I didn't think either of us was going to pass as a church lady.

I parked the SUV in front of the Fleck house and cut the engine. "We're going to be ourselves," I said. "Two professional bail bonds enforcement agents."

"Are you sure that's who we are?" Lula asked.

"That's what it says on my business card."

"I gotta get some of them made up," Lula said.

I rang the bell and a young man answered. About my height, which was five foot seven. Brown hair tied back into a low ponytail. Slim. Baggy jeans and beat-up sneakers and a red plaid flannel shirt, untucked.

"Eugene?" I asked.

"Yeah," he said, looking Lula over. "Only I'm not interested in kinky sex. My mom's going to be home any minute."

"Hunh," Lula said. "What makes you think we'd want to do *you*?"

I stepped in front of Lula so that my foot was halfway into the door frame. "I represent Vincent Plum," I said to Eugene. "You failed to show for your court appearance and I'm going to help you reschedule."

"Okay," he said. "Go ahead and reschedule me."

He made an attempt to close the door, but I was already inside. "We need to go downtown to reschedule. It won't take long and then we'll bring you home."

"I guess I could do that," he said. "As long as it doesn't take too long."

Truth is, he'd get booked in, and because it was early in the day and court was in session, he might be lucky enough to go in front of a judge and have his bail bond set and be given a new appearance date. Then if he could get someone to secure his bail bond, he'd be free to go. If all of this didn't happen, he'd spend some time in lockup.

I put him in the back seat of the SUV. I drove out of the neighborhood and avoided the center of the city by taking Marlboro Street. I stopped for a light by the Catholic church.

"There's a lot of people in front of the church," Lula said. "Don't look like they're dressed up for a wedding."

"There's a homeless camp in the park on the next block," Eugene said. "They come here to get food. The church gives out two meals a day."

"Some of them are waving at us," Lula said. "And they're

yelling something." She cracked her window. "It sounds like they're yelling *Robin*!"

"It's because of all the publicity about Robin Hoodie," Eugene said. "The police found my fingerprints on the truck and charged me with hijacking, and it got to be big news. My picture was all over the television and in the papers, saying I was Robin Hoodie."

"Are you?" I asked.

"No. Of course not, but everyone thinks I am. I can't walk past a homeless person without them telling me they're one of my Merry Men."

"Looks like they're coming over," Lula said. "Looks like *all* of them are coming over."

In an instant the car was surrounded. The Merry Men were cheering for Robin and thumping on the car with their fists. The light changed and I couldn't move because there were Merry Men in front of me. I leaned on the horn, and they started rocking the car.

"This here's a riot," Lula said. "I'm getting nauseous from the rocking." She was rooting through her enormous fake Prada tote bag. "I got a gun in here somewhere. You want me to shoot them?"

"No shooting!" I said. "Call for police."

"I'll already throw up by the time they get here," Lula said.

"They're just excited because they think they see Robin Hoodie," Eugene said. "I could go out and calm them down."

"That's a good idea," Lula said to me. "Don't you think that's a good idea?"

I thought it was a bad idea, but I didn't have any better ideas. "Go out and get them off the road," I said to Eugene, "but don't take too long. We want to get to the courthouse before they break for lunch."

I popped the door lock, and Eugene got out and was swallowed up in the crowd of Merry Men.

"This is working," Lula said. "They're moving away from the car. It's like a herd of homeless migrating back to the church."

"I see the herd," I said. "I don't see Eugene."

I got out of the car and looked around. No Eugene. I got back in the car.

"Looks like the Merry Men got Robin," Lula said. "Just like in the movie. They swooped in and saved Robin."

I drove around a couple blocks, but I didn't see Robin Hoodie or Eugene Fleck. I drove back to the Fleck house. A white Toyota Corolla was parked in the driveway. Mrs. Fleck was home.

I left Lula in the car, and I went to the house and rang the bell. A pleasant-looking woman answered.

"Mrs. Fleck?" I asked her.

"Yes."

"I'm looking for Eugene. Is he home?"

"No," she said. "I'm afraid he stepped out."

I introduced myself and gave her my card. "He needs to reschedule his court date," I said to Mrs. Fleck. "I'm available to help him."

"That's very nice of you," she said. "I'll tell him you stopped by. I'm sure he'll be sorry he missed you."

I returned to the car, drove to the end of the block, and parked.

"I suppose we're doing surveillance," Lula said.

"Yes. Sooner or later, he has to go home."

"It better be sooner," Lula said. "I need to tinkle."

"You're kidding."

"No way. I don't kid about tinkling. It's on account of I drank all that coffee to wash down all the doughnuts. And then I had a couple sodas. They say you're supposed to drink a lot of water, but I can't see it. Water is too thin. I drink soda. It tastes better and it's got bubbles. It's like happiness in a can."

"Can you hold it for a while?"

"How long is a while?"

"An hour," I said.

"Not gonna happen."

"Half hour?"

"Maybe ten minutes," Lula said. "It was a lot of soda."

I gave up on the surveillance and drove back to the office.

# CHAPTER TWO

Connie looked up from her computer when we walked in. "Did you get someone?"

"We got him and then we lost him," I said. "Is Vinnie still here?"

"He left right after you did," Connie said. "He had to go downtown to bond someone out." She handed me a file. "I got a new FTA. It just came through. Indecent exposure in the supermarket. Not a big-ticket bond, but it'll get you pizza money."

I took the file and shoved it into my bag. "Can you get me more information on Bruno Jug?" I asked Connie. "Wives, girlfriends, social clubs, hobbies, vacation houses. Anything."

"You bet," Connie said. "I'll do a search on him, and I'll ask my cousin Carl. Jug isn't in the family, but he moves in some of the same circles as Carl."

Connie is remotely connected to the mob of yesteryear, and she has some current relatives who have unexplained incomes. Carl would be one of them.

Lula reappeared from the back of the office. "What did I miss? What are you talking about?"

"Bruno Jug," I said.

"I could use to miss that conversation. I don't like things that got to do with death."

"I doubt he does his own wet work," Connie said. "He's white-collar. He's a suit."

"I still don't want to talk about him," Lula said. "I want to talk about the hitch. I expected to see a ring when I came in this morning, and all I got was news that there's a hitch. Ranger isn't backing out, is he? That would be real disappointing."

I dumped my messenger bag onto the couch and slouched into one of the uncomfortable plastic chairs in front of Connie's desk.

"It's not Ranger," I said. "He's still in Virginia with his tech guy. They're cleaning up a security breach in an office there."

"Then what?" Lula asked.

"Remember when Morelli came back from Miami and showed up at the crime scene?"

"Yeah, I remember that," Lula said.

"Okay, so we got together after."

"Uh-oh," Lula said. "How together?"

"Just together. Talking."

"And?"

"And he asked me to marry him."

"Holy shit," Lula said.

Connie, the office manager and the most religious of the three of us, which isn't saying much, made the sign of the cross.

"And?" Lula asked.

"And I sort of said yes."

"Holy shit again," Lula said.

Connie's phone rang and Connie sent the call to voicemail. "Keep going," she said to me.

Connie is a couple years older than me, a better shot than me, and caught in a Jersey Shore, eighties time warp with big hair, bright blue eye shadow, and black eyeliner.

"Are you telling me you're engaged to both guys?" Lula asked. "Because if that's what you're telling me, I need a doughnut to calm down."

Connie pushed the bakery box across the top of her desk toward Lula and turned to me. "Who did you choose?"

"That's the problem," I said. "I can't choose. There are extenuating circumstances."

"Like someone's gonna kill someone else?" Lula asked, eating the last stale doughnut.

"No. I don't think it will come to that. The problem is that when I got engaged to Ranger, we celebrated."

"That's to be expected," Lula said. "Anybody would celebrate getting engaged to Ranger. He's smokin', and he's got a full-time housekeeper taking care of him. And she cooks and irons."

"Exactly," I said. "But then I celebrated with Morelli when we got engaged."

"Okay, I get that," Lula said. "Anybody would celebrate getting engaged to him, too."

"Hold on," Connie said. "When you say that you 'celebrated,' do you mean with a glass of champagne?"

"I mean we *really celebrated*," I said.

"So, you *really celebrated* with both men," Connie said.

"Yep," I said. "A lot. First with Ranger and then with Morelli."

"No harm, no foul there," Lula said. "Totally understandable."

"Yes, but when I went to take my birth control pill the morning after Morelli, I found out they'd expired."

"Were they a little expired?" Lula asked. "A little expired would still be okay."

"They were a lot expired," I said. "They should have been thrown away a couple years ago, but they were left in a bathroom drawer with the new pills, and I grabbed the wrong packet. I've been taking the stupid things all month. I don't know why it suddenly occurred to me to look at the date."

"I'd say a combination of guilt and fear," Lula said. "Nobody was wearing a raincoat?"

"No raincoats."

"Maybe you need one of them morning-after pills," Lula said.

"I don't think I want to do that," I said.

Lula went wide-eyed. "You mean you want to have a baby?"

"I think I might."

I couldn't believe I was thinking this, much less saying it out loud. I couldn't cook, and I gagged when I babysat Morelli's dog and had to pick up after him. How was I ever going to take care of a baby?

"For one thing, I'm not getting any younger," I said to Lula. "It could be now or never."

"I suppose," Lula said. "But you haven't gotten any older either. And now or never is one of them overrated motivational ideas."

"You still have to pick a man," Connie said. "Do you know which one?"

"That's the hitch," I said. "If it turns out that I'm not pregnant, I know who I want to marry. If it turns out that I'm pregnant, I can't make a decision until I'm seven weeks in. At seven weeks you can do a paternity test. I googled it."

"So, if you're preggers, you'll marry whoever the baby daddy is?" Connie asked.

"Yes."

"Even if it's not your first choice?"

"Yep. Not a problem. I had a hard time choosing, anyway," I said.

"You got a point," Lula said. "You can't go wrong with either of them. When are you going to know if you're pregnant?"

"I can start testing six days after Morelli and I celebrated."

"That would be four days from now," Lula said. "When is Aunt Flo supposed to show up?"

"I'm not sure. I have almost two weeks of pills left, but I've stopped taking them, so Aunt Flo might be confused."

"Okay, so we have to wait until Friday," Lula said.

"The six-days-after isn't a sure thing," I said. "The ten-days test is more reliable, and the best test is after you've missed a period."

"I can't wait for ten days," Lula said. "As it is, I'm gonna be holding my breath until Friday."

"What about your apartment?" Connie asked me. "I heard you got evicted."

"I did, but I've been reinstated. The management company changed its mind. They realized the fire wasn't my fault. I mean, I can't help it if some wacko firebombed my apartment."

"Yeah, and we caught the wacko, so that has to count for something," Lula said.

I glanced at the doughnut box on Connie's desk. Empty. Damn. Connie kept a flask in her bottom drawer, along with her gun and a can of hair spray. Probably it was too early to take a hit from the flask. I didn't usually drink hard liquor, but in the absence of a doughnut, it served a purpose. I gave up on the doughnut and the liquor and slumped a little lower in my chair.

"Most of the damage was cleaned up by the restoration team," I said. "And if I can bring Jug in, I'll collect enough on his apprehension to buy new bedroom furniture. And maybe a television."

"Are you sure you want to do all that if you're getting married?" Connie asked.

"I can get a mattress and frame overnight for under three hundred dollars. Otherwise, I might be sleeping on my couch for a couple months."

"I see where you're going with this," Lula said. "You've got to keep two guys on the hook, so it's not like you could live with one of them. I don't know how you're going to do this."

"It should be okay for a day or two," I said. "I'll be busy getting my apartment set up. And I've got a couple FTAs that will be a priority. Ranger is out of town, so I only have to deal with Morelli."

"What happens after a couple days?" Lula asked.

"I might get sick. Something contagious."

"That's good," Lula said. "You should say you got COVID. That always works. That's good for at least a week. And then you could get long COVID if you need more time."

I was hoping I wouldn't need more time. I didn't like keeping Ranger and Morelli hanging like this. It felt icky. It wasn't the way I wanted to start a marriage.

"Uh-oh," Lula said to me. "You've got that face."

"What face?"

"The face like you're not happy, where your mouth turns down and your eyes don't have no sparkle."

"I shouldn't have celebrated with both of them."

"Yeah, well, that ship already sailed. You just need to take your mind off it. We should go get the indecent-exposure guy. They're always fun. And they hardly ever shoot at us."

My phone rang. It was Morelli.

"Hey," I said to him.

"Just checking in," he said. "I'm still playing catch-up on paperwork, but I should be done at the end of the day. I thought we could get takeout and you could spend the night."

"That sounds great, but I told my parents I'd be there for dinner. And then Grandma wanted to go to a viewing at the funeral home. And you know how that ends up. I'll have a headache from the carnations and lilies. Maybe tomorrow would be better. I've gotta go. I have another call coming in."

"You're going straight to hell," Lula said to me. "No doubt about it. That was a monster fib."

"I fib all the time. It's part of my job," I said.

"That don't make it right," Lula said.

"Do you fib?" I asked her.

"Hell yeah. I'm a lifelong fibber. One of these days I'm going to confession and get rid of my fibber sins."

"I thought you weren't Catholic."

"Do you have to be Catholic? I'm Catholic by association. I know a lot of Catholics. And I had a bunch of Catholic customers back when I was a ho."

I grabbed my messenger bag and hung it on my shoulder. "Time to saddle up and move out."

"Yahoo," Lula said.

I gave Lula the new file when we were in my Trailblazer.

"Jerry Bottles," she said. "Sixty-two years old. Not an attractive photo. Bald, big belly, has a nose like Captain Hook in *Peter Pan*. Says he's five feet six inches tall and weighs a hundred sixty pounds. Self-employed plumber. Looks like this isn't his first exposure. His last arrest got him community service, but he exposed himself while he was doing his time, working to clean up the duck pond in Greenwood Park, so he was sent for a psychiatric evaluation. He lives in one of those little row houses on the outskirts of the Burg. Seventy-two Wilmot Street."

The Burg is a chunk of Trenton on the other side of the railroad tracks from the center of the city. I grew up in the Burg and my parents still live there with my grandma Mazur. Houses are small. Streets follow no rhyme or reason. The bakeries are excellent. The medical center sits on the edge of the Burg. Vincent Plum Bail Bonds is several blocks away and on the opposite side of Hamilton Avenue.

I drove down Hamilton and made a left turn into the Burg before I got to the medical center. I wound my way through the Burg and found Wilmot. There was on-street parking in front of the row houses. I knew there was also parking in the alley that cut the block.

"That's his house there," Lula said. "The one with the Christmas wreath on the front door. There's cars parked at the curb but none of them looks like a plumber's vehicle."

"What does a plumber's vehicle look like?"

"It's one of those things you know when you see it," Lula said.

I drove around the block and turned into the alley. Some houses had single-car garages in the alley. Number 72 did not. There was a truck parked in the small backyard.

"You see," Lula said. "That's a plumber's vehicle. I knew as soon as I looked at it."

"It says *Bottles Plumbing* on the side panel."

"Fuckin' A," Lula said.

I parked alongside the truck, and Lula and I got out of my Trailblazer and walked to Bottles's back door.

"We should be nice to him," Lula said. "You never know when you'll need a plumber."

I didn't think I needed a plumber who displayed his personal plumbing in public, but I would be nice to him anyway.

Bottles answered on the second knock. He was wearing jeans that sat below his belly overhang and a navy collared shirt that had *Bottles Plumbing* stitched in yellow on the pocket. He had a few greasy strands of hair stretched across his bald head and an outcropping of hair on his large Captain Hook nose. I try not to be judgmental, but by anyone's standards he was not an attractive man.

"Gerald Bottles?" I asked.

"Yeah," he said. "What's up?"

"I represent Vincent Plum Bail Bonds," I said. "You missed your court date. I need to get you rescheduled."

"That's a real pain in the buttocks," he said. "How about we just forget the whole thing. Nothing ever comes from this court stuff anyway. I'm already doing shrink time, which is a total waste. This shrink guy doesn't get it. I think he's got penis envy, but that's just my opinion."

"If you don't want to go to court, why don't you stop whipping it out in public?" Lula said.

"I'd rather stop breathing," Bottles said. "I'd rather gouge out my eyeballs. I'd rather become a vegan."

"So, you'd rather be a dead, blind vegan than give up being a pervert," Lula said.

"I'm not a pervert," Bottles said. "It's that when God gives you something special you got an obligation to make the most of it. I'm not stupid but I'm not real smart either. I don't have a lot of education. I don't have good hair. I got a big nose and a big belly. What it all adds up to is that I'm not exactly a heartthrob. I'm not even good at conversation. No one wants to talk about unclogging a toilet."

"I'm guessing this is going somewhere," Lula said.

"What I've got is a really pretty penis," Bottles said. "And it's a crime against nature not to show it to people."

"Honey, every man thinks his penis is pretty," Lula said. "Even the ones who want it to be bigger still think what they got is pretty. That don't mean everyone can go around waving it like a flag on the Fourth of July."

"Yeah, but mine is exceptional," Bottles said. "I have the perfect penis. Do you want to see it?"

"No!" I said.

"I guess I could take a look," Lula said. "Being that I used to be a professional ho and I've seen my share, I could give an unbiased opinion."

Bottles unzipped and took it out. "There," he said. "What do you think?"

"I gotta admit, that's a damn nice penis," Lula said. "It's a real nice pink color and the skin looks silky smooth. I'm guessing it doesn't get a lot of abuse."

"I take good care of it," Bottles said. "You should see it when it's in all its glory, if you know what I mean. It's stunning."

"We'll take your word for it," I said. "You could put it away now."

"Some people have beautiful paintings that they want people to see. Some people drive flashy cars. Some people live in fabulous mansions. I have a penis," Bottles said. "I can only keep it hidden for so long and then I have to take it out so people can appreciate it. And I mean, let's face it, it's pretty much all I've got."

"I see where you're coming from," Lula said, "but you're a nut."

"Speaking of nuts," Bottles said, "mine are worth a look."

"Not today," I said.

Bottles looked disappointed. “Some other time?”

“Yeah,” I said. “We need to take you into town to reschedule your court date.”

“I’m due on a construction site,” he said.

“If you can make bail, we might be able to fast-track you.”

“No problem. I’m running a tab with Vinnie.”

“I gotta ask you about the Christmas wreath on your front door,” Lula said. “You must be one of them Christmas-all-year-long people.”

Bottles looked surprised. “I have a wreath on my front door?”

“Yeah,” Lula said. “It’s still green so it must be plastic, and it has a big red bow on it.”

“I never use the front door,” Bottles said. “I didn’t know there was a wreath on it. It must have been there when I bought the house two years ago.”

# CHAPTER THREE

I dropped Lula off at the office, walked Bottles through the legal system, and brought him back to his house. I stopped at Giovichinni's Deli, got a turkey club on a brioche roll, and took it to the office to eat.

"Looks like everything worked out with Bottles," Lula said. "We saw that Vinnie bailed him out. So, Bottles must not have exposed himself to the judge."

I dropped my messenger bag on the floor, pulled a chair up to Connie's desk, and unwrapped my sandwich. "I was worried," I said. "I kept him cuffed up to the last minute, and then I rushed him out of the building as soon as the judge set his bail bond."

"I've been thinking about Bottles," Lula said. "It doesn't seem fair that he got stuck with a special penis. I can relate on account of some of my special things gotta stay covered up too. I've got world-class nipples, for instance, and my opportunities to get them appreciated are limited."

Lula is a woman of generously proportioned, perfectly balanced-out booty and boob. Capping off her breasts, which were only slightly smaller than basketballs, were nipples as big as wine magnum corks. The two-sizes-too-small polyester and spandex scoop-neck top she was wearing was stretched to breaking point over the wine corks.

"News flash," Connie said to Lula. "Your nipples aren't exactly hidden."

"Okay," Lula said, "but my light's under a bushel, so to speak. Anyway, that was just an obvious answer. There's other things."

"What other things?" Connie asked.

"Things about ourselves that we keep secret," Lula said. "Don't we all have those things?"

There were two issues to consider here. The first is that it's easy to underestimate Lula. On the surface she's multicolored hair, ho clothes, and *say what?* And then when you're least expecting it, a crack appears in the surface and something profound leaks out. The second thing to consider is that I feared that, unlike Lula, I didn't have anything below my surface. And equally disturbing, I didn't have anything that was special about me, hidden or otherwise. I took some moments to think about it and came up with nothing.

"Anyway, I'm lucky that I got other possibilities going for me," Lula said. "I could be anything I want to be. Someday I might want to be a lawyer or a supermodel or an astronaut. Bottles don't seem to have anything on his agenda but being a plumber. Not that I'm downplaying the value of being a good plumber, but let's face it . . . it don't get the respect like a supermodel."

I ate my sandwich while I read through the information on Jug that Connie had printed out for me. He'd been accused of a laundry list of crimes and convicted of none. Jurors, witnesses, and informants mysteriously died or had bouts of amnesia. Judges ignored evidence and ruled for acquittal.

"I'm surprised he went FTA," I said to Connie. "There's no history of him doing that for any of his other arrests."

"He has a new wife," Connie said. "He just got back from his honeymoon. I imagine the court date was inconvenient."

"So, this might be an easy bust," I said.

"Maybe," Connie said. "I asked my mom about Jug, and she said there's rumors he's senile. Got dementia. Can't remember anything. Combative. Dribbles."

"And he just got married?"

"Yeah. She's twenty-three years old. True love."

"That's nice," Lula said. "He's making the most of his golden years even if he can't remember them."

"Do we have an address for him?" I asked Connie.

"His address has been the same for forty years," Connie said. "He has a house in North Trenton and an office downtown. It's all in your report."

"I'm going to do a drive-by on his house and his office," I said. "Get the lay of the land."

"I'll go with you," Lula said. "Maybe we'll get lucky, and he'll be out walking his dog, and we can snatch him up and drive him to get rebooked."

"There's no mention of a dog in any of the reports I pulled," Connie said.

"Well, you said he's rumored to be senile. It could be a pretend dog," Lula said. "My aunt Bestie was senile, and she talked to an imaginary giraffe. She got arthritis in her neck from always looking up to the giraffe. She had to get a cortisone shot. And then there's that Jimmy Stewart movie about a giant imaginary rabbit named Harvey. Except it's not clear if Harvey is imaginary or real."

I remember seeing that movie for the first time when I was a kid and the idea of a huge invisible rabbit scared the bejeezus out of me. I wasn't comfortable about the Easter Bunny hopping around in our house either. As an adult I've come to love *Harvey*, but I'm still creeped out by the Easter Bunny.

I took North Olden Avenue, crossed the railroad tracks, and followed the GPS lady's directions to Merrymaster Street.

"This here's a nice neighborhood," Lula said. "It's real tidy and respectable with lots of big shade trees. I bet they hardly have any crime here. If I was married and had a kid and a real dog that was named Chardonnay, I would want to live here. Being that I don't have any of those things, I'd rather stick a fork in my eye than live in one of these houses."

Lula rented a small apartment in a house that was currently painted lavender and pink. It wasn't in a high-crime, gang-controlled area, but there was enough crime to keep you on your toes and make life interesting.

"That's Jug's house with the black shutters and quality mahogany door," Lula said. "Number twenty-one."

It was similar to other houses on Merrymaster. Two stories. Nice-size front yard and backyard. Larger than the yards in the Burg, but not so big that you had to spend all day mowing the lawn. Single-car garage. Nothing fancy. Just a solidly built, practical box of a house.

"Connie's report says Jug drives a black Volvo sedan and the Mrs. drives a silver Mercedes EQE sedan. That's a nice car but you gotta plug that sucker in, so I'm guessing she gets the garage. Since I don't see no Volvo in the driveway, I'm thinking Mr. isn't home."

"And I'm thinking you're right. Next stop is his office."

"We gotta go back to town. He's on East Gilbert Street. Jug Produce. Looks like he's got an office and a warehouse there.

According to Connie, he's one of the top produce wholesalers in Central Jersey."

I retraced my steps back to North Olden and let the GPS lady take me to East Gilbert. I was approaching Jug Produce, and Ranger called.

"Just checking in," he said. "Ella tells me you've moved out."

Ranger has a small but perfect apartment on the top floor of his office building. Gourmet food, Bulgari shower gel, fluffy towels, heavenly pillows, freshly ironed expensive sheets, and other niceties are supplied by his housekeeper, Ella. The one-bedroom flat has a neutral, slightly masculine color palette with comfortable, clean-lined, softly modern furniture that Ranger didn't even buy secondhand.

My hamster, Rex, and I had cohabitated with Ranger while my apartment was recovering from the firebombing. I moved out like a thief in the night when I went off the rails and got engaged to Morelli.

"Rex and I went back to my apartment," I said. "I thought I'd take this time to organize since you're out of town."

"And now?"

"Now I'm in the car with Lula, and you're on the speakerphone."

"Babe," Ranger said. And he disconnected.

"He's a man of few words," I said to Lula.

"Yeah, but he says *babe* like it's an invitation to an orgasm."

Jug Produce was housed in a two-story cement-block warehouse. There was a front door on East Gilbert Street that served as a visitors' entrance with on-street parking. Windows on the second floor. Probably offices up there. Connie's notes indicated that the Jug property fronted Gilbert and backed up to the street behind it. I drove around the block and found the back gate to Jug Produce.

"It looks like there's a loading dock behind the building," Lula said. "Everything's nice and secure with chain-link fence. Guess you want to make sure no one's stealing melons and such."

I thought it probably was also handy for delivery of hijacked sneakers and human trafficking.

"I guess we're coming back here tomorrow," Lula said.

"I'd rather try to get him at home. I think it will be an easier apprehension."

"That's going to be early in the morning or at dinnertime," Lula said.

"I'm thinking first thing in the morning. We'll stake out the house, wait for lights to go on, and then we'll go in."

"How early is first thing?"

"Seven o'clock."

"Say what? In the morning? It takes half an hour just to drive there. That's like out of the house at six thirty. I got a beauty routine. I gotta accessorize. Plus, I'll miss my morning doughnuts at the office. It's part of the start-my-day ritual. My body won't know what to do without doughnuts. My body don't like surprises like that."

"I'll bring doughnuts."

"And coffee. Good coffee. Not the kind *you* make."

"Yeah, I'll bring good coffee."

---

I dropped Lula off at the office and drove to my apartment building. Three floors of uninspired brick construction. Not new. Not old. Not luxury living. Not a slum. Affordable and moderately comfortable if you were willing to lower your standards. I parked in the lot and looked up at my second-floor windows. The brick around the windows was still smudged with soot from the fire. I bypassed the unreliable elevator and took the stairs. Men were working in the hall on the second floor, replacing the water-soaked carpet. Some good things come out of a fire, right? Like new carpet.

I let myself into my apartment and glanced into my kitchen. Apart from some smoke damage it was untouched by the fire. My hamster, Rex, was asleep in his aquarium on my kitchen counter. I called hello to him, dropped my messenger bag on my dining room table, and returned to the kitchen to give Rex a snack. Half a Ritz cracker and a peanut still in its shell. The bedding stirred in front of his soup-can den, and Rex poked his head out and twitched his nose. He rushed at the cracker and peanut, shoved them into his cheek pouch, and returned to his soup can. The perfect roommate. Quiet, nonjudgmental, small poop.

The fire had wiped out my bedroom and most of my living room. The fire restoration company had done a decent job, but I needed paint throughout, new carpet and furniture. So far, my redecorating efforts had gotten me a couch, a table lamp, a sleeping bag, and a pillow. I didn't want to spend any more than was absolutely necessary on the essentials. They were temporary. Probably. Hopefully. Maybe.

I sat at my dining room table/desk and opened my MacBook Air. After a half hour I had a queen mattress and frame, an end table, a nightstand, a second table lamp, a quilt, and a set of sheets getting delivered in forty-eight hours. If I brought Jug in, I would be able to pay for it all.

The obituaries were next up. I surfed funeral homes and hit gold right away. Larry Luger was having a viewing at the Burg's premier funeral home. Larry was a big deal in the Knights of Columbus. He was going to draw a crowd. Grandma would be attending. Grandma and her girlfriends' social life consisted of viewings, bingo at the firehouse, and an occasional visit to the Hunk-O-Mania All-Male Revue.

I changed into a navy skirt with a matching jacket and a simple white sweater. I retied my ponytail, swiped on some lip gloss, and I looked at myself in the mirror. "You're supposed to have a glow when you're pregnant," I said to my reflection. I didn't see a glow. Maybe it was too soon. Maybe I wasn't glowing because I was a big fibber. Now I had to go to a viewing tonight with Grandma so I didn't get caught in my fib. I sniffed at my jacket sleeve. Most of my clothes burned in the fire, but a few things, like the skirt and jacket, survived. The survivors smelled like campfire and cremated marshmallows. If Jo Malone could bottle it, I'd buy it. As it was, I had it for free.

I called my mom. "I need to go to the Luger viewing tonight," I said. "I thought I'd mooch dinner off you first."

"I'll have Grandma set a plate. We're having shells in red sauce, and your grandmother bought a chocolate cake at the bakery."

"Great. I'm on my way."

I slipped my phone into my handbag along with a canister of pepper spray and some flexi-cuffs. Just in case I ran into some bad guys. A girl can't be too prepared. I had a gun, but it wouldn't fit in my little bag, and anyway, I didn't have any bullets.

---

My parents live in a modest two-story house that has a postage-stamp front yard and a backyard that's only slightly larger. Hydrangea bushes border the small front porch. Trash and recycling receptacles border the small back stoop. The rooms inside are arranged shotgun. Living room, dining room, kitchen. The furniture is overstuffed and comfy. The end tables are cluttered with framed photos of family. The dining table seats six but has been known to feed twelve. The kitchen is the heart of the house and the sole domain of my mom and Grandma Mazur.

Dinner is always precisely at six o'clock. Everyone had just come to the table when I rolled in and took my seat.

Grandma leaned forward when I sat down. "Let me see!" she said to me. "I bet it's a beauty."

"What's a beauty?" I asked.

"The ring. Let's see the ring."

"I don't have a ring," I said.

"Of course you have a ring. We heard you were engaged."

I got a cramp in my stomach. "Who told you I'm engaged?"

"Everyone," Grandma said.

"Who am I engaged to?" I asked.

"Joseph Morelli," my mother said. "Is there a problem? Did you break up already?"

I shook my napkin out and took some shells and red sauce. "No," I said. "Of course not. I just didn't realize it was public knowledge. It just happened. And we didn't pick out a ring yet."

"How about a date?" Grandma asked. "Do you have a date set?"

"Green beans," my father said. "I need the green beans."

I passed him the green beans and spooned some grated cheese on my shells. "No date yet."

"A Christmas wedding would be nice," Grandma said. "The bridesmaids could wear red."

I poured myself a glass of wine, raised it to my mouth, and stopped. Were you allowed to drink wine if you were preggers?

"Your mother said you're going to the Luger viewing tonight," Grandma said to me. "It'll be a good one. They're expecting a crowd. They're putting him in slumber room number one. Emma Wasneski was going to pick me up, but I can ride with you now. We need to go early so we can get in when they open the doors. I want a seat up front on this one so I can get a good look at the widow. I heard she had some work done by that new cosmetic dermatologist on Hamilton. I've been thinking about giving her a try. They say she works miracles with Botox and fillers."

But then, maybe I wasn't preggers, I thought, my wineglass still poised in midair. I didn't have the glow. And I only felt nauseous when I got a phone call from Morelli or Ranger. I mean, who wouldn't under the circumstances.

"Red sauce," my father said.

Grandma passed him the red sauce and I considered my glass of wine. It would be a shame to waste it.

"You only go to viewings when it's business," Grandma said to me. "Who is it this time? A serial rapist? One of those tattooed gang killers? Do I need my gun?"

My mother went rigid in her chair. "You aren't taking your gun," she said to Grandma. "No one is taking a gun." She cut her eyes to me. "No one."

"Not me," I said. "No gun."

"Well, let's have it," Grandma said. "Who are you hunting down?"

I took a small sip of wine. Surely a small sip was okay. I mean, I didn't even know if I *was* preggers. "Bruno Jug."

"He's a big fish," Grandma said.

My mother made the sign of the cross. "He'll have you killed," my mother said. "He's bonkers. He was bad enough when he was sane, and now he's crazy."

"Lots of people have tried to kill Stephanie," Grandma said. "Her apartment just got firebombed. That was a good one."

I wanted more wine, but I'd had my sip, so I reached for the bread basket. I took a couple chunks and slathered them with butter.

"Most women die from heart disease and breast cancer, but my daughter is going to get killed by Bruno Jug," my mother said. "A bullet to the brain."

"Not necessarily," Grandma said. "It depends who does his wet work. If he uses Jimmy the Pig, she could get bludgeoned. And sometimes people just disappear, and you don't know if they're in the landfill or dumped offshore."

My father stopped eating and picked his head up. "Who's getting dumped offshore?"

"Stephanie," my mother said. "She's going after Bruno Jug. He didn't show up for court and now she's going to put him in cuffs at Larry Luger's viewing."

"Larry Luger died?"

"Aneurysm," Grandma said. "Come on him all of a sudden while he was brushing his teeth."

"Hunh," my father said. "Brushing his teeth." And he went back to eating his shells.

My mother chugged a glass of wine and poured another. "Why me?" she asked.

Grandma tipped her head up and sniffed. "It smells like something is burning. Is anything on the stove in the kitchen?" she asked my mom.

My mom went quiet for a moment. "No," she said. "I'm sure the stove is off. I smell it too. It smells more like someone has a fireplace going."

"There's no fireplaces in these houses," Grandma said. "It must be the Weavers grilling again. It smells like they're toasting marshmallows."

"It's me," I said. "It's my jacket. I can't get the smell out from the fire."

"It makes me hungry for dessert," Grandma said. "Good thing I bought a cake this morning."

---

The funeral home is on the edge of the Burg. For years it was owned and managed by Constantine Stiva. It has since changed hands, but everyone still calls it Stiva's. It's a large white colonial-type structure with a wide front porch, a small parking lot on the side, a newer brick addition, and several garages in the rear. Grandma and I arrived early enough to get one of the prized parking spots in the lot. Grandma hurried off to the front porch so she would be one of the first in line to push through the big double doors when the viewing began at seven o'clock. I lingered in the car. I was in no hurry to go into the funeral home. I especially was in no hurry to encounter Bruno Jug at the funeral home. It would be a spectacle. Fortunately, it was unlikely that he would show. I couldn't see the new Mrs. Jug hanging at the cookie table with Grandma and her pals.

I waited until the last straggler had disappeared inside the building, and then I left my car and joined the viewing.

Grandma and her crew had a viewing routine. First in, grab the good seats up front where you could check out the mourners as they passed in front of the casket. Tonight, they'd also be scrutinizing the widow for signs of Botox. At seven forty-five they would get in line and pay their respects. Then they'd head for the cookie station. Doors closed at nine o'clock. I'd only known Grandma to leave before nine o'clock on one occasion and that was because she had uncontrollable diarrhea from God knows what. So, I was stuck in the funeral home until nine o'clock. This was my punishment for celebrating with two men. I guess it could have been worse. There were cookies. And so far, no Bruno Jug.

I hung out in the lobby, wandering around the perimeter of

the room. There were upholstered benches, but I thought I would look pathetic if I sat on one all by myself. Like the last girl asked to dance at a seventh-grade mixer. People would talk. They'd say, *There's Stephanie Plum. Her apartment got firebombed again. Poor thing.*

Morelli called me at eight o'clock. "Bob misses you," Morelli said. "Do you have a headache yet?"

Bob is Morelli's dog. He's big and orange, and he smiles a lot.

"It's all good," I said. "Grandma and the ladies just got to the cookie table. I have an hour to go."

"And then?"

"If I don't have a headache, I thought I might take a drive over to Bruno Jug's house. He's FTA and if I could bring him in, I would be able to pay off my credit card."

"You don't want to mess with Bruno Jug. He's easily offended. Like if someone tried to cuff him, he'd take it personally and have them soaked in gasoline and set on fire. Let Vinny bring him in."

"Rumor has it that Jug's senile."

"I've heard the rumor. I've also heard a rumor that his new bride is pregnant by their Chihuahua and that the world is coming to an end in thirty-two days."

"They have a Chihuahua?"

"I have to go," Morelli said. "Third period just started. Rangers are down by two goals."

I hung up, turned in the direction of the cookie table, and bumped into Herbert Slovinski. I knew Herbert from high school. He sat behind me in algebra. He mumbled to himself all during class and sometimes he would sigh, and I could feel his breath on my neck. Morelli's breath on my neck was sexy, Herbert's breath not at all. My best friend, Mary Ann, swore she saw him pick his nose and eat the booger. He hadn't changed much since high school. My height. Skinny. Mousy brown hair parted on the side. Big black-framed glasses that kept sliding down his nose. Brown slacks, white button-down shirt that was a size too large, tan cardigan circa 1950.

"Hey, Stephanie Plum," Herbert said. "How awesome is this? Just like being behind you in algebra. How's it going? Is it going great? It's going great for me."

"Gee, that's terrific," I said. "If you'll excuse me . . ."

"I bet you're on your way to the cookie table," he said. "Have you noticed only women go to the cookie table? Why is that?"

"I never noticed."

"That's probably because you don't come here a lot. I come a lot."

I knew I was going to regret asking, but I had to ask anyway. "Why?"

"I'm thinking I might want to be a funeral director. So, I've been scoping it all out. Testing the waters."

"Sounds like a plan. Good luck with it. Nice running into you."

I stepped around him to get to the cookie table but he stuck with me.

"This is amazing, right?" he said. "Here we are talking. We never talked in high school. You always rushed out of class as soon as the bell rang. And you were always ahead of me in the band. The baton twirlers were always up front."

"You were in the band?"

"I played the clarinet. I still play it. I'm awesome on the clarinet. You should come hear me sometime."

"Where do you play?"

"At home. I'm currently living with my parents, and they think I should go pro. Do you want to hear a joke about the clarinet? What's the difference between a clarinet and an onion? No one cries when you chop up a clarinet. That's funny, right? You could come over tonight after the viewing."

"Tempting, but I'm going to pass. Things to do." I kept inching my way to the cookies. "Did I tell you that I'm engaged?"

"No. Wow, that's a surprise. I didn't hear. So, you're not married yet, right? So, no problem. We could still get together. Ordinarily my dance card is full, but there aren't any good viewings tomorrow. We could have coffee or drinks somewhere."

"Not a good idea. My fiancé is very jealous. He's a cop. He carries a gun."

"We should be careful about getting together then. Keep it quiet. I could pick you up in my car. I have a Prius. Are you green?"

"No," I said. "I'm pink. I need to go, and you can't follow me."

"Why not?"

"I'm going to the girls-only cookie table."

"Okay, well I'll call you. We'll make arrangements. Did I mention I have a cat? Her name is Miss Fluff. I hope that won't be an issue in our relationship."

"Herbert, we have no relationship."

"Okay, maybe not now, but I think we could make this work if you would give it a chance."

I muscled my way through the herd of women at the cookie table and blindly grabbed a handful of cookies. Herbert was hanging a short distance away, keeping watch in case I couldn't resist his magnetic pull and rushed back to him.

I was pretty sure God was pissed off at me. How else could you explain Herbert Slovinski? What I lacked in faith I made up for in fear of God's wrath. It wasn't enough to make me go to church on a regular basis, but it gave me an inner grimace from time to time.

---

I parked at the curb in front of my parents' house and Grandma unsnapped her seat belt.

"That was a decent viewing," Grandma said. "Larry looked better than he has in a long time. Too bad Bruno didn't show. I was ready in case you needed backup."

"It was a long shot."

"Are you coming in? The hockey game might still be on."

"I'm going to head back to my apartment. I have some computer work to do."

I watched Grandma disappear inside the house, and I took off for Merrymaster Street. Twenty minutes later I was parked across the street from Jug's house. His lights were off. A single porch light was lit. The garage door was closed. No car in the driveway. Headlights flashed a block away. A car was coming toward me. I ducked down and the car went past me and turned into Jug's driveway. Two people got out and walked to the front door. Minutes later, they were in the house and the house lights went on. Mr. and Mrs. Jug were home. His black Volvo sedan was also home for the night.

Jug had been driving, so obviously his supposed senility didn't affect his ability to operate a luxury vehicle. I hung around for ten more minutes and chugged off to my apartment.

# CHAPTER FOUR

Lula was standing on the sidewalk in front of her apartment house when I pulled to the curb. The sky was getting light, but the sun wasn't up yet. She was wearing a silver bedazzled sweatshirt, a black spandex skirt, and magenta satin pumps with a five-inch stiletto heel. The platinum-blond wig from her Marilyn Monroe collection was crooked on her head. She got into the car, and I took a closer look.

"One of your false eyelashes is missing," I said to her.

"Are you sure?"

"Yes."

She checked herself out in the visor mirror and peeled the remaining eyelash off.

"Good thing I'm a natural beauty," Lula said, "or else I'd be feeling insecure without a boost in the eyelash department."

"Yeah. Lucky you."

"You got coffee?"

"In the console cupholder. The extra-big one is yours. Doughnuts are in the box on the back seat."

"Soon as I get some coffee in me, I'm gonna be ready to kick ass. I got my running shoes on in case we gotta chase down the old crazy guy."

"I can see that. Wouldn't want you to try to run in sneakers."

"Hell no. I can't get no push-off in sneakers."

"And you're wearing a rad hoodie."

"I figured it would be chilly until the sun gets up, so I'd need something warm."

"It's got a lot of sparkle."

"That's the good part. All the sequins work as insulators when it's dark and then when the sun comes up the heat bounces off me. Except when I first grabbed it, I thought it might not be appropriate for an early morning takedown on account of the glamour level. What do you think?"

"I think when the sun hits those sequins anyone standing next to you is going to go blind."

"I never thought of that, but that's another good thing about this hoodie," Lula said. "When I got this hoodie on, I'm like a stun grenade. I'm a walking flash-bang. I'm a nonlethal weapon." She grabbed the white pastry box off the back seat and chose a chocolate-covered cream-filled doughnut. "You got a good selection of doughnuts in this box. There's no loser doughnuts here."

I stopped for a light and picked out a doughnut with pink frosting and colorful sprinkles.

"I drove past Jug's house last night," I said to Lula. "I saw him come home and park in the driveway. If the black Volvo is still there, we can be pretty sure Jug is inside the house."

"Okay. Then what? We gonna go in and get him out of bed like gangbusters? That wouldn't be my first choice. I got my running shoes on, not my door-bashing-down shoes."

I turned into Jug's neighborhood and parked across the street from 21 Merrymaster. "It's not my first choice either," I said. "I'd like to approach him when he leaves his house and walks to his car."

"You got that worked out?"

"Yes. When we see activity in the house I'll move across the street and stand by the SUV that's parked next door. When I confront Jug, you can drive my car into the driveway and block his exit."

"That's a good plan," Lula said. "I've seen people do that on television shows and it always works. Of course, last time we tried it you got your car all smashed up, but that might have been one of those freak occurrences."

Curtains were drawn in the Jugs' upstairs windows. At seven thirty a slim bar of light flashed on between the curtains.

"Showtime," Lula said.

Fifteen minutes later lights went on in the Jugs' kitchen. I left my Chevy Trailblazer and nonchalantly walked over and stood by the neighbor's SUV. Jug's front door opened and a fat Chihuahua waddled out onto the porch. The door closed and the Chihuahua made its way down the steps to the lawn. It wandered around in circles, hunched over, and pooped. It saw me standing by the SUV and moseyed over.

As they say, better to be lucky than good. Jug was going to come out to get his dog and I would bring the dog over to him. Done and done.

"Hey," I crooned to the dog. "Aren't you a cutie. One of my fiancés has a dog. He's a lot bigger than you. His name is Bob."

I crouched down and let him sniff my hand. "You're a friendly little guy." I scratched him behind his ear, and he leaned into it. If he was a cat, he'd have been purring. I picked him up and kept doing the ear massage thing.

After a couple minutes the front door opened, and Jug stepped out onto the porch. He was wearing pajamas, and he had a piece of toast in his hand. He looked side to side, not seeing the dog.

"Mr. Big," he called out. "Big!"

"Is that your name?" I asked the Chihuahua.

The dog didn't say anything. It was concentrating on the ear scratches. I moved out from behind the van and walked toward Jug. Mr. Big was happily cuddled up in my arms, snuggled against my chest.

"Hi!" I said to Jug. "Is this your puppy? He wandered over to me."

"He doesn't usually leave the yard," Jug said, "but he's always had a weakness for pretty girls."

I'd have been more flattered if this hadn't been said to me by some old mob guy with a glob of oatmeal on his pajama top.

"You're Bruno Jug," I said.

"Yeah, and who are you?"

I put Mr. Big down on the ground, reached into my pocket, and pulled out cuffs. I clapped one on Jug's wrist, and Lula drove my Trailblazer into his driveway.

"Stephanie Plum," I said. "Apologies for the cuffs, but it's protocol. I work for Vincent Plum Bail Bonds, and you missed your court date. Lula and I will be happy to take you into town to get you rescheduled."

"What the fuck," he said. "I'm in my pajamas."

Lula was out of the SUV and standing next to me.

"I can get a robe or a coat from your wife," Lula said.

"What about my breakfast," he said. "I'm not done."

"This won't take long," I told him.

"My oatmeal will get cold. Tell Vinnie I'll reschedule when I'm ready to reschedule."

"I need to bring you in now," I said.

"Take a hike," he said, and he turned toward the house.

I grabbed his pajama top and yanked him back, and two buttons popped off. Jug stared down at the damaged top for a beat, looked at the bracelet on his wrist, and shifted his full attention to me.

"Uh-oh," Lula said. "He got crazy eyes."

I took a giant step back. "Sorry about the pajamas."

Jug unclenched his teeth and glared at Mr. Big. "*Kill!*"

Mr. Big lunged at me and sank his Chihuahua teeth into my leg just above the ankle.

I instinctively kicked my leg out. Mr. Big lost his grip, flew through the air, and bounced once on the lawn about fifteen feet away. He jumped to his feet and came at me again. This time he snagged the bottom of my jeans.

Mrs. Jug popped out of the house. "What's going on?"

"Trespassers," Jug said. "Get my gun."

Mrs. Jug turned on her heel and disappeared back into the house.

"Guns aren't necessary," I said, using my most trust-inspiring, soothing voice. "This is a simple matter of rescheduling."

"You ruined my breakfast and favorite pajamas," Jug said, eyes narrowed, jaw muscles bulging, precisely enunciating each word.

"It's impressive how you can talk with your teeth gnashing together like that," Lula said to Jug. "And you might not know, but your face is real red. You might feel better if you take a blood pressure pill."

"I'll feel better when I shove my foot up your pussy," Jug said, launching himself at Lula, his hands reaching for her neck.

Lula stumbled back and swung her giant tote bag at him, catching him square in the face, knocking him off his feet.

"What the hell!" Lula said. "What the freaking hell!"

Jug was spread-eagle on the ground, stunned. His nose was spurting blood, his fingers were twitching, his eyes were unfocused.

"He's gonna be real unhappy when he comes to and sees all that blood soaked into his favorite jammies," Lula said.

Mrs. Jug ran out of the house onto the porch, gun in hand, and gaped at Jug on the ground. "You killed him," she shrieked, squeezing off a bunch of rounds in our direction. "You killed my Juggy!"

Time stood still for a beat and then adrenaline took charge, and we all went into save-yourself mode. Big ripped off a piece of my jeans and ran into the house with it, and Lula and I jumped into the Trailblazer and hauled ass out of the driveway, out of the neighborhood. I checked my rearview mirror and saw that my back window was shattered. A couple bullets had pinged off my side mirror before I got out of range, but Lula and I were okay.

"You don't think we really killed him, do you?" Lula asked.

"No," I said. "He was just stunned."

"He shouldn't have threatened my pussy like that. You know how sensitive I am to that sort of thing. I don't tolerate violence against my pussy."

"Or any other body part," I said.

"Damn skippy. Good thing the Mrs. is such a bad shot. There was bullets going everywhere. It's because she was all excited and rushing things in the beginning. She settled in once we were in the car. Still, even then she only took out the rear window and a side mirror, and it could have been by accident." Lula looked down at my torn jeans. "That vicious dog took a bite out of you. You got some blood dripping off your ankle."

"I thought he liked me," I said.

"Yeah, but he was a trained killer. He was no doubt trained to ignore personal emotions when it comes to obeying a command. Now what are we doing? Are you going to the ER to get a rabies shot?"

"No. I'm going back to the office to get a Band-Aid."

---

Connie was at her desk when we walked into the office. "Did you get Jug?" she asked.

"Almost," Lula said. "Stephanie got attacked by his killer dog, and then his wife shot at us a bunch of times."

"What kind of dog does he have?" Connie asked.

"Chihuahua," Lula said. "Dog would rip your heart out. Of course, you couldn't be more than two feet tall. Or maybe if you were laying on the ground."

I went to the bathroom, washed the blood off my leg, and put a couple giant Band-Aids over the tooth marks. I stopped at the coffee machine and settled into one of the uncomfortable chairs in front of Connie's desk.

"What's new?" I asked Connie.

"I've been here for thirty-seven minutes, and I've taken three phone calls for you. All from someone named Herbert Slovinski. He said you were expecting him to call."

"If he calls again tell him I died."

"Cause of death?" Connie asked.

"Constipation."

The front door to the bail bonds office opened and Morelli

walked in. All conversation stopped and all eyes were on Morelli. Most of the plainclothes guys wore suits and dress shirts. Morelli wore jeans, boots, and a dress shirt or sweater with sleeves rolled. When Morelli put on a suit he looked like a casino pit boss.

He smiled and nodded at Lula and Connie. He crooked his finger at me in a *come here* gesture. I followed him outside and we stood looking at my SUV.

"Someone took out your window and your side mirror," Morelli said.

"Mrs. Jug."

"She had a reason?"

"She thought I killed Mr. Jug."

"And?" he asked.

"I didn't."

"Good to know. Exactly how close did you come to killing him?"

"I ripped two buttons off his pajama top."

"That's serious stuff," Morelli said.

"Yeah. He turned his dog loose on me."

Morelli looked down at the shredded cuff on my jeans. "Big dog?"

"Chihuahua. And then Lula hit Jug in the face with her tote bag and sort of knocked him out a little."

"She knocked him out with her tote bag?"

"She was carrying a Glock, a stun gun, and a can of hair spray. The bag had some weight to it."

"Okay. What happened next?"

"Mrs. Jug showed up with a gun, she saw 'Juggy' lying on the ground and thought we killed him, so she started shooting at us. That's when we left."

"I'm assuming you left without Jug."

"You assume right. It was one of those 'save your own ass before all else' situations. How did you know about my car?"

"I'm on my way to a blood and guts display a couple blocks from here. Domestic dispute gone very bad. Saw your car and thought I should stop to see if you were bleeding."

I pulled my torn pants leg up so he could see the Band-Aids. "I did my own triage."

Morelli's phone buzzed, and he looked at the display. "I have to go. Try to stay safe. Send Jug some replacement pajamas and tell him to get in touch with you when he's ready to reschedule. And stay away from his wife."

I waved Morelli off and looked down at my belly. No baby bump. Too soon. Not too soon to be more careful . . . just in case. It was a sobering thought that there might be more at stake than my own life.

"Well?" Lula asked when I returned to the office.

"Morelli said I should send Jug some replacement pajamas."

"That's not a bad idea," Lula said. "A nice gesture like that is always appreciated. It could go a long way in mending fences."

"I don't want to mend a fence," I said. "I want to do my job."

"Okay, but it could confuse him into thinking we're friendly and he'd drop his guard," Lula said. "And then it would be easier to sneak up on him."

"She has a point," Connie said.

"I'll even go get them," Lula said. "I'm good at any kind of shopping, and I figure this could qualify for a petty cash expenditure. I could go get something now."

"It's early," I said. "The shopping center isn't open yet."

"We don't need a shopping center," Lula said. "We got Walmart. Walmart's got everything and it's right up the street on Nottingham. Walmart's always open when you need it."

"If you're going to Walmart, I need snack mix for the office and a curling iron," Connie said.

"We can take my car since your car is in need of some repair," Lula said.

Lula drives a classic red Firebird that she keeps in pristine condition. It has a faux-leopard cover on the steering wheel and a sound system that gives me heart arrythmia when it's cranked up to full volume.

---

It was almost ten o'clock when we pushed our cart out of Walmart. We had a year's worth of snack mix for the office plus at least six months of peanut-butter-filled pretzel rolls, Connie's curling iron, a huge jug of sea-salted cashews, a frozen sheet cake with yellow roses, a family-size variety pack of meat sticks in case we needed emergency protein, fluffy pink slippers for Lula, a small lamp for my nightstand, a new dish drain for Lula, Jug's jammies, and a gift bag for the jammies.

"We did good on the jammies," Lula said, loading everything in her trunk. "They're quality jammies and they were on sale. Jug's gonna look good in these jammies, and the buttons looked real secure, like they wouldn't pop off if someone snatched him from behind. You just have to write a nice little note to go with them."

I should never have agreed to buy pajamas for Jug. His dog bit me, and his wife shot at me, and I'd just bought the man pajamas. Stupid, stupid, stupid. And wrong. Only good thing that came out of it was my new lamp. Tomorrow I would have a nightstand to put it on and my bedroom would be cozy. If I used a forty-watt bulb I wouldn't be able to see that the room needed painting.

Lula turned off Nottingham, followed Hamilton to the office, and parked behind my Trailblazer. "What the heck," she said, staring at the new rear window on the SUV. "Looks like the window fairy's been here."

I unclipped my seat belt and got out of the Firebird. "Maybe Connie got it fixed."

My phone rang with an unknown number.

"Hi!" the caller said. "Are you okay? Connie said you were dead, but I knew she was joking. She's a big joker, right? I can take a joke. It's one of my good points. I have a lot of good points. Are you back at the office? Did you see your car? I saw the broken window, so I had it fixed. I called one of those mobile glass people and they came right out. I didn't know what to do about the side mirror. I can take your car to an auto body shop if you want."

"No! Thank you for the window. That wasn't necessary, but it was thoughtful. Send me the bill and I'll get a check out to you."

"No way," Herbert said. "Heck, when I'm in a relationship it's all the way."

"We aren't in a relationship. I'm engaged. I'm not interested in another relationship."

"I sent you flowers in case you really were constipated. It's always nice to get flowers when you're constipated, right? I have to go now because I'm at work, but I'll call you later when I get a break."

I yelled "No!" into the phone, but he had already disconnected.

Lula had the carton of pretzel rolls in one hand, and she was holding the sheet cake with the other hand. "This cake is starting to defrost," she said. "We should eat it. Good thing we got those meat sticks and peanut butter pretzels so we can have a balanced diet."

# CHAPTER FIVE

Lula parked her Firebird in front of Jug Produce and cut the engine. I was sitting next to her with the gift bag on my lap and my seat belt still cinched.

"I feel sick," I said to Lula. "I can't do this."

"Uh-oh, that's a sign that you're preggers. You got morning sickness."

I thought it was a sign that I had to stop eating cake and washing it down with meat sticks and peanut butter pretzels.

"I shouldn't have eaten that big yellow rose on the cake," I said.

"You'll feel better once you get moving," Lula said. "You got a mission. You got cuffs in your pocket, right?"

"Yeah."

"And your stun gun in your other pocket?"

"Yeah."

"Then you're all set. And I'll be right behind you in case things get ugly."

"Things aren't going to get ugly. This is going to be very civil. And I want you to stay here. I don't want this to look like a takedown."

"Okay, I'm on it," Lula said. "You want me to keep the motor running in case you need to make a fast getaway?"

"No. I won't need a fast getaway. I'm not delivering a bomb. I'm delivering a gift bag."

I left the Firebird and walked into the building. The lobby was small and dated. The woman at the desk reminded me of Connie. I would bet money that she had a can of hair spray and a semiautomatic in her bottom drawer.

"I have a gift for Mr. Jug," I said to the woman.

"You can leave it here and I'll make sure he gets it," she said.

"I'd prefer to deliver it in person."

"He's a very busy man," she said. "Is he expecting you?"

"No, but I'm sure he'll want to see me. I accidentally ripped his pajama top this morning, and I wanted to apologize." I held the bag up. "I bought him some new pajamas."

"There's a story here," she said. "Name?"

"Stephanie Plum."

Her eyebrows raised ever so slightly. "You want to let me see what's in the bag?"

I gave her the bag. "It isn't a bomb."

"Just checking," she said, returning the bag to me. "Hey, Lou," she yelled. "Stephanie Plum is here to see Mr. Jug."

There were footsteps in the hall behind her and a very large man walked into the lobby. He was in his fifties with a fat roll stretching the fabric of his three-button knit shirt, hanging over the waist on his dress slacks. He was balding, and he had a face like a bulldog.

"Mr. Jug is a busy man," Lou said.

"She's got a present for him," the woman said. "Pajamas."

"You can give them to me," Lou said. "I'll make sure he gets them."

"I'd rather give them to him myself," I said. "It's personal."

Lou nodded at the desk woman, she made a phone call and nodded back at Lou.

"He's gonna see you," Lou said to me, "but he's busy so make it quick."

I followed Lou up a flight of stairs and down a short hall. Jug's office door was open, and Jug was at his desk. Three men were in the office with him. One was standing next to Jug and the other two were seated on a large leather couch.

"This is Stephanie Plum," Lou said to Jug. "She has a present for you."

"I know who she is," Jug said.

I handed him the gift bag. "Wear them in good health."

Jug pulled the pajamas out of the bag and gave a bark of laughter. "Hah! Good one. But I still might kill you."

I gave him my card. "Let me know when you want to reschedule your court date. I'll give you a ride to the courthouse. If you kill me, you'll have to drive yourself."

"Hah! Another good one." He turned to Lou. "Give her one of those fruit baskets we just got in. The one with the pears."

"Come on, cutie," Lou said to me. "Visit's over. Mr. Jug is a busy man."

"Hah! Busy man," Jug said.

I followed Lou down the stairs, he gave me a fruit basket, and I left the building.

"What's with the fruit basket?" Lula asked when I buckled myself in.

"Jug gave it to me. It has pears."

"Pears are good. Personally, I only eat them if they're covered in chocolate or salted caramel. Still, he must have liked his pajamas if he gave you pears." She pulled away from the curb and made a U-turn. "I guess he didn't want to re-up today?"

"He's a busy man."

"Yeah, he's got a lot of irons in the fire what with the human smuggling and money laundering and selling protection, not to mention selling fruit. Plus, he might not have all his marbles. That could slow you down."

Connie called and I put her on speakerphone.

"Are you returning to the office any time soon?" she asked. "I have a new FTA and Robin Hoodie is back in the news."

"What did he do this time?" I asked.

"He stole a food truck and drove it to the big homeless encampment by the river. By the time the police arrived, he was long gone, and everyone was stuffed full of pulled pork sliders."

"You gotta give Robin Hoodie credit," Lula said. "He's got some good ideas about helping the homeless."

"The owner of the food truck didn't think it was a good idea," Connie said.

"That's the unfortunate downside to Robin Hoodie's good deeds," Lula said. "It's not like he's robbing Prince John and the sheriff of Nottingham. Those guys deserved to get robbed. They were overtaxing the peasants. And Prince John didn't even need more money. He owned the castle free and clear. He didn't have a mortgage or anything."

"We'll drive by the Fleck house," I said to Connie. "Eugene was next up on my to-do list anyway."

---

The white Toyota Corolla was parked in the Flecks' driveway. Lula pulled in behind it, and we walked to the front door and rang the bell.

Mrs. Fleck answered. "Oh dear," she said. "I'm afraid Eugene isn't home."

"Do you know where he is?" I asked.

"I don't know exactly, but I imagine he's with Kevin. Kevin picked him up this morning. Kevin is Eugene's best friend. They've been friends since grade school. They're both a little geeky. They're both gamers."

"Where does Kevin live?"

"He has an apartment over his parents' garage. Martino Auto Body and Dog Wash. It's on Liberty Street."

"I know where that is," Lula said. "It's next to Jenny Lou's Tattoos. I was going to get a tattoo there once, but in the end, I decided my skin was perfect as is without injecting ink into it."

"What kind of car does Kevin drive?" I asked Mrs. Fleck.

"Goodness, I don't know," Mrs. Fleck said. "It's always something different."

"Does Eugene have a car?"

"No," she said. "He has his driver's license, but he never had any interest in owning a car. He rides his bicycle everywhere. He'll probably be home for dinner if you want to try to talk to him then. We're having tacos tonight. Taco Tuesday. Eugene never misses tacos."

Lula and I got back into the Firebird, and Lula drove to Martino Auto Body. The body shop consisted of four bays. A couple dented cars were parked in front of the bays. Another car was on a lift in one of the bays. There was a single door on the far side of the building. There were windows above the bays.

Lula parked on a side street, and we went to the door on the end of the building. No doorbell. No window in the door.

"What do you think?" Lula asked me.

"I think this has to be it." I knocked on the door. No answer. I pounded on the door. No answer.

"They could be inside, sleeping off the pork slider party," Lula said.

"Or they could be out and about following the Amazon truck around, collecting goodies for the underprivileged."

"You want me to open this door?"

"Yes," I said. "Do it."

Lula put her hand on the doorknob and turned it. "This is disappointing," she said. "The door isn't locked. Takes all the fun out of doing a B & E."

We took the stairs leading up to the second floor. There was a small landing and another door. This door was locked.

I knocked a couple times. I called out to Kevin. No answer.

"Okay," Lula said. "Stand back."

She took a hammer and a screwdriver out of her tote bag and bumped the lock. I walked in and shouted, "Bond enforcement," just in case someone was there, or, more important, we were caught on a security camera.

We were standing in one large room with a single door at the far end, which I assumed led to the bathroom. There was a studio-apartment-size kitchen tacked onto the back wall. Sink, refrigerator, freezer, four-burner stove, microwave, coffee maker. Overhead cabinets. A small square table with four chairs was positioned in the kitchen area. There was a cereal bowl and a coffee mug in the sink. A box of Cheerios was on the counter. A couple giant beanbag chairs on the floor. Huge flat-screen TV. A brown leather couch that had seen better days. A bed had been pushed up

---

I drove the short distance to my parents' house and carted the fruit basket into the kitchen.

"What's the occasion?" Grandma asked. "Is someone sick? Did someone die?"

"I offered to take Jug to get rescheduled and he declined, but he gave me this fruit basket."

"It's a beauty of a fruit basket," Grandma said. "Except it looks like it's got a lot of pears."

"What's wrong with pears?"

"They aren't an everyday fruit. An apple a day keeps the doctor away, but you never hear a rhyme like that about pears. And I don't have a recipe for a pear pie."

My mom came over and examined the fruit basket. "You have all kinds of good things in here," she said. "Kiwi fruit, apricots, little oranges, dates, there's an avocado and a block of cheese."

"Do you want the basket?" I asked her. "I can't eat all this stuff."

"I guess I could take a couple of the little oranges and the cheese," she said.

"We were just getting lunch together," Grandma said. "We have leftover meatloaf if you want a sandwich. Or there's liverwurst and Swiss cheese."

"A meatloaf sandwich sounds perfect."

Grandma put an extra place setting on the kitchen table and sat down. "Help yourself. We got lots of meatloaf. I'm feeling like liverwurst today."

My mom came to the table and decided to have meatloaf. "I saw on the news that Eugene Fleck was at work feeding the homeless again."

"They don't know for sure that it was Eugene Fleck," Grandma said. "He got arrested on suspicion of burglary for that delivery truck heist, but I heard from Angie Krisenski, who heard from her daughter who does police dispatch, that it's not an open-and-shut case. *Robin Hoodie* fed the homeless today." Grandma assembled her sandwich. "I checked just before lunch and there's no video up yet. It's going to be hard to top the UPS truck, but this should still be good."

I tucked into my sandwich. "Are you talking about local news?"

Grandma looked at me like I had sprouted two heads. "I'm talking about YouTube. Haven't you been following Robin Hoodie? Half the world is following him. Even your father is following him. Last week he broke into the Nike store at the mall and then he live-streamed delivery of about forty boxes of Nikes to a bunch of homeless drug addicts camped out on a sidewalk somewhere. I almost started bawling watching those addicts trying shoes on. I was happy they got shoes, but it was a horrible sight to see. One of them still had a needle stuck in his leg. I had to turn it off and watch BTS videos to get a grip on myself."

I had a chunk of meatloaf sitting halfway down my throat, not going anywhere, thanks to the mental visual of an addict with a needle stuck in his leg.

"It was an unusual video," Grandma said. "Usually, Robin Hoodie's videos are more fun, with people opening packages and being happy, like they're at a party."

My next mental flash was of Kevin's loft apartment with the GoPro cameras and stash of cardboard boxes.

"Do you get to see Robin Hoodie in these videos?" I asked Grandma.

"Once in a while you get to see a glimpse of him, but you can't really see him because he's wearing a hoodie, and he always has a mask on under the hoodie."

So when Eugene was arrested and had his picture printed in the paper and flashed across the television screen on evening news shows, he became the face for Robin Hoodie, I thought.

I finished my sandwich and skipped dessert for obvious reasons. After a morning of full-on doughnuts and Walmart cake, I was afraid I'd go into a diabetic coma if I had more sugar. I gave my mom the little oranges and the block of cheese and carried the fruit basket back to my car. I'd planned to stake out the Fleck house after lunch, but I went to my apartment instead.

A glass vase holding a massive amount of cut flowers was in front of my door. A small pink envelope was tucked into the flowers. I opened the envelope and read the message.

*Hope you aren't constipated anymore. Love, Herbert.*

I unlocked my door and shoved it open. I wrapped one arm around the flowers and tightened my grip on the fruit basket in the other arm. I staggered in and put the flowers and the fruit basket on my kitchen counter. I sliced off a small chunk of pear and dropped it into Rex's food bowl. Rex rushed out of his soup can, looked like he'd won the lottery when he spied the piece of pear, stuffed it into his cheek, and scurried back into his can. God bless Rex. I'd finally found a creature who appreciated free fruit.

I brought my messenger bag into the dining room, sat at the table, and opened my laptop. I went to YouTube and searched for Robin Hoodie. Bam. There he was. I scrolled down and pulled up the UPS truck video. It started with an aerial view of the homeless camp. It cut away from the aerial and picked up the truck approaching a collection of tents. Robin Hoodie got out from behind the wheel, opened the back door to the truck, and started pitching boxes out. Almost instantly the truck was surrounded by the homeless. They were ripping the boxes open and pulling out their contents. Cheers went up when someone got an iPad. More cheers for a North Face winter jacket. I had to admit, it was mesmerizing. I couldn't stop watching. I looked at a couple more Robin Hoodie videos after the UPS truck. Robin Hoodie always remained a shadowy figure. He never showed his face. He was always alone, but clearly he had a partner. Maybe he had a whole crew. He was wearing a GoPro, but there were times when there was a second camera angle. And someone was flying a drone. In one of the videos, gloved hands were opening packages that I presumed had been swiped from people's porches. They were opened on a folding table that looked a lot like the ones in Kevin's apartment. They were given close-ups and then repackaged in large boxes and dropped off at soup kitchen locations and small encampments. There was a whole box of kids' toys that went to a family shelter. No one ever spoke in the videos but sometimes there was music.

Wow. I couldn't think beyond that one word. Wow. I pushed back in my chair and took a moment to step away from the videos. It was almost impossible not to love Robin Hoodie. All those happy homeless people. All those desperate substance abusers. All those kids with new sneakers and toys. Then there were all those shadowy images of someone with Eugene's build pitching boxes out to people. And there were all those photos I took of video equipment, empty cardboard boxes, drones, and GoPros in Kevin's loft. Not to mention Eugene's fingerprints on the UPS truck. Hard to believe that Eugene wasn't Robin Hoodie. Not impossible, but difficult not to believe.

I called Connie. "Do you know about Robin Hoodie?" I asked her. "Have you seen the videos?"

"There are videos?"

"YouTube."

"I don't watch a lot of YouTube," Connie said. "Only when I can't figure something out. Like, how do I shut my iPhone off."

"Let me talk to Lula."

"Hey," Lula said. "What's up?"

"Robin Hoodie. Have you seen his videos on YouTube?"

"No. I watch the music videos and I like Jeff Goldblum and the kid who sells sneakers."

"Take a look at Robin Hoodie on YouTube and call me back."

Twenty minutes later I got the phone call.

"Holy crap," Lula said.

"Do you remember when I had to bring in that ninety-three-year-old woman who was in assisted living? Everyone hated me."

"Yeah, that was ugly. The other residents came after you with their canes and scooters," Lula said.

"This could be worse."

"I see what you're saying," Lula said. "This Robin Hoodie guy is a hero. He's got his own YouTube channel. He's a celebrity. Even people who think what he's doing is wrong are still gonna be pissed off because he's good watching and you're gonna end all that. And the people who are in favor of the homeless and orphans and such are gonna look at you like you're the sheriff of Nottingham carting the savior of the poor and downtrodden, Robin Hood, off to jail in chains. You'll be lucky if you don't get your apartment firebombed again."

"Do you think Eugene is Robin Hoodie?"

"I guess it's possible," Lula said, "but it would be disappointing. I already got a fantasy going, and my fantasy Robin don't look like Eugene."

"Eugene's mom expects him to be home for dinner, so I thought it would be a good time for us to make a capture."

"I guess that would be okay," Lula said. "I don't have any dinner plans for tonight."

"Mrs. Fleck said they always eat at six o'clock."

"Are you going to try to snag him going in or going out?"

"I thought I'd go in while they're eating. He doesn't seem like the sort of person who would make a scene in front of his parents. I'll meet you at the office at five thirty."

I hung up and called Morelli. "What do you think of Robin Hoodie?" I asked him.

"Not much, but my mom and grandma love him."

"Have you seen his videos?"

"A couple."

"Do you think Eugene Fleck is Robin Hoodie?"

"I think it's possible. The body type is similar. His prints were found on the truck."

"Robin Hoodie always wore gloves in the videos I watched. I got the impression he was careful not to leave incriminating evidence."

"He also had help. There was a second cameraman," Morelli said. "Why are you interested in Eugene? Are you a Robin Hoodie fan?"

"Eugene is FTA. I need to get him rescheduled."

"And?"

"I'm new to Robin Hoodie, and I don't get it. What sort of person would do this? Why would someone do this and risk jail by putting out videos?"

"Money," Morelli said. "Robin Hoodie is worth millions. He's been building his channel for a little over a year. He went global with the UPS truck and moved into the big time. He gets paid for the number of hits on his channel, and he has advertisers."

"I don't see any indication that Eugene has money. He's living with his parents and riding around on a bicycle."

"Then maybe he does it for the rush. He could be a thrill junkie. Or he could do it for the fame. Or he could really believe in the cause."

"What do you think?"

"I don't think anything. It's not my case. No blood involved. I don't know all the details."

"Yes, but it's fascinating. Aren't you fascinated?"

"I'm going to be fascinated tonight when I'm watching the Rangers beat Boston. That's fascinating. Are you going to be watching with me?"

"Maybe. It depends on how it goes with Eugene."

There was a beat of silence. "Are you getting cold feet on the marriage thing?"

"No! Definitely not. I've just got a lot going on. And I've got a cash flow issue. I need to get Bruno Jug and Eugene."

"Honey, you've always got a cash flow issue. That never stopped you from catching a Rangers game or spending the night with me."

"You're right. I expect to be done with Eugene by the time the Rangers get on the ice, and Jug can wait."

"That's good, because I have something special for you."

People were yelling in the background.

"I have to go," Morelli said. "I'm in the middle of something here."

He disconnected and I broke out in a cold sweat over the something special. What if it was an engagement ring? What would I do? I looked down at my stomach. "Anybody home in there?" I asked. No one answered, and the cold sweat morphed into a hot flash. Hard to tell if it was from panic or hormones. Okay, calm down, I told myself. Breathe. You can take the pregnancy test on Friday. You just have to make it to Friday. At least Ranger was still out of town, so I had that going for me.

A text message buzzed on my iPhone. It was from Ranger. *Wrapping up business here. Be home tomorrow.*

Crap!

# CHAPTER SIX

Lula was standing on the sidewalk in front of the office when I pulled to the curb. The platinum wig was on straight and even from a distance I could see that she was wearing two eyelashes.

"Connie left early," Lula said, sliding in next to me. "She said not to forget about the new FTA."

"I haven't looked at it yet. It's in my bag. Pull it out and read it to me."

Lula found the file and flipped it open. "Zoran something. I can't pronounce his last name."

I joined the traffic on Hamilton and headed for the Fleck house on Elm Street. "Spell it."

"D-j-o-r-d-j-e-v-i-c."

"Okay, we'll call him Zoran."

"He's Caucasian," Lula said, "five foot ten, forty-six years old, brown hair, brown eyes, divorced. Owns a laundromat. And he's a vampire."

"That's different," I said. "We don't get a lot of vampires."

"Maybe never," Lula said. "We had a couple werewolves, but I can't remember no vampires."

"What's the crime?"

"According to the police report, he's accused of biting a woman in the neck and trying to drink her blood. There's a picture here of her neck with fang marks in it."

"Is there a picture of him?"

"Mug shot," Lula said. "He looks angry. Got a lot of hair. Description said brown but it looks black and shot with gray in the picture."

"Any priors?"

"Bunch of parking tickets."

I drove down Elm Street and idled in front of the Fleck house. The white Corolla was parked in the driveway and a silver Nissan Sentra with a bashed-in right fender was parked at the curb. I pulled in behind the Sentra and cut the engine.

"Do you know what would be good?" Lula said. "We should have body cams. GoPros or something. Then we could put this on YouTube and get rich and famous for taking down Robin Hoodie."

"That would be a nightmare. Remember how you said I'll be lucky if I don't get my apartment firebombed again?"

"Oh yeah. I forgot that part. Maybe I can get a selfie with him just for my own personal remembrance. It could be a historic moment."

"No selfies. No request for an autograph. No sneaking a souvenir into your tote bag. We aren't arresting Robin Hoodie. We're arresting Eugene Fleck."

"But he might be Robin Hoodie," Lula said.

"Forget Robin Hoodie. Our job is simple here. Eugene is

in violation of his bond, and we're bringing him back into the system."

"Boy, you aren't any fun now that you're pregnant. You got a lot of rules."

"We don't know if I'm pregnant."

"Remember how you said you would marry the baby daddy? Suppose you have twins and they each have a different daddy. It could happen, right? What would you do?"

"I'm pretty sure that only happens with rabbits, but if it did happen, I guess I'd be a single mom with twins," I said.

"I'd be their auntie," Lula said.

That kind of choked me up. "Yes," I said. "You would be their auntie."

"Okay, now that we got that settled, let's go ruin the Flecks' dinnertime."

I got out of the Trailblazer and went to the sidewalk. "It's our job."

"Damn straight it is," Lula said, joining me. "Are you going to ruin their dinner big-time with cuffs and everything or are you gonna try to be classy?"

"I'm aiming for classy."

"I got classy in fucking spades."

I rang the doorbell and Mrs. Fleck answered it.

"Stephanie and Lula," she said. "What a nice surprise. We were just sitting down to dinner. It's Taco Tuesday. Would you like to join us? I always make extra."

"Hell yeah," Lula said. "I love tacos."

"Actually, we're here to reschedule Eugene," I said.

"Of course," Mrs. Fleck said. "He's at the table. His friend Kevin is here as well. Take a seat and I'll add two more place settings."

Mrs. Fleck went to get plates and I grabbed Lula by the back of her shirt.

"We didn't come here for dinner," I said. "We came to arrest Eugene."

"Yeah, but he hasn't eaten his dinner yet. You said we were gonna be classy and seems to me it would be rude not to let everyone eat dinner before you drag Eugene's skinny ass out of here. Especially after Mrs. F. went to so much trouble. She's got sour cream and shredded cheese and lettuce and hot sauce and all kinds of stuff on the table. I can see it from here."

I cut my eyes to the dining room. Everyone was watching us. Eugene did a little wave.

"That must be the Mr. at the head of the table," Lula said. "He looks like he could eat a lot of tacos."

Go with it, I told myself. Take a seat and wait for the moment. These are nice people. No reason to cause any more stress than is necessary.

I went to the table and sat in the seat next to Eugene. "I'm sure you know why we're here," I said to him.

"Not a problem," he said. "I was going to get in touch with you anyway. I got swept away by the Merry Men. They were so happy to see me that I didn't have the heart to tell them I wasn't Robin."

"Are you sure you aren't Robin?" Lula asked from across the table. "I've been watching Robin on YouTube, and you look like you could be Robin." She turned to Kevin, sitting next to her. "You look like you could be Robin, too. Put a hood on you and be hard to tell the two of you apart. Without the hood it's easier on account of you have all that curly red hair. I've got a wig with hair just like yours."

Kevin rolled his eyes up, as if he could see his hair. "This is mine," he said.

Kevin's build was slim. His skin was pale and freckled. His voice was quiet, barely above a whisper. He looked like a red-haired ghost sitting next to Lula.

Mrs. Fleck returned with plates and silverware. "Everyone help yourselves. There's more in the kitchen."

Lula filled her taco shell and did a taste test. "This is real good chicken," Lula said to Mrs. Fleck. "I bet you marinated it to get it this tasty."

"I have a secret recipe," Mrs. Fleck said. "I have a special sauce for my beef tacos too."

"I'm impressed that you take your tacos seriously," Lula said. "That's an admirable quality."

"Thank you," Mrs. Fleck said. "It's nice to have young ladies at the table. Eugene has never had a girl visit him before this."

"Jeez, Mom," Eugene said. "That's embarrassing. And anyway, they came to arrest me. They're from the bail bonds agency. You're going to have to bail me out again."

"You should have remembered your court date," Eugene's father said. "This is going to cost us more money. And it's irresponsible."

"I had reasons," Eugene said.

"How does this rescheduling work?" Mrs. Fleck asked. "Is it done online? Do we sign more papers and give you a check?"

"I have to go to the police station with them," Eugene said. "It's after court hours, so I'll have to spend the night in jail, and then in the morning I'll go before a judge, and he'll give me a new trial date and set a bail bond amount."

"That's terrible," Mrs. Fleck said, her voice raised, clearly upset. "I had no idea. You didn't have to stay in jail last time."

"Court was in session when he was brought in last time," I said. "We were able to write an immediate bail bond."

"This is terrible," Mrs. Fleck said. "He's been accused of a crime he didn't commit. He can't even go out in public without people pointing him out and wanting to take a selfie with him. And now he has to get locked up in jail!"

Oh boy. This was going south fast. I pushed back in my chair and stood, reaching for my cuffs. "It's just overnight."

"Overnight!" she shrieked. "No. That's terrible. He hasn't even finished his taco."

"Hold on here," Lula said. "Let's all calm down a minute and consider things. Do you got dessert?" Lula asked Mrs. Fleck.

"Of course," Mrs. Fleck said. "Chocolate cake and vanilla ice cream. It's our tradition on Taco Tuesday."

"Did you hear that?" Lula said to me. "Chocolate cake. It would be a shame for Eugene to miss having chocolate cake. Look at how skinny he is. And I bet he was thinking about having a second taco after he finishes the one he's got. I bet we were all thinking about that."

"There's always next Tuesday," I said.

"Yeah, but there might not be a next Tuesday if he gets a speedy trial and conviction," Lula said. "Something like that's never happened before in Trenton but you never know."

"I've never been in jail overnight," Eugene said. "It sounds scary. It would be great if you would let me stay home tonight and reschedule tomorrow. I swear, I'll be at the courthouse first thing in the morning."

"I wasn't thinking of anything so drastic," Lula said. "I was just thinking of not rushing through the meal with dessert and all. A night in jail isn't that bad. I spent a bunch of nights in jail. They usually give you a Happy Meal. If you're lucky it could even be a Big Mac. And you get a blanket, and you get to meet new people if you're in the tank. Sometimes you even get to bunk with an old friend. When I was a ho it was like girls' night out in the tank sometimes."

Kevin did a nervous giggle and everyone else looked horrified. Even I was horrified. I went into damage-control mode, sucked in some air, and sat down.

"You're absolutely right," I said to Eugene. "There's no reason why we can't all enjoy our tacos and reschedule you tomorrow."

"Amen," Lula said. "Could someone pass me the hot sauce?"

---

"That went well," Lula said when we were back in the Trailblazer. "I was afraid for a minute there that it wasn't gonna be our finest hour, but it turned around and turned out okay. This was a satisfying evening."

"We didn't apprehend Eugene."

"No, but we got chocolate cake," Lula said. "Sometimes you gotta go with the way fate evens things out."

"What do you think the chances are that Eugene will show up tomorrow morning?"

"There's a lot of things to take into consideration on that, but I'd say fifty-fifty."

"I'm getting a bed delivered tomorrow. What do you think the chances are I'll have the bed repossessed if I can't make the minimum payment on my credit card because I didn't apprehend Eugene?"

"They don't usually repossess a bed. They'll just put you in collection and ruin your credit score and make your life a living hell," Lula said.

I drove to the office, dropped Lula off at her car, and drove home. Morelli was expecting me to spend the night with him but that wasn't going to happen. Truth is, I would have loved to spend the night with him. I missed him. I missed the easy comfort of being with him and Bob. Unfortunately, the easy comfort would turn into something more intimate, and that would be terrific but not good.

Rex was running on his wheel when I let myself into my apartment. I said hello and told him about the taco dinner party while I searched through the fruit basket. I found a bag of caramel-coated popcorn and gave some to Rex along with another slice of pear. I turned to go into the dining room and spotted Herbert Slovinski standing in my foyer.

"You didn't lock your door," Herbert said. "You should be more careful. Anybody could walk in. There are crazy people out there."

"I always lock my door," I said. "How did you get in and what are you doing here?"

"I was worried about you being constipated. After I sent you the flowers, I thought I should have sent you stool softeners instead. Or I should have sent you both. Are those my flowers in your kitchen? Do you like them? I didn't know what flowers were your favorites. Some people don't like lilies. Lilies are best if you cut their sex parts off. I know that sounds terrible, but I don't think lilies mind. I see you have a fruit basket. That's the best thing for constipation. I should have thought of that but it's a good thing I didn't since you already have one." He stepped away from the door and looked into my living room. "This is the first time I've seen something that was firebombed. I thought there would be more damage . . . like a room that was gutted and charred black. Whoever did this probably was an amateur. I mean, if you're going to firebomb something you should at least do a good job of it, right? It looks like your furniture didn't even get burned." He adjusted his glasses. "You haven't got much furniture. I expected you would have more. You look like a more-furniture person."

"This is new furniture. The fire was mostly contained in my bedroom and living room and none of the furniture survived."

"Gee, that's too bad. I could help you get furniture if you want. I have a lot of connections. I can get anything practically for free."

"Thanks, but I have furniture ordered."

"How about a television?" Eugene said. "I bet you don't have a television ordered. I can have one here for you tomorrow. A big flat-screen. Where do you usually put your television? Not that it matters. I'll get you a nice big console to go under it. Then you can hang it or put it on the console. Do you want one for your bedroom too? Lots of people like a television in their bedroom."

"No. Really not necessary." I looked down at my watch. "Gosh, look at the time. I need to be somewhere."

"That's too bad. I thought we could do something fun. Do you like Scrabble? I'm a Scrabble genius. I'm good at all board games. I always win at Monopoly. I have a whole collection of games. I even have Candy Land. I bet it's been a while since you played Candy Land."

"Yeah, forever," I said, inching back to the door. "I hate to rush you out of here, but I'm already late."

"Do you need a ride? I have a Prius."

"Thanks again, but I need to take my own car."

"Where are you going?"

I stared at him for a beat. Where was I going?

"I'm going to my boyfriend's house," I said.

"The one you're engaged to?"

"Yes. The cop with the gun."

"That's too bad. We could have played a game or something. Did your games all get burned up too?"

"I'm not much of a games person." I had the door open.

"Thanks for stopping by," I said, physically moving him into the doorway.

He leaned toward me, coming in for a kiss, and before he could get close enough, I shoved him into the hall and closed and locked the door.

"Okay then," he yelled on the other side of my door. "Good visit. We'll have to do this again sometime soon, right?"

I looked into the kitchen at Rex. He was stopped on his wheel, staring at me with his shiny little black eyes. Even Rex was appalled. I gave him a couple Froot Loops and told him not to worry. Everything was okay. The weird guy was going away. I went back to my door and looked out the peephole. No Herbert. That was a good sign. I went to a living room window, peeked out, and saw Herbert walk out of my building and go to his car. He got in and sat there. I watched for a couple minutes, and he didn't drive away. I went to the kitchen and got a bottle of water. I took the water to the couch and checked my emails, text messages, and socials.

Morelli called. "Are we still on for tonight?"

I went to the window and looked down at the parking lot. Herbert was still there. I closed my eyes and rested my forehead on the windowpane. Nothing short of a bullet was going to discourage this doofus. If he didn't see me drive off, he was going to be back banging on my door asking me if I needed bathroom aids.

"Yep," I said to Morelli. "I'm on my way."

I said goodbye to Rex, locked up, and went straight to my Trailblazer. I didn't look in Herbert's direction. I left the parking lot and two blocks later I turned onto Hamilton Avenue. I glanced at my rearview mirror and saw Herbert behind me in his Prius. The moron didn't even have enough sense to put a car between us. I wondered how much damage I would sustain if I put my car in reverse at the next light and rammed him. Tempting but not a good idea, I told myself. It would involve another annoying conversation with him, and at the very least I'd need a new rear bumper.

Ten minutes later I parked at the curb in front of Morelli's house and Herbert idled at the corner. I traced down his phone number and called him.

"Hello," he said. "Gosh. This is great. I didn't expect a phone call so soon."

"What are you doing?"

"What do you mean? I'm in my car."

"I know you're in your car. I can see you. Why are you following me?"

"I wanted to make sure you were okay. You didn't look too good at the end of our visit."

"I'm fine. I would be even better if you'd go away. Forever."

"Hah! That's funny. I was just waiting to make sure you got in the house okay. I mean, it's not like I don't have anything else to do tonight. There's a viewing at Harrison Funeral Home in Mercerville that I might catch. It's not my favorite funeral home but once in a while I check it out."

I hung up, got out of the Trailblazer, and let myself into Morelli's house. Bob rushed at me, put his giant paws on my chest, and knocked me back against the closed door.

"Good boy," I said. "Good Bob."

Morelli sauntered over and took Bob's place against my chest. "Rangers are up by one," he said.

He kissed me and I got all warm inside. "Rangers are going to have a good year."

"Yeah. Me too," he said. "What would you like? Wine? Beer?

Have you had dinner? Want a quickie? Rangers are between periods."

There it was! The ultimate out.

"None of the above," I said. "Speaking of periods . . ."

Morelli looked stricken. "No."

"Yes. Sorry."

"I might be able to ignore it."

"No way."

"Cramps?"

"Big-time," I told him. "Like childbirth."

# CHAPTER SEVEN

I woke up thinking that the night had been pretty good and could have been a lot worse. I didn't get caught in my fib, and I didn't totally have full-on sex. Just some making out, which under the circumstances seemed reasonable. The sun was shining, and Bob was in bed next to me. Morelli was long gone. He was an up-at-the-crack-of-dawn person. He was already locked and loaded and on the job. I got dressed in yesterday's clothes, grabbed a banana and a protein bar from the kitchen, and drove back to my apartment. No Herbert in my rearview mirror. No Herbert in my parking lot. Yay. Rex was asleep in his soup-can den when I walked into the kitchen, so I blew him a silent kiss and didn't disturb him with the details of my evening. I made coffee and took a cup into the bathroom. An hour later I was clean top to bottom, mildly caffeinated, and ready to start my day. I had a text message that said my furniture would be delivered between one o'clock and four o'clock. This gave me the morning to make a capture that would allow me to pay at least the minimum amount on my credit card.

I left my apartment, got into my Trailblazer, and drove to the office. Still no sign of Herbert.

Connie was at her desk and Lula was slouched on the couch when I walked in. Lula had a lot of pink hair today, plus she was wearing a garlic necklace and a chain necklace with a large wooden cross.

"I'm ready to go after the vampire," Lula said. "I've been reading about them and there's a lot of conflicting information. There's old-fashioned vampires that are the living dead. They come out of their graves when it's dark on account of they don't do good in the sun, so they do their bloodsucking at night. They aren't real attractive. Then there's more modern vampires that know enough to wear sunscreen so they can suck blood any time they want. Some of them can't cast a shadow or be photographed and it turns out we don't have a good picture of Zoran Whatshisname. Just look at his mug shot. It's all blurry because he's a vampire," Lula said. "And he's a widower. I looked it up in the obituaries, but it didn't say what his wife died from so I think that's real suspicious. Dollars to doughnuts he drained his poor wife dry sucking her blood all the time."

"Vampires aren't real," I said. "They're folklore and fiction."

"Do you know that for sure?" Lula said. "What about that guy in *Buffy the Vampire Slayer*? He looked pretty real."

I went to the back room and got a giant cup of coffee in a to-go cup. "That was a television show."

"Yeah, but it was excellent," Lula said. "And it was almost like reality TV."

"I'd planned to look for Zoran this morning, but I'm not going out with you dressed like that," I said.

"Like what?"

"Like wearing all that garlic."

"It's to ward off the vampire," Lula said. "I'm sensitive about losing my blood and vital body fluids."

I looked over at Connie. "Talk to her. Please."

"I don't remember Buffy always wearing garlic," Connie said. "That might be one of those outdated precautions."

"I guess I could see that," Lula said. "There's garlic in everything these days. Vampires would have a hard time ordering out. So, they might have adapted." She took the garlic off and dropped it into her tote bag. "Still, I'm going to leave my cross necklace on. It complements my skin tone, and it never hurts to have God on your side."

I pulled the file out of my bag and paged through it. "Zoran manages a laundromat. We should check that out first."

"Okay, but if he has fangs, I'm pulling the garlic out of my bag," Lula said.

I handed the file to Lula. "If he has fangs, we will pretend not to notice because he obviously needs an orthodontist."

Lula followed me out of the office. "If it's all the same to you, I'd appreciate taking your car so mine doesn't get contaminated with vampire cooties."

"Not a problem." I got behind the wheel. "Where are we going?"

"It says here that the laundromat is on Freemont Street. Another reason not to take my car. My baby doesn't get parked in that neighborhood."

Freemont Street was one street over from Stark Street. Stark started out okay and ended up as no-man's-land. Freemont wasn't up to Stark Street's crime-ridden standards, but it wasn't Rodeo Drive either.

I pulled away from the curb. "What block on Freemont?"

"Second block."

The second block of Freemont was small businesses at street level and subpar apartments and rooms to rent on the second and third floors. The gangs were ever present, but the murder rate was minimal on the second block. If I left my car unattended, it had a 50/50 chance of getting carnapped.

"So, how's things going with you?" Lula asked.

"Going good," I said.

"How good?"

"Just good."

"'Cause you got that look."

"What look is that?"

"Like you got some," Lula said.

"Excuse me?"

"You always look all relaxed and smiley when you had a night of horizontal refreshment. You know, like you got some color to your cheeks on account of your blood oxygen level is at a hundred percent."

"That's ridiculous."

"Nuh-uh, it's science. You can't argue science. Okay, so in the past some government officials have tried to fabricate science, but I know a orgasm glow when I see one. Although, I guess it could be a bun-in-the-oven glow. What's happening on the baby front?"

"Nothing is happening on the baby front."

"Okay, so then you did the deed with someone, and it had to be Morelli because Ranger isn't in town. Unless you did the deed with yourself. Except in my experience, that isn't usually as glow producing."

"Jeez Louise."

"This is a good address for a laundromat," Lula said, looking through the file. "No one in that neighborhood has their own washer and dryer, so either they're dunking their undies out in the kitchen sink or else they gotta go to a laundromat."

"Has this guy had any priors other than the parking tickets?"

"Nope. None that are listed here."

"Any details on the crime?"

"Just that he bit this woman in the neck, and he said it was because he was a vampire."

"Did they do a wellness check? Take him to psychiatric?"

"Not that I could tell. Arresting officer verified that the suspect appeared to be a vampire."

"Did they take the arresting officer to psychiatric?"

"See, you're implying that you have to be crazy to believe in vampires. That's because you don't got a lot of *maybe* or *what if* in you. You doubt your imagination. That's the part of you that's constipated. Your imagination is all clogged up inside of you and nothing can come out. You got imagination constipation. You don't want to believe the unbelievable. You probably don't believe in aliens from outer space either. Or ghosts or flying squirrels."

"Flying squirrels are real."

"Maybe vampires are real. I bet the arresting officer looked at this guy with blood dripping off his fangs and he said, *Hell yeah, this here is a vampire.*"

"And you're willing to believe in vampires because your imagination isn't constipated?"

"You know it. If anything, my imagination got diarrhea."

There was no doubt in my mind that this was true. I took Hamilton Avenue to Broad and Broad to State Street. I drove through center city and turned onto Freemont. The laundromat was squashed between a store selling gently used clothes and a tattoo parlor.

"Look at this," Lula said. "You could take your pick of parking spots. There's hardly any cars parked here. Only that one in front of the tattoo parlor."

"The one up on cinder blocks because its wheels have been removed?"

"Yeah, that's the one. The one that's all spray-painted with gang slogans."

Here's the thing. I'm not all that brave, and I'm not genius brilliant. I think I get by because I have some common sense and I persevere. And common sense told me that most self-respecting gangbangers weren't out stealing cars and shooting people at this hour of the morning. So, the risk of theft and death was greatly diminished.

I parked at the curb, and Lula and I walked into the laundromat. It was standard fare with a row of washing machines and clothes dryers on one side, folding tables in the middle of the floor, and a row of plastic chairs on the other side. There were some vending machines and a couple closed doors at the back of the room. No one was out and about. The place was eerily quiet. Lula and I walked down the row of chairs to the machines dispensing detergent packets, soda, and candy bars.

"Looks like nobody's home," Lula said. She knocked once on a door that said LADIES AND GENTS, pushed it open, and looked inside. "Nobody home here either."

The door next to the candy bars was closed. *Office* had been written on it with a permanent marker. I opened the door, and Lula and I stepped inside. A woman was sprawled on the floor. Her eyes were open and fixed. Her mouth was open, but her screams were silent. She had a wound on her neck and blood was everywhere. A man dressed in black was bending over her. He looked up when we entered and hissed at us. He had blood on his hands and blood was dripping from his mouth. He catapulted over the woman, shoved Lula out of his way, and ran out of the room and out of the building.

"Holy hell," Lula said. Her eyes rolled back into her head, and she crashed to the floor.

My heart was beating hard in my chest. I instinctively put my hand to my belly in a protective gesture and sucked in air. I fumbled in my pockets, located my phone, and called Morelli.

"I'm in a laundromat on Freemont Street," I said, "and there's a woman dead here and there's blood all over and the vampire knocked Lula out of his way and ran out of the building."

"Are you pranking me?"

"N-n-no," I said.

"This for real? Are you okay?"

"I'm sort of shaky, but I don't think I'm going to throw up. Lula fainted, and she's still lying here."

"Step away from the crime scene," he said. "I'm on my way."

Lula was mumbling and her eyes were open, but she wasn't coherent. I grabbed her feet and managed to pull her out of the office.

"Wha . . . ," Lula said.

"You fainted," I told her. "Stay down until the paramedics get here."

"Wha?"

I heard sirens and saw the cop car angle-park. Two uniforms came in. One went to Lula. The other went into the office and closed the door. A fire truck rolled to a stop and the paramedics came in.

I pointed to Lula. "She fainted," I said to a paramedic. "I don't know if she hit her head on the floor."

I moved to the row of seats and sat down. Lula was still on

the floor, getting oxygen. I felt like I could use some oxygen, but I didn't want to look like a wimp.

Morelli walked in and came directly to me. "Are you okay?"

I nodded. "Mostly," I said. "I need a Snickers bar."

"That's my girl," Morelli said.

"No, really. Get me a Snickers bar. The machine is in the back."

Morelli yelled at one of the uniforms. "Jake, get me a Snickers bar from the machine." He turned back to me. "Talk to me."

"I got an FTA who was charged with assault. Bit a woman in the neck and said he was a vampire. His name is Zoran something. Owns this laundromat. Lula and I got here, and the place was empty. We went to the office and found this guy bending over a dead, bloody body. He had blood all over his hands and dripping from his mouth. He bolted when he saw us. Knocked Lula aside and ran out."

"Maybe we should talk about our future and you retiring," Morelli said.

"Now?"

"Later."

Jake came over with the Snickers and a Coke.

"I don't need to retire," I said, peeling the wrapper away. "I just need a Snickers."

Lula was on her feet. They walked her over and sat her down next to me.

"I could use a couple candy bars," Lula said. "They got any Mounds or peanut butter cups?"

Morelli went to the office and minutes later came back to me. "Can you give me a description of the vampire?"

"I didn't get a good look. He was moving fast once he saw us. I'd say average height and build. Dark brown hair, shot with gray. Caucasian. Dressed in black. Bloody. Fit the description of my FTA."

"He looked me right in the face when he shoved me out of his way," Lula said. "His mouth was open, and his tongue was sticking out. And he had fangs. And his eyes were red. I don't know if vampires are supposed to have red eyes, so he might just be a pothead. It was horrible." Lula looked past Morelli. "Where's my candy bars? I need candy bars."

Jake came with more candy and helped Morelli get Lula and me out to my car.

"Are you okay to drive?" Morelli asked me.

"Yeah," I said. "I'm good. I just had a moment back there."

"Not every day you interrupt a vampire at feeding time," Morelli said.

"Do you think he's really a vampire?"

"No," Morelli said. "Do you?"

"No," I said. "I think he's a crazy person with large canines."

I buckled myself in, Morelli kissed the top of my head and closed my door. I gave him a small smile and wave and drove away. I got to the corner and looked at Lula, and I knew we were thinking the same thought. What if he really was a vampire?

"I feel better now that I got some sugar in me," Lula said. "What's next?"

"I was thinking we could drive by Zoran's house. Maybe he went home to get clean clothes."

"And he could be exhausted after killing that lady. And probably he isn't so hungry anymore," Lula said. "I got my garlic, but we should go to the hardware store and get a stake to drive into Zoran's heart before we go into his house."

"Heart impalement isn't in my skill set," I said to Lula.

"Ordinarily I might be able to pull it off, but I'm just recovering from fainting right now," Lula said.

"Exactly, so we'll skip the hardware store and go straight to Zoran's house."

Lula paged through the file. "He lives a couple blocks from the laundromat. Exeter Street. I know that street. It's got a bunch of small bungalow-type houses that are kind of nice."

I drove to Exeter, found Zoran's house, and parked across the street.

"Now what?" Lula asked.

"We wait."

"What are we waiting for?"

"We're waiting for the police to arrive and search the house."

Ten minutes later, two cop cars and a plainclothes car showed up. Not Morelli. His partner, Jimmy. They walked around the house. Tried the door. Looked in some windows. They couldn't enter, but I could. Zoran had signed his rights away when he got his bail bond from Vinnie. I could forcibly enter a building if I thought Zoran was in it. I left Lula in the car, and I walked over to Jimmy.

"Do you want me to go in?" I asked him.

"Morelli would ban me from his weekly poker game if I let you go in there," Jimmy said. "I'd never get any more of his mother's lasagna. Anyway, I'm pretty sure Djordjevic isn't home. We looked in all the windows and there's no blood trail. No Zoran. No blood on any of the door handles. His car is parked in his driveway. He's only a couple blocks from the laundromat. He probably walked to work. I'm going to leave two guys here to question the neighbors and keep an eye on things."

"He's FTA," I told Jimmy. "I'd appreciate a call if you find him."

"Sure thing," Jimmy said.

I went back to my Trailblazer and got behind the wheel. "The perp's name is pronounced 'Georgiavich.'"

"It doesn't look like it sounds," Lula said. "It's not one of those phonetic names, and I don't see it being a stellar name for a vampire. Georgiavich sounds too happy to belong to a vampire. It makes me think of Georgia peaches. Zoran is a better vampire name. He should just go by Zoran. There's a bunch of people who just use one name. Dracula for starters. Then there's Cher and Zorro and Chewbacca, and my favorite is Jungkook."

"Actually, it's Count Dracula," I said.

"Yeah, but his friends call him Dracula."

I started the car. "Jimmy said there's no sign that Zoran is in the house. He's leaving a couple guys here to canvass the neighborhood, so we might as well move on."

"I'm thinking I need to move on to lunch," Lula said.

"You just ate five candy bars."

"They made me jittery. I need some bread and grease to even out the sugar. I need anti-vampire food like a Taylor pork roll sandwich and fries and slaw."

"Taylor pork roll is anti-vampire food?"

"Hell yeah. You want to be Jersey strong? Eat Taylor pork roll. It's made in Trenton. It's full of nitrates so it increases your shelf life. You eat enough and you could live forever. Pino's makes pork roll on a bun with a fried egg and cheese. I could probably kill a vampire with my bare hands after eating a couple of those babies."

"That seems like a stretch."

"I might have exaggerated," Lula said.

I drove to Pino's, and we were able to get a booth in the family section. We ordered and I leaned forward, elbows on the table. "Just to review," I said. "We have Eugene Fleck. He was supposed to show at the courthouse this morning." I looked at my watch. "There's still time. He's got thirty minutes before the court breaks for lunch. Then there's Bruno Jug. Waiting on a call from him."

"Could be a long wait," Lula said.

I nodded. "I can close out Jerry Bottles and his magnificent member. And that leaves Zoran."

"I can't get excited about our to-do list," Lula said. "Eugene Fleck is a sweetie pie, but then you've got a mobster who kills people and a vampire who kills people. I'll probably feel better after I eat my pork roll, but right now a job driving Uber sounds pretty good."

I called Connie and asked her to check on Eugene. She called back just as our lunch was set on the table.

"Eugene didn't check in at the courthouse," Connie said. "And he isn't answering his phone."

I moved the call to speakerphone so Lula could hear. "Anything new on Robin Hoodie?"

"He posted a short video this morning. He hijacked a truck filled with cookies last night and unloaded the cookies at two encampments. The police said the truck was full when it was driven off the Blue Moon Diner lot at 10:30 p.m. and found empty in the Walmart parking lot at midnight."

"Do you know about Zoran?" I asked Connie.

"Only that dispatch sent all hands to the laundromat."

"Lula and I walked in on a man bending over a dead woman who was bleeding profusely from a wound on her neck. He bolted when he saw us."

"And you think it was Zoran?"

"The man fit Zoran's description and they were in Zoran's office at the laundromat."

"Was Lula wearing her garlic?"

"No. It was in her tote bag."

"Just sayin'," Connie said.

"I hear you." I hung up and dug into lunch, starting with the slaw. "It sounds like Eugene and Kevin were busy last night," I said to Lula.

"Yeah, but you didn't ask any of the right questions. Like how big was the truck and what kind of cookies are we talking about? If it was a Keebler's elves eighteen-wheeler, that would be one thing, and I would expect there were some Chips Ahoy! and Oreos and Lorna Doones. Or it could have been a Famous Amos truck and then it would have been just chocolate chip. If I was going to hijack a truck to feed to the homeless, I'd look for the Keebler truck because of the variety. Some of the homeless might get migraine from chocolate chips. It's a common allergy. Although I have to say Amos makes a good cookie." Lula finished her sandwich and moved on to the French fries. "What's next on our schedule? I'm voting we go after Eugene, being that he's the only one who might not want to kill us. And you can see how it all worked out for the best. If we dragged Eugene, off to jail last night, he wouldn't have been able to redistribute the wealth to the needy today."

I glanced at my watch. "I have a furniture delivery coming between one and four o'clock. Eugene will have to wait until I get my bed."

"I'm okay with that," Lula said. "You can drop me at the office. I want to catch up on Robin Hoodie handing out all those cookies, and it's better when you watch his videos on Connie's big monitor. He's more heroic looking on her monitor than when you see him on your phone and he's only a half inch tall."

# CHAPTER EIGHT

It was a little after two o'clock when my furniture arrived. I made my bed, plugged my nightstand lamp in, and put my living room lamp on the new end table that was placed next to the couch. I told myself that it was cozy, and it was home, but the truth is, it didn't feel like home. Home had been firebombed one too many times. I went into the dining room and packed up my messenger bag, and Ranger called.

"What's the status report?" he said.

"I'm in my apartment and I'm about to go out looking for fugitives."

"Anyone interesting?"

"Robin Hoodie, Bruno Jug, and a vampire."

"Nice. Do you need help?"

"Not at the moment."

"Babe," Ranger said. And he hung up.

I called him back. "Are you in Trenton?"

"Yes."

"Excellent." And I hung up.

Ranger doesn't usually need to say a lot because I get all the information I need from *babe*. It can be loving, sexy, questioning, cautionary, or simply hello. And in this instance, the less said the better, because I wasn't forced to fib or explain my absence. Unfortunately, this get-out-of-jail card wouldn't last long. When my number came up on Ranger's list of priorities, he'd want answers.

I grabbed my messenger bag and a sweatshirt, and I left my apartment. It was still early enough in the day that court would be in session. So, there was a chance that I could get Eugene bonded out without an overnight stay, if I could find him fast enough. I got all green lights on my way to the office. A sign that maybe my luck was changing and there wouldn't be any more bloody bodies in my immediate future. I parked in front of the office and Morelli called.

"Just checking in," he said. "Are you okay?"

"I'm good. I'm at the office. I need to find Eugene and get him rebonded."

"And tonight?"

"It's Wednesday," I said. "It's your poker night. We don't usually get together on poker night."

"Yeah, but it's at Marty's house. His wife kicks us out at ten o'clock."

"And you want me to take up the slack time after that?"

"Think of the poker game as the opening act."

"And then I'm the main act? The big event?"

"Yeah."

"I'm flattered but I'm going to pass. I'm not up to the big event. I'm going to bed early. I need my beauty sleep. Anything new on the vampire?"

"The ME lists cause of death as head trauma and loss of blood. It looks like you walked in on a fresh kill. Time of death was placed at about the time you were parking your car."

My stomach turned at the memory. Morelli faced this sort of thing every day and had learned how to deal with it. I was barely holding it together. Truth is, I didn't want to learn how to deal with it. I didn't want that kind of horror to be a regular part of my life.

"I ran into Jimmy earlier," I said. "Did he turn anything up on Exeter Street?"

"Nothing useful. The neighbors all agreed that Zoran is a wack job, but he keeps his lawn cut and doesn't play loud music, so there's never been a problem."

"Did his neighbors mention to Jimmy that Zoran is a vampire?"

"Yeah, but Jimmy said they were just glad he didn't think he was the Easter Bunny and hopped around leaving chocolate eggs on their front lawn."

"Or he could think he was Robin Hood and swipe their Amazon packages off their porch."

"Exactly," Morelli said. "I have to go back to work. Let me know if you change your mind about tonight."

Lula was on the couch, surfing on her phone, when I walked into the office. I nodded at her and took a seat in front of Connie's desk.

"Lula told me about the scene at the laundromat," Connie said. "She told me she fainted."

"It was terrifying and disgusting and beyond description," I said.

"Are you okay?"

"No," I said. "I can't stop seeing it."

"Did you get your furniture?"

"Yes. I made my bed and plugged my lamp in and it's starting to look more homey."

I heard the front door open, and I turned to see Eugene push his bike into the office.

"I'm sorry I'm late," he said. "I had stuff to do this morning." He shrugged out of his backpack and removed a round tin. "My mom baked some cookies for the office. They're chocolate chip. They're her specialty."

Lula was on her feet, examining the cookies. "They look homemade." She took a cookie and tasted it. "It's homemade all right. I thought it might have come off a truck, but I was wrong. This is a real nice gesture. You've got a good mom."

"I know," Eugene said. "I'm lucky like that. Is it too late to get rebonded?"

I looked at Connie. "What do you think?"

"Is your mom putting up the bond again?" Connie asked Eugene.

Eugene tipped his head down a little. "My dad wouldn't let her. He said I had to learn a lesson."

"You need something to secure the bond," Connie said.

Eugene had a grip on his bike. "I was hoping I could use this. It's a good bike and I keep it in top shape."

We all looked at the bike. Eugene was going to be short about a thousand dollars. Maybe more.

"It's a pretty nice bike," Lula said.

"Doesn't look like it has any dents or scrapes," I said.

Connie rolled her eyes. "Don't anyone tell Vinnie I did this." She cut her eyes to Eugene. "It's a deal."

"I'll take him," I said. "With a little luck we should get him to court in time."

"No," Connie said. "It'll save time if I take Eugene."

This made sense. I can make apprehensions, but I'm not qualified to write a bond. Only Connie and Vinnie can write a bond. If I got Eugene to court, Connie would have to come downtown anyway to do the paperwork.

"I'll watch the office while you're gone," I said.

Connie and Eugene left, and I took Connie's place behind the desk.

"You look serious over there," Lula said. "What are you doing with Connie's computer?"

"I'm searching for information on Zoran."

"Why?"

"I'm going after him."

"Oh, no. No, no, no, no. Bad idea. Double-doody idea. And not necessary. The police will find him. They'll lock him up in a nice, padded cell and shoot him full of Thorazine. And here's the good news. He'll get free dental. He can get his fangs filed down so he fits into the prison population better."

I sent a file to Connie's printer. "This is a sick person. He needs to be found before he kills someone else. And it's what we do, right? We find people."

"Yeah, but we aren't all that good at it," Lula said. "And I'm not sure he's a people."

"When Connie returns, I'll have her run a more complete search. Right now, I'm printing out his credit report, his work history, and an article from the Trenton paper. The headline is *Love Bite Lands Vampire in Jail.*"

"I'm not in favor of this," Lula said. "I'm gonna be real unhappy if I get killed by a vampire."

"You have to at least be curious about this guy. You're the one who always has to slow up to look at a car crash. This is like a car crash."

"Nuh-uh. That's you. I'm the one with my eyes closed. You're the one who rushed out to see some idiot jump off a fourth-floor ledge."

"That was official business. He was FTA. And he didn't jump. He slipped." I took the pages from the printer. "Zoran's credit history is clean. No litigation or derogatory comments. He has an AmEx card and a Costco Visa. No investment history. His house is mortgaged. Looks like he pays on time. No mention of him owning a laundromat. Drives a Chevy Colorado pickup. It's on a lease."

"That makes sense," Lula said. "He probably needs a truck to cart his victims off to the landfill."

"The article is interesting. They interviewed Zoran's parents. Leo and Pat. His father worked for Boeing in Seattle for twenty-three years. He retired four years ago, and they moved to Jamesburg to be closer to Pat's family. Zoran's mother works part-time as office help for the Methodist church. Zoran is an only child. Blah, blah, blah. He got good grades in school. Always had an interesting imagination."

"Maybe he didn't have an imagination," Lula said. "Maybe his parents thought he was imagining being a vampire except he wasn't imagining."

"I'm at a dead end until Connie returns and I can go to Jamesburg. I don't have any other leads."

Lula dragged one of the plastic chairs over next to me. "Connie won't be back for at least an hour. Pull up the Robin Hoodie videos. I want to see the new one about the cookies again. And there's another good one where he opens the back of the truck and it's full of toilet paper. That's the fun thing about hijacking. You don't always know what you're gonna find inside."

---

It was almost four thirty when Connie returned.

"I had to do some fast talking, but I managed to get him

rescheduled and bonded," Connie said. "I dropped him off at his parents' house. His new court date is in two weeks and we're going to track him down the day before and lock him in his room until it's time to escort him to the courthouse."

"He hasn't got any wheels," Lula said. "He's going to have to loot a bike store. That's going to be a good video, watching all those homeless guys who are probably still jacked up on cookies, riding around on a bike."

"Jeez," Connie said. "Maybe I should give him his bike back."

"No way," Lula said. "Bikes for the homeless is an excellent idea. It's a way for them to get exercise instead of nodding off on the sidewalk at all hours or sitting around in their tent all day. I don't know why people didn't think of this sooner. It'll let them get to a variety of soup kitchens and detox clinics, and it'll enlarge their panhandling ability."

I narrowed my eyes at Lula. "And the real reason you want to give bikes to the homeless?"

"Okay, so I want to see the video, but you can't blame me for that. Admit it, you'd want to see the video. I mean, who wouldn't want to see that video. It would be an award winner if there was an award for YouTube videos." Lula's eyes almost popped out of her head. "OMG! That's my best idea yet. A YouTube award show!"

"They might have one," Connie said. "Sort of."

I hiked my messenger bag onto my shoulder. "I'm out of here. I'm going to Jamesburg to talk to Zoran's parents." I turned to Connie. "I got a credit report, a work history that didn't say much, and a newspaper article off the net. I could use more info on Zoran."

"I'll see what I can dig up," Connie said.

I looked at Lula. "Are you on board?"

"I guess," Lula said. "One of us has to carry the garlic."

I took Route 1 north to County Road 522 and followed the directions given by the GPS lady. We rolled into Jamesburg in thirty-five minutes start to finish.

"This is kind of nice," Lula said. "Lots of grass and trees and white houses with black shutters and front porches. And there's a sign for a country club. I wouldn't mind joining a country club. I would fit right in. I could learn how to play golf and tennis. I could see myself in one of those little tennis outfits. I'd be looking good, whacking the ball in my little white skirt and thong."

"They probably wouldn't let you wear a thong."

"What do you mean? Everyone wears a thong."

"Not on a tennis court."

"How about in France?"

"I don't know about France."

"They probably got naked tennis in France," Lula said. "And Denmark."

The GPS lady told me to turn left into Green Garden Estates. A sign said that it was a community for active senior living.

"What's active senior living?" Lula said. "How active do you gotta be to live here? Do they give you a test? Like, could you get in if you could only do two or three jumping jacks? Suppose you're in a coma? You probably couldn't live here."

I turned onto Whippoorwill Lane and stopped in front of number 25. "This is it."

"These are all one-story ranch houses on this street. I'm guessing this is the street for people who have low activity expectations and can't climb stairs," Lula said. "So, when they say active seniors, I'm thinking the bar might be set pretty low."

"Here are the rules," I said to Lula. "When we go in to talk to

Zoran's parents, you will let me do the talking. You will not take your garlic out of your bag. You will not ask them if someone in a coma can live here."

"Hunh, there you go with the rules, again. It's like you don't trust me to say the right thing."

"Exactly. And I also would appreciate it if you didn't shoot anyone or threaten to shoot someone."

"Okay, I guess I could see that."

We went to the door, and I rang the bell. A woman opened the door a crack and peeked out. She looked to be very fit and in her sixties with a short brown bob and minimal makeup.

"Yes?" she asked.

"I'm looking for Zoran," I said. "Is he here?"

"No," she said. "What is this about?"

I gave her one of my business cards. "I work for his bail bond agent. Zoran missed his scheduled court date, and I would like to help him reschedule. Are you Pat? Are you his mom?"

"Yes," she said. "I'm Pat. I don't know where Zoran is right now."

"If he doesn't reschedule, he'll be considered a felon," I told her. "Do you have any idea where I might find him? I've already tried his house and the laundromat."

"You've been to the laundromat?"

"Yes."

"The police were just here. They said there was an accident at the laundromat."

I nodded. "A woman was killed."

"Terrible," Zoran's mom said. "Just terrible."

"I don't feel good," Lula said. "I don't like talk about killing. I feel dizzy. I gotta sit down."

Lula staggered in front of me, leaned against the door, pushing it wide open, and stumbled into the house. I scrambled after her, leading her to a chair in the living room.

"Maybe some water?" I said to the woman.

"Of course," she said, hurrying into the kitchen.

"Am I good, or what?" Lula whispered to me. "Did you see how I got us into the house with my award-winning acting?"

The woman returned with a glass of water and handed it to Lula. Lula drank some and sprinkled some on her face.

"I feel better now," Lula said.

"It must be nice to live close to Zoran," I said to his mom. "Do you see him a lot?"

"Not so much since we moved to Green Garden," she said. "Zoran works long hours at the laundromat, and we have so many activities here that we don't get to Trenton very often."

"How long have you lived here?" I asked her.

"We've been at Green Garden for four years."

"Previously you were living in Trenton?"

"When Leo retired from Boeing, we left Seattle so we could be closer to his parents in Trenton. They were aging and having medical issues. We really were full-time caregivers for a couple years, and then when they passed, we moved here."

"Did Zoran move to Trenton with you?"

"Yes. He was also working for Boeing, but there was the tragedy with his wife, and he wanted to move away from the memories, so he came east with us. He wanted a new start and the laundromat seemed to be a good fit for him. He has an engineering degree, you know. He's very smart, but he wanted to try something different from engineering."

"Zoran owns the laundromat?"

"Oh no. He doesn't have that kind of money. His uncle owns the laundromat. Zoran is the manager."

"Do you know any of Zoran's friends? I might be able to get in touch with him through one of them."

"He had a friend named Goofy. He would talk about him sometimes. He said Goofy always made him laugh. I don't know Goofy's real name, but I think he must live close to the laundromat."

"Any girlfriends?"

"Nothing serious. There was a girl named Rosa that he was seeing for a while. And a very pretty girl named Julie. He never brought any of his friends home to meet us, but I saw a picture of Julie on his phone."

"This has been helpful," I said to Pat. "If Zoran gets in touch with you, please tell him that he needs to reschedule his court date."

Lula stood and hiked her tote bag onto her shoulder. "Was there anything unusual about Zoran?" she asked Pat. "I couldn't help but notice the picture of him you got on your end table, and he has a couple big sharp teeth."

"It's a family trait," Pat said. "The Djordjevic men are very proud of their unique teeth." She took a second framed photo from the end table and handed it to Lula. "This is Zoran's dad when he won the tennis tournament last year. It's a little blurry but it's still a good picture. It's hard to get a picture of the Djordjevic men. They're always on the move."

"Holy hell," Lula said, handing the picture back to Pat. "He's a real good-looking man, and I can see the family resemblance with the teeth and all." Lula clutched her tote bag to her chest and looked around. "Where is the big guy? He isn't home, is he?"

"He ran out to the store for a few things. He should be back any minute."

"Any minute? Jeez, that's too bad that I'm going to have to

miss him, but I gotta go now. I got an appointment somewhere. I got something to do."

I followed Lula out of the house and down the sidewalk. She was already buckled in by the time I got behind the wheel.

"Did you see him?" Lula said. "It's a whole family of freaking vampires. Am I the only one noticing these things? These people got fangs. They could eat a steak while it's still on the cow. I mean, I try not to discriminate on the way people look, and I'm all in favor of inclusivity, but I'd have to think twice about playing tennis with a vampire."

"It's still early," I said. "Let's see if we can find Goofy."

"How are we going to do that?"

"I'm going to drop you off at the laundromat and you're going to walk up and down the street and ask about Goofy."

"You want me to use my natural charms."

I drove out of Green Garden Estates. "Yeah. I'd do it, but your charms are bigger than mine."

---

Lula walked the length of Freemont Street. She briefly stepped into a bar. She spoke to an old man who was sitting on a stoop and a group of guys hanging on a corner. She went into a deli and came out with a soda. She did all this on the opposite side of the street from the laundromat because the area around the laundromat was cordoned off with yellow crime scene tape. She sashayed up to the Trailblazer, and I popped the locks so she could get in.

"Goofy is a bartender at Lucky Linda's. It's on the third block on Stark," Lula said. "No one knows his real name. No one knows where he lives. Everyone likes him."

"I don't suppose he works the day shift?"

"Lucky Linda's don't have a day shift. Goofy comes on at nine o'clock."

Great. Nothing I wanted to do less than visit a bar on the third block of Stark Street after dark.

# CHAPTER NINE

Connie was getting ready to close up shop when Lula and I rolled in.

"Just in time," Connie said, handing me a folder. "I printed the background reports for you. The laundromat is owned by Zoran's uncle. Sergei Djordjevic. He owns seven other laundromats in Central Jersey and four car washes. I gave you his address. He lives in North Trenton. Ludlow Street. There's also some information on Zoran's deceased wife. And just for giggles I ran a search for missing women in Zoran's neighborhood and came up with three in the past six years."

"Any of them named Rosa or Julie?"

Connie froze for a beat. "Rosa Sanchez and Julie Werly. The third is Marianne Markoni. I included the police report that was filed for missing persons. Sanchez and Markoni were hookers working Stark Street. Rented rooms in a tenement on Freemont. One block from the laundromat. Werly was a schoolteacher.

Second grade. Lived with her parents two houses down from Zoran."

"I'm not liking this," Lula said. "This is freaking me out. We got a serial vampire on the loose."

"I need to close the office," Connie said. "Mom needs a ride home from mahjong at the senior center and then we're going to House of Chen for dinner. Vinnie came by while you were out, and he's making noise about bringing Bruno Jug in. Apparently, he's getting pressure from Harry. Turns out Vinnie shouldn't have bonded Jug out in the first place. From what I could piece together, Harry made a remark about Jug's dog and as a result didn't get invited to Jug's Christmas party. The result is that Harry and Jug make the Hatfields and McCoys look like best buds. It also seems that they're now stepping on each other's toes crime-wise."

The bail bonds office was a legitimate business, but Harry had his finger in other pies that were questionable and some that were not even close to legitimate.

"I'm waiting for Jug to call me," I said. "We have an arrangement."

"If Jug doesn't call in the next two hours, that arrangement is going to have to be reorganized," Connie said.

I tucked the folder into my messenger bag. "Got it."

"It's my quitting time too," Lula said. "I got a dinner date tonight with my honey."

"Are you still seeing the guy who renovated your apartment?" I asked her.

"You bet I am," Lula said. "He might even be *the one*."

"What about the guy who lives next door to you in your apartment house?" Connie asked. "The one who looks like Sasquatch."

"He's the *other one*," Lula said.

So far, I didn't have a dinner date and that was the way I wanted it. I was on a countdown to Friday, when I could take a pregnancy test. We all left the office, got into our cars, and drove off in different directions. I took Hamilton to South Olden and crossed Route 1. I was on my way to Zoran's uncle's house in North Trenton. Zoran couldn't go home. Where would he go? To a relative? To a friend? He needed to change out of his bloody clothes. He needed to eat and to find a place to hide out and sleep. Transportation was limited. He didn't have use of his truck. He'd have to walk or steal a car or use public transportation. Public transportation would be awkward being that he was soaked in blood.

I turned onto Ludlow Street and parked in front of Sergei Djordjevic's house. It was a two-story house that was most likely built in the thirties or forties by someone with a young family and a modest income. It was slightly larger than my parents' house, but I was guessing the interior layout was similar. The house next door was an exact structural replica, but the owner had fancied up the front of his house by adding a fake brick exterior.

Lights were on in all the houses. The occupants were in pre-dinner mode. Kids doing homework. Televisions spewing news. Dinner was in the microwave.

I knocked on Djordjevic's door and a man answered. He was wearing a dress shirt with the top button open. No tie. Drink in his hand. Some kind of whiskey on the rocks. Fangs showing.

"Sergei?" I asked.

"Yes."

"If I could have a moment, I'd like to talk to you about your nephew Zoran."

"Are you police? Newspaper? I've already talked to the police. I have nothing more to say."

I gave him my card. "I know this is a bad time, but Zoran missed his court date. If he doesn't reschedule, he'll be considered a felon."

"Is that a problem?"

"It's reason to arrest him."

"The police told me that Zoran is a *person of interest* in the laundromat tragedy," Sergei said. "I'm sure you already know this."

"I knew there was a murder. You're his uncle, and he works for you. I thought he might have come here to get away from everything."

"Not on a Wednesday," Sergei said. "Everybody knows we have pot roast on Wednesday." He cut his eyes in the direction of the kitchen. "My wife burns it black. She says it makes dark gravy that way." He sipped his whiskey. "She's a terrible cook."

"Do you know where I might find Zoran?"

"No. He's a loner. Doesn't share a lot, but he's a good man and an excellent employee. Keeps the laundromat clean and the machines in order. He's been my manager for almost six years. I'm sure he had nothing to do with what happened to that woman."

I knew he had everything to do with what happened to *that woman*, but I wasn't going to argue with a man who had fangs. "If you happen to talk to Zoran, let him know that I'm available to help him reschedule. It would be in his own best interest."

I left Sergei to deal with his charred pot roast, and I headed home. I had a brief moment when I considered stopping at Bruno's house, but I decided against it. Better to deal with Bruno's office henchmen than his trigger-happy wife.

---

I walked into my apartment and found Herbert in my kitchen.

"Hi," he said. "I bet you're surprised to see me here. I didn't call you ahead or anything because I wanted to surprise you. You're surprised, right? Wait until you see what I did!"

"Oh jeez. Don't tell me you did something."

"Not all by myself. I could have done it by myself, but it would have taken longer, and I thought you would want to have it done right away. If it was me, that's what I'd want. I'm not good at waiting to get things done. It's not like I'm impatient or anything, it's just that I'm not a procrastinator. I only allow myself to have good qualities. Nicky and Walter helped me. They just left. If you'd gotten home fifteen minutes sooner, you could have met them."

"What did you do?"

"I painted your apartment. You can tell, right? There aren't any more black fire smudge marks. They were hard to cover but we did it. Your bedroom is Sea Salt. It's the most calming bedroom color. The rest of the apartment is a cream with a hint of yellow. It's a neutral but it's sunny during the day and cozy at night. That's what it said in the advertisement in the paint store."

I walked into the living room. It was transformed. "Wow," I said. "I can't believe you did this. It's beautiful."

"We didn't get paint on any of your furniture either. And the new-paint smell masks the campfire smell. I hope you weren't attached to the campfire smell. We used water-based paint, but it still has a little new-paint smell to it. I like the new-paint smell, but I understand that it's not everyone's favorite."

I walked into the bedroom. Herbert was right about the calming effect. It was a very peaceful, restful color.

"Now that we're in your bedroom maybe you'll have sex with me," Herbert said. "I'm very good at it. I've read a lot of books and watched a lot of videos and I've had some hands-on experience, if you'll excuse the pun. I'm especially popular with older women."

"It was nice of you to paint my apartment, but I'm not having sex with you. Ever."

"Ever is a long time. I won't hold you to ever. And you'll feel different when the carpet arrives."

"Carpet?"

"Don't worry, I'll be here to accept delivery tomorrow and check it all out. You can be here too, if you want, but I know you have work to do. My work hours are flexible. Sometimes I work in the morning and sometimes I work in the afternoon and sometimes I work at night. You'll like the carpet. It's a nice dense-weave poly in a neutral color. I got a good deal on a bulk roll. There's enough for your whole apartment. I even walked on a sample with my bare feet to make sure it felt good. Some carpets can be scratchy. I don't like those carpets."

"How are you getting into my apartment?"

"You left your door open."

"My door was locked when I left."

"Are you sure? Because I was able to walk right in."

"It was locked."

"Maybe the building super let me in, now that I think about it. He was happy to hear we were painting. And I might have bribed him a little."

"You have to leave now."

"Without sex first?"

"Get out."

"Okay, how about dinner if you don't want to have sex? I have connections to get fast service at many restaurants."

"OUT!"

He looked at his watch. "I have things to do anyway. I guess I'll go now, but you should eat something. You'll feel better after you eat something. I always feel better after I eat. I'm not one of those people who likes to feel hungry."

I maneuvered him to the door, shoved him out, and closed and locked the door.

"I can have something delivered," he yelled through the door. "How about Chinese? Or maybe sushi or a burger. You can't go wrong with a burger and fries. I like Swiss on my burger but some people like cheddar."

"I don't want something delivered," I yelled back. "Do not have something delivered. I have dinner plans."

"Me too, now that I think about it," he said. "People are always wanting to have dinner with me."

I leaned against the door and looked at my apartment. It was shockingly better. Herbert and his friends did a really good job. Probably I should have been more grateful. I mean, would it have killed me to have dinner with him? The answer was *maybe*. Maybe a bullet in the brain would have been less horrible than dinner with Herbert. I went to the kitchen and looked in the fridge. Stale bread, peanut butter, and olives. Perfect.

I had dinner on my dining room table while I read the information Connie had printed out for me. Rosa Sanchez disappeared a year ago. She was working the night shift on Stark Street and never returned to her two-room apartment. It was as if she vanished into thin air. No sign of violence on the street or at her rooming house. Marianne disappeared three years ago. Same deal. Just vanished. No clues left behind. Julie Werly was a different story. Six months ago, her parents came home from dinner out with friends and found a trail of blood from the couch in the living room to the back door and out into the backyard.

Forensics came back positive that the blood belonged to Julie, but her body was never found. No murder weapon was found. The case was still open but inactive. I needed to talk to Morelli about Julie Werly. I checked the time. It was almost seven o'clock. Morelli would be at the poker game. Not a good time to call him. It would have to wait until the morning.

Zoran's deceased wife was next up. Elena Stockard Djordjevic. She lived in Seattle all her life. Graduated from Cal Tech. Worked at Boeing. She was married to Zoran for fourteen months and didn't come home from work one day. Her car was found parked at a scenic overlook rest stop. It was locked. No sign of violence. The missing persons report was filed two days later. A massive manhunt had combed the area around the rest stop, but nothing was found. Three weeks later, the remains of a leg washed up on a beach and DNA identified it as belonging to Elena.

Gross! Yuck! I was going to have nightmares. I took my MacBook Air to my couch and searched for a movie. I settled on *Coneheads*. One of my all-time favorites. After *Coneheads* I watched some *Bridgerton* episodes. I crawled into my new bed a little after eleven. I turned my bedside light off and lay perfectly still in the dark room. I'd hoped to bring *Bridgerton* into bed with me, but my mind was stuck on bloody women and severed limbs.

The message app flashed on my phone. I grabbed the phone off the nightstand and read the text. *I'm coming in.* Crap! It was Ranger, thoughtfully assuring me that I wasn't having a home invasion by a random molester. Instead, I was having a home invasion by Ranger. The news produced a rush of panic in me that was equal to what the random-molester panic would have been. Bad enough that Ranger was at my door, but it was even worse that I was in bed wearing nothing more than a silky camisole and panties because I hadn't gotten around to replacing my cremated pajamas. Not a problem, I told myself. Just stick to the script. It had worked with Morelli, right? Sort of.

I didn't have to get up to let Ranger in, and I couldn't keep him out. The man of mystery was a security expert. He was able to open two dead bolts, a slide chain, and a bump-proof lock without breaking a sweat. I switched my light on and sat up in bed. I heard my front door open and close, and I heard all the locks click back into the locked position. Moments later, Ranger walked in. He was wearing Rangeman black fatigues, a Kevlar vest, and a gun belt.

"Long day?" I asked him.

"There was an incident at one of my accounts."

"And?"

"It's been resolved. I was in the area, so I thought this was a chance to get together. I wasn't going to stay long. I have paperwork backed up on my desk, but now that I'm here I'm thinking the paperwork can wait one more day." He tossed his vest into a corner of the room and dropped his gun belt on top of it. "I'm assuming we're still engaged."

"Sure," I said. "Do you still want to be engaged?"

"At this exact moment I'm a hundred percent in."

Ranger removed his shoes and unbuttoned his shirt. He was of Hispanic descent and had skin the color of a deep tan. His body was perfect. Hard muscle in all the right places. Six-pack abs. Nice butt. Exquisite privates. He took the shirt off and unzipped his cargo pants, and I felt my nipples tingle. I looked down and saw that they were standing at attention, poking into the silky camisole. Jeez Louise! I grabbed the quilt and pulled it up over my tinglers.

"Hold on," I said. "There's something I have to tell you."

Ranger's phone buzzed and he checked the screen. "It's going to have to wait. The incident I just resolved has turned into an explosion and raging inferno. I need to get back there."

I was saved by the inferno. Huge relief. I didn't have to tell another fib. I watched him get dressed and had a twinge of regret that he hadn't gotten past the cargo pants.

# CHAPTER TEN

It was five in the morning when Ranger returned to my bedroom. He smelled slightly smoky, and he had a five o'clock shadow that was a combination of beard and soot.

"Is there anything left of your account?" I asked him.

"It's now a vacant lot. This was a major screwup on my end. We obviously missed an incendiary device when we cleared the building. I have an early morning briefing, but I need to talk to you."

"Okay," I said. "Talk."

"Do we have a marital schedule?"

"No."

"Do you want one?"

"Not right now," I said. "I have a lot going on."

"That works for me," Ranger said. "I'm behind at Rangeman. I need to hire two more men and an office assistant. And now I need to find out what went wrong tonight. To be honest a wedding ceremony isn't important to me. Having you in my apartment when I finish my day *is* important."

"It's important to me too," I said. "I miss Ella."

"If I fired Ella, would you still want to marry me?"

"I'd have to think about it."

That made him smile. His teeth were very white in his dark, sooty beard. "Are you making any progress with Bruno Jug and the vampire?"

"I have an agreement with Bruno. The vampire is disturbing and complicated."

"Do you need help?"

"Yes. I want to interview a bartender on Stark and I don't feel like enough of a brute to do it alone."

"So, you need Rent-A-Brute?"

"Yes."

"I'm your man. When do you want to do this?"

"Any time after nine thirty tonight."

"I'm not sure of my schedule. I'll text you a half hour ahead. It'll probably be around ten."

Ranger left. I went into the kitchen and stared into the fridge. The bread had grown a blue splotch of mold while I'd been sleeping. No milk. No juice. Small amount of peanut butter. I got a spoon and ate the remaining peanut butter.

"I'm pathetic," I said to Rex. "I might be pregnant and the major food group in my diet is doughnuts. That's irresponsible." I looked around my kitchen. "What's worse is, I don't even have any doughnuts."

Rex was asleep in his soup can and didn't respond.

I called Morelli. "Are you still home?"

"Yep," he said. "I just got out of the shower. Did you pull an all-nighter? Is everything okay? I've never known you to be awake at this hour."

"I'm good," I said. "I'm coming over. I need breakfast."

Fifteen minutes later I was at Morelli's little kitchen table, and he was making scrambled eggs. I had coffee with real half-and-half, a small glass of orange juice, and a wheat bagel with cream cheese. He brought our eggs to the table and sat across from me.

"What's going on?" he asked, adding Tabasco to his eggs.

"I've decided to get healthy. From now on I'm going to get up early, get some exercise, and eat good food."

"Did you get exercise today?"

"I took the stairs instead of the elevator and then I walked to my car."

Morelli grinned. "That's a start."

"Baby steps," I said, and I did a mental grimace at the unintentional double meaning. "I want to talk to you about Zoran Djordjevic."

Morelli forked in some egg. "Points for pronouncing his name right."

"I think it's possible that he's a serial killer."

Morelli stopped eating and gave me his full attention. "What have you got?"

I gave him the chronological history of the four missing women, beginning with Zoran's wife and ending with Julie Werly.

"I wasn't the principal on any of the locals," Morelli said, "but I'm familiar with them. All dead ends."

"Interesting though, right?"

"Jimmy was the principal on Werly. It was a big deal. Horrible crime. Everybody was broken up about it. She was really well-liked.

Her students loved her. My understanding is that her parents refuse to believe she's dead."

"No body."

"Right. The body and the murder weapon were never found. I'll talk to Jimmy about it."

I finished my breakfast and stood. "This was great. Thanks."

"Will I see you tonight?"

"Not tonight," I said. "I'm doing a stakeout."

Morelli rinsed his coffee mug and put it in the dishwasher. "Tell me it isn't dangerous."

"It isn't dangerous," I said.

Morelli wrapped his arms around me and kissed me. "Be careful."

---

The next stop was the supermarket. It didn't open until seven o'clock, so I sat in the lot and made a food list. After the food list, I reviewed what I knew about Zoran, which was very little. He was dripping blood when he ran out of the laundromat. I decided I should go back to the scene of the crime and see where the blood trail stopped. And I should ask Ranger if his tech guy could tap into any video feeds in the area. The police would also have that ability, but they wouldn't tell me what they found.

A small clump of early shoppers had gathered in front of the store. The doors opened and the shoppers rushed in. I left my car, got a cart, and followed at a more sedate pace. I looked for things that were appropriate for someone who had no talent in the kitchen. Baby carrots, snap peas, green beans. All prewashed and sealed up in bags. And I could share them with Rex. Salad greens. Prewashed and sealed up in a plastic box. I was on a roll. I could do this. I added blueberries, strawberries, bananas, a couple apples, and cherry tomatoes. I considered buying potatoes but decided it might be beyond me first time out. I got shelled walnuts and almonds for Rex and me. Swiss, cheddar, provolone, and American cheese slices. Instant oatmeal. Pop Tarts. Lots of them. Peanut butter and almond butter. Honey. Lots of olives. Wheat bread that said it was healthy and full of seeds. Burger buns that had no real nutritional value. A variety of condiments. Milk, half-and-half, vanilla yogurt, Irish butter, orange juice, eggs. I got to the meat counter and drew a blank. I didn't know what to do with meat but it seemed like I should buy some, so I got a large packet of ground beef. I did a left turn and went down the frozen-food aisle. I couldn't cook but I could defrost and reheat. Frozen veggie burgers, frozen beef patties, frozen chicken nuggets. Bags of frozen vegetables. Frozen rice and pasta meals. Frozen waffles and bagels. Seemed like a good start.

I checked out, took all my groceries home, and put them away. I spent a moment staring at the inside of my fridge, thinking it looked nice with food in it. I took a shower, blasted my hair with the hair dryer, and got dressed in the usual uniform of T-shirt, jeans, and sneakers.

Lula and Connie were already in the office when I strolled in.

"We've still got some good doughnuts left," Lula said. "Connie got extra Boston cream today."

"I'm going to hold on the doughnut. I already had breakfast this morning. I want to take a look at the laundromat crime scene."

"I guess I could go with you," Lula said. "Not much going on here."

I drove to Freemont and parked across from the laundromat. The crime scene tape was still in place. The street was empty.

"What are we looking for?" Lula asked, following me to the taped-off area.

"Blood. I want to see if there's a blood trail."

"There's splotches coming out the door," Lula said. "The splotches end but there's footprints on account of he must have stepped in the blood. And there's some little dribbles going down the sidewalk in the direction of the clothes store."

We got to the clothes store and the dribbles ended.

"Hold on," Lula said at the curb. "I think there's a footprint here but it's hard to see. It looks like he crossed the street, but there was a lot of traffic here when the cops and EMTs arrived. Everything got run over."

We went to the other side of the street and searched around.

"If I was Zoran, I'd go through that alleyway on the side of the grocery," Lula said.

We took the alleyway and came out on Stark Street. There was a bar on one side and a narrow, three-story rooming house on the other. The front door to the bar was open. The interior was dark. We stepped inside, and I was knocked over with the stench of stale beer and pot. A skinny guy in a tank top was standing holding a mop on the far side of the room.

"Something I can do for you ladies?" he asked.

Lula was rocking a red Raquel Welch wig and a scoop-neck top that was two sizes too small and showed about a quarter mile of cleavage. "You want me to take point on this?" she asked me.

I nodded. "Yup. Go for it."

She stepped forward so the mop guy could get a good look. "We're businesswomen," Lula said. "One of our clients was supposed to meet us on the corner about a half hour ago, and he hasn't shown up. We thought he might have been thirsty and stopped in here."

"Nobody been here this morning but me." The mop guy looked at Lula and then at me. "He supposed to do business with both of you?"

"He's a regular," Lula said. "We give him a twofer. Maybe you know him. His name is Zoran."

"I don't know anybody named Zoran."

"He works at the laundromat on the next street," Lula said. "White guy with weird teeth."

"That's Fang," mop guy said. "Everybody knows him as Fang. You make a comment about his teeth to his face, and he tells you he's a vampire. Like he's real proud of it. I heard he got hungry during work hours and killed a customer."

"Did he come in here a lot?" I asked mop guy.

"Not a lot. Once in a while. Some of the street vendors conduct business in the alleyway, and we get some trade from it. This is a shitty bar but it's the only one open in the morning. If you're a morning freak and want a place to sit and do your thing, this is it."

"And Fang comes in to do his thing?"

"I guess you'd have to do some kind of substance abuse to get through hanging out in a laundromat all day," Lula said. "What is Fang into?"

"He was old-school," mop guy said. "Liked the psychedelics. Shrooms, acid, pot, special K. A couple times I saw him with roofies. Not that it's any of my business, but I figured with his dental problems he probably needed Scooby Snacks to get a cooperative date."

"I don't like men who take advantage of a woman with that kind of stuff," Lula said.

"I hear you," mop guy said. "I guess Fang found a better way, right? Spend time with you ladies." He smiled, showing a large gold tooth in the front with a small diamond embedded in it. "What would it take to get a twofer from you? I got a back room here, and I could pay you in liquor. You could take your pick."

"That's real appealing," Lula said, "but we're on the clock, and we gotta be back on the corner for a pickup. We'll stop in when we got more time. You don't want to rush a twofer with us."

"You know where to find me," mop guy said.

"What time do you open?" I asked him.

"I come in to clean up around seven o'clock."

Lula and I left the bar. We moseyed around a little looking for signs of blood, but we didn't spot any dribbles or footprints. We gave up on the tracking project and took the long way back to my SUV, avoiding the alleyway. The state's mobile crime lab was parked in front of the laundromat. A squad car was parked behind it in the exact spot where we'd seen a footprint.

"Looks like the cops are busy obscuring evidence," Lula said.

Morelli and Jimmy had both been on the scene yesterday. They were good cops. They were smart. The initial blood trail was obvious, and I was sure that the footprint had already been documented. I was also sure that they knew about the alleyway drug market. The twofer ladies had the advantage over Morelli and Jimmy when it came to getting information out of the mop guy.

"I've still got some friends on the street," Lula said. "One of them might know something, but they don't get up this early. I could talk to them after lunch."

"Good thinking," I said. "In the meantime, I'm going to visit Bruno Jug."

"Are you sure that's a good idea? He said he'd call *you*. Do you at least have a present for him? Last time you brought him a present."

"No present. Just me, offering him a ride."

"Maybe you should get dressed up a little," Lula said. "Spruce up your makeup. What kind of makeup are you wearing anyway?"

"Eyeliner and a little mascara," I said. "And lip gloss."

"Everyone's wearing false eyelashes now. You should try it. It would add drama to your face. And you'd look good with eye shadow with some glitter to it."

"Anything else?"

"A dress would be good. And heels. Heels with your jeans might be a good look if you put on a tank top and maybe a little leather jacket over the tank top."

"I'm not asking him out on a date. I'm offering him a ride to the police station."

"Just sayin'. Sometimes you want to sweeten the deal."

I thought Lula raised a good point about my clothes. I couldn't see myself doing the job in a dress and heels, but I thought I could look more professional. I was wearing the few emergency things I'd bought after the fire. A comfortable hoodie, sneakers, and some inexpensive girly T-shirts. The jeans were nice. I'd spent money on the jeans.

"If I could bring Jug in, I could buy some clothes," I told Lula.

"As I see it, that's a lot of motivation," Lula said. "Let's go get the crazy old coot."

---

I drove to East Gilbert Street and parked in front of Jug Produce.

"I hope you aren't planning on leaving me in the car again," Lula said. "I want to see what a fruit tycoon's office looks like."

"It's not that impressive."

"I imagine it's not as fancy as the Oval Office, where the president works. I saw a picture of the Oval Office, and it had a big blue rug with an eagle in the middle of it. I don't know if I could live with an eagle in the middle of my rug, but I guess if you're the president you have to put up with that sort of thing. Like, it's his cross to bear."

I had my own carpet cross to bear. It was named Herbert. He was going to be in my house today supervising rug installation. I did a mental head slap. I should have been more adamant about not wanting the carpet. Stupid, stupid, stupid!

"Are you okay?" Lula said. "You're making a funny face like you just ate something awful and you might throw up."

"I'm good," I said. "Just a touch of indigestion."

"That's on account of you didn't have your usual doughnut in the morning. Once you get your body used to doughnuts, it's not happy with anything else."

I suspected Lula was right about the doughnuts, but this morning my gastric reflux was being caused by Herbert. I got out of the SUV, crossed the sidewalk, and went into the building with Lula tagging along. The small foyer was empty. No one behind the desk. I could hear voices not far off. I walked past the desk and took the stairs to the second floor. I walked down the short hallway and stopped at Jug's office. The door was closed but I could hear talking inside. I knocked on the door and Lou answered.

"Hi," I said. "Remember me? You gave me a fruit basket."

"What do you want?"

I stepped to the side and peeked around him, spotting Jug at his desk. "Hi, Mr. Jug," I called out. "It's Stephanie. I'm the one who brought you pajamas."

Lula elbowed Lou aside so she could see into the room. "And I'm Lula," she said. "I picked the pajamas out. You got a real nice office here."

Lou tried to move Lula back into the hall.

"Hey!" Lula said to Lou, pulling herself up a couple inches, getting into his bulldog face. "You watch your hands. You get your hands off me. No one touches Lula 'less she wants them to. Did I give you permission to touch me? No, I did not."

"What's going on?" Jug asked. "What's with the ladies?"

"You see?" Lula said to Lou. "There's a gentleman sitting behind that desk. He called us ladies."

"Sorry, Bruno," Lou said. "I don't know how they got up here."

"We walked up the stairs, you moron," Lula said. "We came to see Mr. Jug. And I wanted to see his office because he's a fruit tycoon, and I never met a fruit tycoon before."

The fruit tycoon was wearing a giant baby bib over his dress shirt, and he was eating what looked like a big bowl of ice cream.

"A fruit tycoon," Jug said. "That's a good one. Let the ladies in. Maybe they'd like a picture with me."

Lula gave me her cell phone and hustled over to Jug for her picture.

"Maybe we should take his bib off first," Lou said.

There were four more men in the room. They all rushed over to get the bib.

"It's peach ice cream," Jug said. "I'm testing it out. We're thinking of expanding our fruit business."

"That's real smart," Lula said. "Everybody loves ice cream."

"We have a lot," Jug said. "They made a whole batch of it. Do you want some?"

"Sure," Lula said. "I'd never pass up ice cream."

"Get ice cream for the ladies," Jug said.

"Your office is a lot more classy than the Oval Office in the White House," Lula said. "I like that you have an oriental rug on your floor. It has a lot going on in it, and if you spill ice cream on it, you'd never notice."

"My dog peed on it a couple times, and it soaked right in, and you couldn't see it at all," Jug said.

"You're a smart man," Lula said. "You know how to make good decisions about rugs and stuff."

"You bet your ass," Jug said. "That's why I'm the boss. Right, Lou?"

"Right, boss," Lou said.

A man handed bowls of ice cream to Lula and me.

Lula dug into her ice cream. "This is excellent," Lula said. "It's nice and creamy. And it tastes real peachy. You know what would be good in it? Chocolate chips."

"Chocolate chips!" Jug said. "Of course. I knew it was missing something. It needs chocolate chips." He turned to Lou. "Why didn't you think of that?"

Lou shrugged. "I don't think of things like that."

"I came to talk to you about your court date," I said to Jug. "I thought this would be a good time to get you rescheduled."

"Why is this a good time?" Jug asked.

"Do you have anything better to do?" I asked him.

Jug looked at Lou. "Do I?"

"Yeah," Lou said. "There's the thing."

"What thing?"

"The thing we always do on Thursday," Lou said.

"Haircut," one of the other men said. "You need a haircut."

"And a massage," Lou said. "You always like the massage."

"It would be more fun to go with Stephanie and me," Lula said to Jug.

"Do you give happy endings?" Jug asked.

"Not anymore," Lula said. "I gave that up. We let Vinnie take care of the ending now. Sometimes Connie."

"Connie would be okay," Jug said.

Lou rolled his eyes and the other guys looked like they were trying not to laugh.

"This isn't gonna take long, is it?" Lou asked me. "You got

everything set up? We walk into the court, get the papers signed, and we're out of there, right?"

"Right."

"And there better be something at the end that makes Bruno happy. Cupcakes or something."

"Absolutely," I said. "Primo cupcakes."

They got Bruno dressed in his jacket, asked him if he had to use the little boys' room, and escorted him down the hall and down the stairs.

"Lula and I can take it from here," I said to Lou.

"Not gonna happen," Lou said. "We all go."

"All five of you?"

"Yeah. We're going out the back way. We'll take our car."

"That isn't necessary," I said. "This is a simple procedure."

"It's necessary," Lou said. "This is the way we do things. You're going with us."

"Their car is probably more comfortable anyway," Lula said to me. "I bet it's an Escalade. That's the gangster car of choice. And we don't have to worry about driving through any bad neighborhoods because they're all carrying."

We followed Lou to the loading dock, where two cars were waiting. Both cars had drivers. One of the cars was a big Mercedes sedan. Lou got in the front and Lula and I got in the back with Jug between us. The four remaining men got into an Escalade.

"I told you they'd have an Escalade," Lula said. "They always have an Escalade in the movies."

We moved out through the Jug Produce gate, with the Escalade following. I called Connie and told her we were on our way, and she needed to bring cupcakes with her when she came to bond out Jug.

"I'm not bonding him out," Connie said. "Remember I told you there's a feud going between Harry and Bruno? Vinnie wasn't supposed to bond him out the first time."

I lowered my voice. "I'm with five armed soldiers who are going to be very unhappy to hear this."

"Maybe it'll be enough if I bring the cupcakes," Connie said.

"They better be damn good cupcakes."

I hung up and smiled at Lula.

"Everything good?" Lula asked.

"Yup," I said. "It's all good."

"Where are we going?" Jug asked.

"We're going to the courthouse to get your court date rescheduled."

"And then I get to have a happy ending?"

"Yep," I said. "Connie will be there and she's bringing cupcakes."

"I like cupcakes a lot," Jug said. "Where are we going again?"

"The courthouse."

Lou's phone rang. "Un-huh," he said. "Un-huh, un-huh, un-huh." He tapped the phone off and turned to his driver. "Abort. We're going to the chopper in Bucks."

The driver made an instant U-turn with the Escalade following his lead.

"What?" I said, leaning forward. "What's happening?"

"Change in plans," Lou said. "Bruno has decided to take a short vacation."

"I'm sitting next to him. He didn't say anything about a vacation."

"Sit back and relax," Lou said. "You aren't in any immediate danger."

"Immediate? Like I will be in the future?"

"Are you girls carrying?" he asked.

"Damn right I'm carrying," Lula said.

"Good to know," Lou said. "Just make sure you don't shoot me in the back, because the boys in the Escalade behind us wouldn't like it."

Lula and I turned to look out the back window. The Escalade was right on our bumper. We cut through downtown and went over the Stark Street bridge into Pennsylvania. We followed the road along the river for what seemed like an eternity but was really more like thirty to forty minutes. The car turned off Route 32, and the river was behind us. We were almost instantly in an area that was heavily forested, interspersed with cut fields. We passed a couple driveways leading into the woods and an occasional house. It was a curvy road, and we made a few turns before the car stopped at a private gated drive. The gate opened and we wound our way through the woods. The woods gave way to paddocks for horses and a stone house that could only be described as a mansion. Several cars were parked close to the house. We drove past the house, following a single-lane paved road that led to an open field and a Sikorsky S-76 helicopter. Mrs. Jug was standing to one side, flanked by two large men. One of the men was holding Mr. Big.

"You don't know where you are, right?" Lou asked me.

"Nope," I said. "Haven't a clue. Don't want to know."

"Me either," Lula said. "I'm dumb as a box of rocks."

Lou helped Jug get out.

"What about the cupcakes?" Jug asked me.

"Next time," I told him. "Promise."

The Jugs got on the helicopter with Lou and two of the men from the Escalade. The helicopter lifted off and disappeared. One of the remaining men got into the Mercedes to ride shotgun and we headed back to Trenton. No one said anything. We were on the Stark Street bridge and Connie called me.

"I'm at the courthouse with cupcakes," she said. "Where are you?"

"I'm in Bizarroland," I said. "I'm on my way back to the office. I'll meet you there. Make sure you bring the cupcakes."

# CHAPTER ELEVEN

"Okay, let me get this straight," Connie said. "You were on your way to the courthouse and there's a phone call and all of a sudden you're on your way to a private airfield in Bucks County."

I selected a second cupcake. "Yep. Not exactly an airfield. I just saw the one helicopter. By the way, these cupcakes are fantastic. I just had one with custard inside it."

"And then they put Jug on the helicopter . . . ," Connie said.

"A big one," Lula said. "With Mrs. Jug and the dog."

"It said 'Sikorsky S-76' on the side of it," I said. "And it took off and I don't know where it went. They drove us back to Trenton and here we are."

"They didn't take us back to Jug Produce either," Lula said. "They had Stephanie's SUV waiting for us in one of the municipal lots downtown. We aren't sure how it got there because they didn't have the key."

"I imagine there are people at Jug Produce who have skills beyond unloading crates of oranges," I said.

"This isn't good," Lula said. "We only got one FTA out there and it's a vampire that I'd just as leave stay far away from. And we don't know where he is anyway. What's wrong with this town? It used to be full of crime. And now there's nothing."

"There's crime," Connie said. "There just aren't any FTAs. Everybody is showing up for court."

"Well that's a real bitch," Lula said. "How's Stephanie gonna buy new clothes if there's no work for her?"

"The two guys who are out there are high bonds," I said. "If I could find them, I'd be in good shape."

"One just flew off in a helicopter," Lula said. "The other is probably sleeping it off in a coffin somewhere."

"I want to know where Jug went," I said. "Helicopters are short range, so either it took Jug to an airport to connect with a plane or else it took him to someplace relatively close."

Connie googled the Sikorsky. "It says here that it has a range of three hundred air miles and can fly for about two and a half hours."

"Run some checks on Jug," I said to Connie. "Where does he have real estate? Check family and close friends. That helicopter took him somewhere perceived as safe. And see if you can find the estate where the helicopter touched down. We went over the Stark Street bridge and drove along Route 32, heading for New Hope. We were on that road for maybe a half hour before it turned off and went into an area of mixed forest and fields, and eventually, we turned right onto a paved gated driveway that ended up at a horse farm with a large stone house and circular drive. The Sikorsky was in a large, flat grassy field at the end of a single-lane paved drive."

"Hold on," Lula said. "I got the news streaming on my phone

and they're talking about Jug. Some woman is saying she got a video of him with her fourteen-year-old daughter and they're doing the nasty. According to the mom, Jug drugged her kid with a date-rape piece of fruit. She didn't say what kind of fruit, but my money's on a banana."

"That's disgusting," Connie said. "That's sick."

I didn't have a high opinion of Jug, but a sex crime involving a fourteen-year-old took things to a new low.

"And here's a shot of the front of Jug Produce with a bunch of crazy reporters and camera guys and a channel twelve satellite truck. That's probably why Stephanie's car got moved. They didn't want to drop us off in the middle of the circus. We were parked right at the front door."

And I thought they probably didn't want us talking to the press about a possible sex crime after Bruno had just asked us about a happy ending. Truth is, while I was horrified, I was also relieved. My fear had been that I'd stumbled into a mob turf war that could have been fatal for Lula and me. An ugly scandal was manageable.

"One mystery solved," I said. "And since Mr. and Mrs. Jug aren't in residence, I think this would be a good time to break into their house. Maybe there's a clue about their hidey-hole."

"And?" Lula asked.

"And then we could go get Jug and bring him back here and I could pay off my credit card. The alternative is to go door-to-door on Stark Street, looking for Zoran."

"Okay then," Lula said. "Let's do some B & E."

I drove to Merrymaster Street, parked around the corner, and Lula and I walked back to Jug's house. I went to the front door and realized that the house had a Ring doorbell. We were on camera. There were glass panels on both sides of the door. I looked in one and saw an alarm unit with a blinking light.

"Nobody home," I said to Lula. "We'll come back some other time."

We left the house and walked back to the car.

"That was a bust," Lula said.

"I should have known he'd have a security system. The back door might not have a camera, but we would set off the house alarm."

"I'm not doing plan B," Lula said. "I got no protection against vampires. I used part of my necklace in spaghetti sauce last night."

"I'm not going door-to-door, but I'm going to drive down the first three blocks of Stark. I know he's there."

"I guess that would be reasonable as long as we aren't getting out of the car. And then after we drive down those three blocks we're going back to the office, right? It's way past lunchtime, and I'm thinking about those cupcakes we left behind. Not that we would have them for lunch, but we could have them *after* lunch. I know you're trying to be healthy for the little tyke. Have you thought of a name?"

"No! I'm not even sure I'm pregnant."

"When can you take the test?"

"Tomorrow is the earliest to see if I'm pregnant. I can't take a paternity test for six more weeks."

"Six weeks is a long time. How are you going to do that?"

"I don't know. One day at a time."

I left North Trenton, did a slow cruise down Stark Street, and didn't see Zoran.

"I'm thinking we stop at Cluck-in-a-Bucket on the way back to the office," Lula said. "I'm feeling like a Double Clucky Burger."

---

We spread the food out on Connie's desk. Fries, Clucky Burgers, coleslaw, and shakes.

Connie unwrapped her Clucky Burger. "I didn't get to run all the search engines, but I got some decent information. I printed out a map and drew a circle showing the helicopter's range without refueling. Then I looked for possible safe houses that could accommodate a helicopter. I came up with four locations. There's also a good chance that the helicopter ferried him to an airport and he's on his way to South America."

"I don't want to hear that," I said. "I don't want to go to South America." I looked at the printout of the map. "So he could be in Vermont, New Hampshire, the Outer Banks, or Long Island."

"Or any place in between," Lula said.

"Tell me about Vermont," I said to Connie.

"Jug has a cousin in Dorset. She lives in a school bus with her husband and five cats. They have ten acres of flat field where theoretically a helicopter could land. I think this one is a long shot."

"Yeah, I think we can cross the cousin off the list. What about New Hampshire?"

"Jug has a son in Portsmouth. He grew up with his mother. Wife number two. He gets along okay with Jug. He's a chef. Single. Works at a restaurant in town. Rents a little house out in the country. Google Earth shows it sitting in the middle of an open field that's next to a dairy farm. Zillow says the house has two bedrooms and one bath. Wouldn't be ideal for the new Mrs. Jug."

"Agree. Outer Banks is next up."

"This ties with Long Island," Connie said. "It's a big house on the ocean with some property around it. Got a tennis court, pool, four-car garage. A helicopter could easily land on the lawn leading up to the house. Jug grew up with the guy who owns the house. The guy's in real estate. Jug and wives number one and two used to visit. Zillow says the house has a four-bedroom guest wing. And I found a picture of Jug on the guy's boat. Seventy-five-foot Hatteras. Jug was holding a fish. Some kind of tournament two years ago. I have a report for you with more information on the guy, including his address."

"And Long Island?" I asked.

"It's a small vineyard on the North Fork. It's owned by Jug's lawyer. Actually, it's owned by a holding company, but for all purposes it's the lawyer's property. I found an article about it in one of those food and wine magazines. The lawyer uses it as a weekend getaway. Has a large stone house and a two-bedroom guesthouse. The vineyard isn't open to the public, but it does some private tasting parties to benefit local charities. It sits on a good-size chunk of land, and it has a helicopter pad."

"It gets my vote," I said.

"It's also the closest," Connie said. "It's a three-and-a-half-hour drive. One hundred and forty-nine miles by helicopter. Well within the Sikorsky's range."

"Do we know anyone on Long Island who can check it out for us?"

Connie finished her burger. "I'm working on it."

"Did you have any luck locating the house in Bucks County?"

"I haven't gotten to that yet. If you have time, you might go to Google Earth and see if you could zero in on it. My afternoon is crammed. I have an appointment with the bookkeeper in fifteen minutes."

"In that case, I might take a cupcake and go have my nails done," Lula said. "They don't match my mood anymore. I got Trenton nails and I'm thinking I might need Long Island nails."

I had do-it-yourself nails, at least until I paid off my credit card. They were currently short and wearing Kyoto Pearl quick-dry polish. They matched my toes. My hair was also professionally neglected, but there was no way I was cutting my own hair. Good thing God invented the ponytail.

I drove to my apartment building on autopilot, thinking about Bruno Jug. Suppose I actually found him on Long Island. Was it unrealistic to think that Lula and I could bring him back to Trenton? He'd gotten on the Sikorsky with Lou and two men from his office. If they'd stayed on the property with him, it would make things much more complicated.

I parked in my building's lot and took the stairs to the second floor. I got a shot of adrenaline when I got to my apartment and found the door unlocked and open a crack. The adrenaline rush was replaced by a knot in my gut when I remembered that Herbert was installing carpet today. The fact that he was in my kitchen did nothing to ease the cramp in my intestines.

"Did you come home for lunch?" he asked. "You have lots of good food here now. I made myself a sandwich. I hope you don't mind. You got healthy bread. I like to eat things that are healthy. I eat a lot of carrots. I saw that you bought carrots. I washed them and put them in a plastic baggie. It said they were prewashed, but I always wash them anyway. I gave one to your hamster. That was okay, right? I googled it first to make sure it was okay. I could make you a sandwich if you're hungry. I make good sandwiches. I'm good at almost everything. You probably already noticed that. Except ice-skating. I can't ice-skate because I have weak ankles."

"I already ate lunch," I said. "I came home to do some work."

"It looks like you work on your dining room table. I noticed your computer there. I could get you a desk, if you want. I have connections. You could put it in your living room area. I noticed you still don't have a television. I could get you one of those too. Then we could watch television together. Except sometimes I work at night. And if I decide to go into the mortuary business, I suppose I would be working a lot of nights, but only until nine o'clock."

I felt my shoulders slump. Herbert was exhausting. He was one more problem on top of all my other problems, and I was having no luck getting rid of him. It would have been easier if he was a horrible person—if he was mean, and abusive, and violent. Unfortunately, he was just obnoxious and annoying and clueless.

I walked out of my kitchen and into my living room and was gobsmacked. The living room and dining room had been carpeted. It was amazing. The carpet was a neutral cream that made my inexpensive couch look wonderful. It felt soft underfoot and the carpet didn't even have any stains. It was new! The door to my bedroom was open and I could see two men working in there.

"They're finishing up in your bedroom," Herbert said.

"It's beautiful," I said, "but I can't afford this."

"No problem," Herbert said. "Sometimes in my business I come across things that are looking for a home, and I do favors for people who would like to return the favor, and this is one of those things."

"What *is* your business?"

"I'm an entrepreneur," Herbert said.

"Is that another way of saying you don't exactly have a real job?"

"I've never thought of it that way. *Entrepreneur* is such a great word. It sounds European."

"You live with your parents."

"They like me. And it cuts down on my overhead. I could live someplace else if I wanted to. I have lots of money. Not as much as Jeff Bezos or Oprah. I might be in the Martha Stewart range. I don't really know exactly how much money I have, but it's a lot."

Okay, I get this. Chances of Herbert finding someone, other than his parents, who likes him are slim to none.

"I have work to do," I said to Herbert.

"I'll make sure no one bothers you."

"Thanks. That would be great."

I moved into the dining room and sat at the table. I opened my laptop and waited while it came to life. Herbert sat across from me.

"What are you doing?" I asked him.

"I'm watching you."

"No. You aren't going to watch me. That's creepy."

"Suppose I watched you from the living room. I could sit on the couch and watch you."

"No."

"Okay then, I'll watch Mike and Manny finish the carpet. I'd watch television but you don't have one."

"Don't you have something to do? Entrepreneurial stuff?"

"Not at the moment. I did some work this morning. I get up early. I don't need much sleep."

I pulled up a map of Trenton and zeroed in on the Stark Street bridge and Pennsylvania. I imagined myself being driven over the Delaware River into Bucks County. We turned right onto Route 32. We drove past Washington Crossing and after maybe a mile we turned off 32 and moved away from the river. I had a satellite view on my map, so I could see trees and fields and houses. Jug was talking, asking Lula questions about ice cream, while we were driving through this area, and I wasn't always paying attention to scenery details.

I slowly scrolled through the map, looking for the house with the circular drive, horse paddocks, and an open field. I could see why Connie passed this over to me. There was a lot of ground to cover. A lot of circular driveways and a lot of open fields. And after we left Route 32, I hadn't been sure of the direction. The road had twisted, and we made a couple turns. Finding the house was like looking for a needle in a haystack. This was going to take time and require some luck.

I stood and stretched and walked into the kitchen. I ate a couple baby carrots and returned to my laptop. Carrots were okay but they'd never replace a whoopie pie. I continued to search, and I heard the men leave my bedroom. There was some chatter at my door. Herbert told one of them that he'd see him later tonight. The door closed and Herbert came into the dining room.

"They're done," he said. "The rug looks good in your bedroom. Do you want to come look at it with me?"

I had a flashback to the last time I was in my bedroom with Herbert. "I'm not going to sleep with you," I said.

"Okay, how about just sex?"

"No. Especially not sex. No sex."

"I guess it must be that time of the month," Herbert said. "Otherwise, women always want to have sex with me. I have animal magnetism."

"I'm in the middle of something here. I'll look at the rug as soon as I'm done. I'm sure it's wonderful."

"Maybe I can help. I'm excellent with computers. I'm like a computer guru."

"Thanks for the offer, but this isn't difficult. It's just time-consuming."

"I guess I'll go then. I have a couple errands to run, and I need to go home and get ready for tonight. Martin Goodman's viewing is tonight at the funeral home on Hamilton. Maybe you'd like to go with me. I could pick you up in my Prius. Have you ever ridden in a Prius? They're excellent cars."

"No. Sorry. I have plans for tonight. I'm meeting a friend."

"That's too bad," Herbert said. "I think this will be a nice viewing. Martin Goodman made a fortune in pharmaceuticals. The legitimate kind. He had wealthy friends. I expect the flower arrangements to be exceptional. I'm not a big flower person, but some people are, and it's an important part of the death ritual. I'll text you when I get home and fill you in on the viewing. Unless you want me to come over later and I can tell you about it in person."

"Coming over wouldn't be a good idea. I'm not sure when I'll be getting home."

"I stay up real late sometimes. You could call me anytime if you want me to come over."

"I'll keep that in mind," I said, walking him to the door.

He stepped out into the hall. "I'll sleep with my clothes on just in case you call and I need to get over here fast."

I had no idea how to respond to this, so I gave Herbert something between a smile and a grimace, closed the door, threw the dead bolt, and slid the chain across.

I looked into the kitchen. "He's gone," I said to Rex. "Everyone is gone, and it will be quiet now." Rex didn't say anything. He was inside his soup can, snuggled into his bedding. Rex had the good life.

I returned to the dining room and slumped in my chair. This wasn't working. I should have found the house by now. I opened the file Connie had printed out for me. There were a bunch of pages paper-clipped together with a sticky note on the top page. *Credit bureau profiles on the four safe house prospects. Haven't had a chance to read them.*

I pulled the profile on the lawyer. Anthony Bordelli. No litigation. No derogatory comments. No car loans. No mortgages. Good credit score. Sixty-seven years old. Married to Charlotte Loch Bordelli. Two adult children. No mention of the house in North Fork, Long Island. Office in Trenton. Residence was listed as 1762 Loury Road, Makefield, Pennsylvania. Holy crap. I'd been scrolling through Makefield. I typed the address into Google Maps and there it was in the perfect location. I must have passed over it a dozen times. The problem might have been that the gated driveway was completely obscured by trees and the horse paddocks weren't obvious. The house with the circular driveway, the garages, and the paved single-lane road that ended at the open field were just as I remembered.

So now I was pretty sure I knew where they'd taken Jug. The big question was, how long would they keep him hidden? And the next question was, how bad did I want to make the capture? If I could grab the vampire, I could afford to wait awhile for Jug. If I didn't bring one of them in, I was looking at financial disaster.

I went to a couple streaming news feeds. Nothing helpful there. It looked like everyone was still camped out in front of Jug Produce. Just for giggles, I mapped out the drive from Trenton to the vineyard on Long Island. It was no surprise that it was an ugly trip with horrible traffic. At least it was manageable in one day if everything went right. It was too late to go today, and I had Ranger scheduled for tonight. If by some stroke of luck I found Zoran tonight, I was golden. If not, I'd set off for Long Island tomorrow morning.

I read through the rest of Connie's background material and did some research on the vineyard and the lawyer. At five thirty I pushed back from the dining room table and went into the kitchen to make myself a nutritious meal. After five minutes of staring into the refrigerator, I called my mom and said I was coming over for dinner.

---

My father looked at the casserole dish in the middle of the table. "What's this?"

"We tried something new," Grandma said. "It was on television on one of those cooking shows and it won the award."

"It looks like dog food," my father said. "It's all brown. Where's the potatoes? Where's the meat?"

"That's the good part," Grandma said. "It's all there, mixed together. It's a one-pot-wonder recipe."

"Food isn't supposed to be mixed together," my father said. "It's supposed to be all separate on the plate. You got the meat, the potatoes or pasta, and the corn or peas or beans. That's the way it is. And there's supposed to be gravy. I like gravy."

"What about lasagna?" Grandma said. "It's all mixed together."

"It's in different layers," my father said. "You can see the meat and the pasta. And the peas are separate."

"There's peas in the casserole," Grandma said. "If you look close you can see them."

"I don't want to look close," my father said.

My mother was at the other end of the table self-administering anesthesia in the form of whiskey. The casserole was directly in front of me, so I took my father's plate, spooned food onto it, and gave it back to him.

"Good news," I said to my father. "I saw an apple pie in the kitchen."

I helped myself to some mystery meal and passed the casserole dish to my mother. "What's this called?" I asked Grandma.

"Humdinger Helper," Grandma said. "You're supposed to make it in one of those giant iron skillets, but we don't have any."

I took some for a test drive. "It's good," I said. "Actually, it's delicious."

"It has elbow macaroni and cheese and lean ground beef in it," Grandma said. "It's got all the essential food groups."

My father had his head down, forking in the Humdinger.

"Have you been watching the news about Bruno Jug?" Grandma asked me. "They say he's missing. Is that because you put him in jail?"

"No. He disappeared before I had a chance to deliver him," I said.

"Nobody knows where he is," Grandma said. "I think he's in the landfill. Did you look in the landfill?"

"Ketchup," my father said. "I need ketchup."

Grandma jumped up, trotted off to the kitchen, and returned with ketchup.

"There's been a lot of talk about Jug since this story broke," Grandma said, topping off her wineglass. "He was known to like the ladies too much, but there's never been word of him drugging someone or molesting young girls. Some people are saying it's because he's not *all there* anymore. What do you think?" she asked me.

"He's a little odd, but it's hard to tell if it's an act, just his personality, or the beginnings of dementia. What do you think?"

"I think it's *all* of those things," Grandma said. "And I think there's something fishy about the story of him drugging a fourteen-year-old girl and raping her. Jug wouldn't drug a kid. He'd buy her. Anyway, I expect to learn more tonight. Mildred

Senski is having a viewing tonight at Stiva's. She's in slumber room number two because Martin Goodman grabbed number one. I wouldn't necessarily go to the Goodman viewing but seeing how things have turned out, I wouldn't miss giving my respects to Mildred Senski. Her cousin, Grace, is married to a Jug. Grace will know all the good stuff."

"Take notes for me," I told Grandma. "See if Grace knows where Jug is hiding out."

# CHAPTER TWELVE

I was on my parents' couch, watching hockey with my dad, when Grandma came home from the viewing.

"I got a real scoop for you," Grandma said. "I'll tell you in the kitchen. I need a piece of pie. The Goodman crowd ate all the cookies and by the time I got to the table there was nothing but crumbs. It's like they never saw a cookie before. It's because all those women who are friends with the Goodmans are nothing but skin and bones. Stick-figure bodies and big bobbleheads. Probably never have a cookie in the house. All they got in their refrigerator is kale and those green blender drinks. And then when they go out, they eat everyone else's cookies. They don't even eat them normal. They nibble and break them into pieces like they aren't going to eat the whole thing."

Grandma took the pie out of the fridge and cut a piece for herself and a piece for me. I took a tub of vanilla ice cream out of the freezer and put it on the table, and Grandma and I sat down and dug in.

"Here's the deal," Grandma said. "Grace told me that Jug and his slut wife and vicious dog are on *vacation*. She was happy to tell me all this because she's not a fan of the wife or the dog and she's not all that crazy about Jug, either. Plus, I think she'd had some cocktails before the viewing. She said the family felt it was best to get Jug out of town until they paid off the mother of the fourteen-year-old."

"Did Grace say how long this would take?"

"They're negotiating. Grace said everyone is being very protective of Jug. She did a lot of eye-rolling when she said this."

"He has some serious tax evasion charges waiting for him in court."

"I don't think the family is worried about that. The judge and jury will all get fruit baskets. The family is mostly worried about Jug having a heart attack from a Viagra overdose. Anyway, Grace didn't know where they were keeping Jug, but he's going to be there for a while and it's not the landfill."

We finished the pie and ice cream and Ranger called.

"Are we still on for tonight?" he asked.

"Yes. Is that okay?"

"I'm down a man so I'm taking the night shift with Tiny. He'll ride shotgun with us. I'm not expecting any problems so we should have time to take care of business. I'll pick you up in half an hour."

"Perfect."

Ranger had high-end clients who paid a premium to get superior protection. He kept several fleet cars in constant motion 24/7 patrolling those clients. Tonight, he was riding patrol with one of his men. This was good for me. There would be no pressure tonight and tomorrow I could take my test.

I left my parents' house, pulled into my building's parking lot, and saw lights flash behind me. I parked and went to the Rangeman SUV. Ranger was driving, and Tiny was in the back seat. If Tiny was green, he could easily pass for the Hulk. I got in next to Ranger, said hello to Tiny, and buckled myself in.

"We're going to Lucky Linda's on the third block of Stark Street," I said to Ranger. "Zoran, the vampire, seemed to be friends with, or at least an acquaintance of, the bartender."

Ranger pulled out of the lot and headed toward the center of the city. "What's the bartender's name?"

"Goofy. No one seems to know his real name."

"Do you have any other Zoran contacts?"

"Yes, but they all dead-ended. He hasn't gone back to his house on Exeter Street. His parents say they haven't seen him. His uncle who owns the laundromat says he hasn't seen him. This morning, Lula and I followed blood tracks from the laundromat. They crossed the street and took us through the alley to Stark Street. That's where they stopped."

"That alley is used as a drug market," Ranger said.

"It was empty when we went through it, but we talked to a guy on Stark who remembered Zoran as Fang. He said Fang shopped in the alley."

Ranger stopped for a light. "Fang's drug of choice?"

"Shrooms, acid, pot, special K, occasionally roofies."

"He likes to trip out," Ranger said. "Needs help getting a date."

"I think he's still on Stark Street somewhere."

"And you want him because he failed to appear for his court date?"

"I saw him moments after he killed that woman. He was hovering over her with blood dripping out of his mouth. It was terrifying and unbelievably, sickeningly horrible. I think he's killed before. I suspect he's killed four other women. Maybe more."

"And he needs to be stopped," Ranger said.

"Yes," I said. "He needs to be stopped."

"Did you tell Morelli?"

"Yes. They're working on it."

"But you can't let it go," Ranger said.

"I'd love to walk away. This guy is insane. He scares the bejeezus out of me, but I have a responsibility to make an effort to capture him. I only have two FTAs right now. It's not like I'm on case overload."

"Your other FTA has disappeared," Ranger said.

"I'm pretty sure I know where he is. Lula and I will be going after him tomorrow. Maybe."

"Maybe?"

"One day at a time."

Ranger turned off State Street, onto Stark.

"Do you know what Zoran looks like?" I asked Ranger.

"More or less. His mug shot was blurry."

"That's because vampires don't photograph well."

"Yeah," Ranger said. "I thought it was something like that."

We cruised past the drug alley and did a slow drive-by on Lucky Linda's.

"It's early," Ranger said. "Not a lot going on. I'll make one more pass and then we'll park."

When we came around the second time there was a Lincoln Navigator in front of Lucky Linda's. Ranger parked behind the Navigator, and we all got out. Tiny took point, standing guard in front of the Rangeman SUV, and Ranger and I went into the bar.

It was appropriately dark, with a bunch of high-top tables in the front and a horseshoe-shaped bar toward the back. A small, raised stage with a couple of poles had been placed inside the horseshoe. Two mostly naked women were writhing and twerking against the poles. Bump-and-grind music competed with the televised ball game at one end of the bar. A wasted couple nursed drinks at one of the high-tops and four men were at the bar, hands wrapped around their bottles of beer. They had a lot of gold chains and tats, and I assumed the men arrived in the Navigator.

Ranger and I slid onto bar stools at one end of the horseshoe, and Ranger signaled the lone bartender. Ranger doesn't wear his weight in gold. He doesn't have a tattoo. He doesn't have a diamond stud in any of his teeth. His hair is perfectly trimmed. His body is perfectly muscled and toned. His gun is perfectly hidden under his perfectly tailored jacket. He only wears black. He says it makes his choices simple in the morning. I think it's for effect, because it's a power look and it's sexy as hell. He's former Special Forces, and if you're foolish enough to mess with him, he's deadly.

The bartender was young, medium height, and had a lot of curly red hair and a showstopping, brilliant white smile.

"What can I get you?" he asked.

"Are you Goofy?" I asked him.

"Usually," he said.

"I'm looking for someone. His parents said you might know where to find him."

"What's his name?"

"Zoran," I said. "I understand he also goes by Fang. He works at the laundromat on Freemont."

"Whoa. Yeah. I know the dude. He thinks he's a vampire."

"Have you seen him lately?"

"Not since he sank his canines into one of his customers. Are you cops?"

"No," I said. "We're working for his family. They want to find him."

This wasn't a lie. His parents had put up his bond money. So, in a way I was working for them.

"His family," Goofy said. "Are they like . . . vampires too?"

"Let's just say they have dental problems and leave it at that," I said.

"Look," he said. "I don't want any trouble. This dude is scary. I only know him as a customer. I entertain him just like everybody else. It's my thing. I'm Goofy. I'm everybody's friend. I can laugh like Goofy. *Haw ah haw ah haw.*"

"That's pretty good," I said.

"Yeah, it gets me a lot of tips. Especially after people get drinking. On a good night I can make more than the girls."

"He comes in here and he drinks and sometimes he's high and he talks to you," I said. "Think about it. What have you got for me?"

Ranger put a fifty-dollar bill on the bar, under a coaster. Goofy reached for it, and Ranger very quietly said, "Not yet."

"Okay, why not," Goofy said, "it's not like I'm a lawyer or a doctor with client privilege. He lives close. In a house. I don't know the street. He has a truck, but he never drives it. He walks from his house to the laundromat and here. He's always alone. I don't think he has any friends. I started working here two years ago and he's sort of a regular. He comes and goes. I think he goes back to check on the laundromat and then he comes back here and has tequila. Always tequila. Once he said he liked blood. He liked the way it smelled and tasted. He looked over at the girl on the pole and licked his lips, and I almost threw up. Then he gave me a ten-dollar tip and left."

"What about your other regulars? Did he ever talk to them?"

"He might have tried but talking about blood is pretty much a turnoff, even for the gangbangers and dopers. It's just weird. And then there are the fangs. It's not a good look."

"Let's assume he didn't go far. Where would he be hiding?" I asked him.

"I don't know. There are some condemned buildings when you get farther up the street. Housing is sketchy on this block. There are dopers who would take him in. Maybe you should just go door-to-door and see if you smell rotting flesh."

That got a very small smile out of Ranger. He gave Goofy a business card with a phone number on it. No name. No address. Just a phone number. "If you have more information," Ranger said.

"Who do I ask for?"

"Just identify yourself as Goofy."

We left the bar and returned to the Rangeman SUV.

"Thanks for being Bruteman," I said to Ranger. "I didn't learn anything new, other than that he drinks tequila, but it's possible that you'll get a phone call."

"It's a process," Ranger said.

---

It was almost midnight, but I couldn't sleep. I was freaked out over the whole vampire thing. The ugliness of it. The insanity. I got out of bed, put my sweatshirt on over my T-shirt, and went into the kitchen. Rex was awake and running on his wheel. Oblivious to everything awful. I gave him fresh water and refilled his food cup. I went into the dining room and checked my email and text messages. I downloaded the GPS directions to the North Fork of Long Island to my iPhone. I studied the satellite picture of the vineyard.

I was ready to give sleep another try when I heard noise in the parking lot. Car radio, I thought. Some drunken idiot coming home, blasting his lame music. I shut my computer down and got myself a glass of milk and a Pop-Tart. I ate the Pop-Tart and drank the milk, and the noise continued. High-pitched squawking. Sounded a little like Paul Simon's "Graceland" followed by "Do-Re-Mi" from *The Sound of Music*. I walked into my dark living room, looked out my window, and sucked in some air. It was Herbert, standing in the parking lot, under one of the overhead lights, playing his clarinet. A cop car turned into the parking lot and stopped just short of Herbert. Two cops got out and walked over to him. There was a short conversation, Herbert pointed up at my window, and I instantly jumped out of sight. The jumping away from the window was instinctive and most likely not necessary since my living room was dark and I wouldn't be visible from the parking lot. I peeked out and saw Herbert get into his Prius and drive away. I felt kind of bad that someone called the cops on Herbert, but at the same time, I was happy to see him leave. I padded back to my bedroom, crawled into bed, and fell asleep with "Do-Re-Mi" playing in my brain.

# CHAPTER THIRTEEN

I parked in front of the bail bonds office and saw Lula and Connie at the big storefront window. They were still on their feet when I walked in.

"Well?" Lula said. "Today is the day. What is it? We've been waiting for you to get here. We thought you'd never show up. What's the result?"

"It was a negative result, which is meaningless at six days. I'll try again at ten days."

"You're killing me," Lula said. "I can't wait four more days to find out if I'm going to be an auntie. Are you sure the test was negative? Maybe you should take another one just in case you got a defective pee stick."

"The tests are expensive, and anyway, I don't have time. I'm going after Jug today. I'm ninety-nine percent sure he's at the vineyard on Long Island. I want to get on the road at nine or ten o'clock, so I miss the worst of rush-hour traffic."

"I guess I'm going with you," Lula said.

"I guess you are," I said. "I'm counting on this being a day trip. It's a three-and-a-half-hour drive, so it'll be a long day, but it's better than staying overnight."

"Do you have a plan?" Lula asked.

"Not exactly. We need to find out how many people are in the house with him. And we need to do surveillance, but the way the house is set on the property is going to make it difficult to see anything."

The front door opened and closed, and Herbert walked over. "I saw all the cars out front so I thought I would come in to say hello." His eyes went to the open doughnut box on Connie's desk. "Are those bakery doughnuts? I love doughnuts. There's nothing like a doughnut in the morning. I mean, I try to eat healthy, but there's nothing wrong with a doughnut once in a while, right?"

"Help yourself," Connie said.

"I'm a sprinkles kind of guy," Herbert said. "This is a problem because there's one with chocolate sprinkles, and one with rainbow sprinkles, and one with pink sprinkles. I'm secure in my manhood so I could eat the pink sprinkles if I wanted but I'm not sure I'm in a pink-sprinkles mood today."

"Oh, for the love of Pete, just pick a doughnut," Lula said.

Herbert snatched up the doughnut with the rainbow sprinkles. "This doesn't mean that I'm gay," he said. "Not that there's anything wrong with being gay. I have some friends who are gay."

"Nobody cares," Lula said.

"I heard you talking about planning your day when I walked in," Herbert said. "You said you were going after Jug. Is that Bruno Jug, the pervert? I heard about him on the news last night."

"Yeah, but he hasn't been proved to be a pervert yet," Lula

said. "He's just up on tax evasion charges. He's a tycoon in the fruit business and we know him personally."

"I see his trucks all over the place," Herbert said. "I wouldn't mind meeting him. I never met a fruit tycoon."

"We're going after him, but it's a secret," Lula said. "He's hiding out and nobody knows where he is but us."

"Wow. That's so cool. Can I go with you? I wouldn't be any trouble. I'd just stand back and watch. Is this going to be a takedown like on *Dog the Bounty Hunter*? That was a great show. I used to watch that all the time. It was almost my favorite show. So, what's the plan? How are we going to get this guy?"

"We don't know," Lula said. "Stephanie hasn't told us yet. We got a problem on account of it's a vineyard with a mansion and maybe bodyguards."

"You need to do surveillance," Herbert said.

"Yes!" Lula said. "That's exactly what Stephanie was thinking, but she don't know how. The property setup is a problem."

"You need a drone," Herbert said.

We all went raised eyebrows. He was right. We needed a drone. "Anyone know how to fly a drone?" I asked Lula and Connie.

"I tried once," Lula said. "It isn't that easy."

"I can fly a drone," Herbert said. "I'm an expert drone flyer. People are always complimenting me on my drone flying. I use one for work sometimes."

"What kind of work do you do?" Lula asked.

"I'm an entrepreneur," Herbert said. "I do a little bit of this and a little bit of that. Sometimes I'm thinking about a new project, and I want to see its surroundings, so I put a drone up."

Just shoot me. An entire day with Herbert. Could life get any worse? An image of Zoran flashed through my head. Yes, I thought. Life could get worse. I could be the woman on the floor in the laundromat. I took a moment to make a mental adjustment. This won't be so bad, I told myself. I could endure a day with Herbert if it meant capturing Jug. And to that end, a drone would be hugely helpful. So, take a deep breath and get on with it.

"We think Jug is at a location on Long Island," I said to Herbert. "I was planning on leaving now, and depending on how things go, we might not get back to Trenton until late tonight."

"Oh boy, this is going to be great," Herbert said. "A road trip. I always wanted to see Long Island. A lot of rich people live there. I'm interested in rich people. I'll go home and get my drone and I'll be right back. I don't live far away. I could bring my clarinet, too. I came to your apartment building to serenade you, but I'm not sure you heard me. The police came and made me leave. I guess it was pretty late for some of the people in your building, but still, who doesn't like to hear a clarinet? I was playing show tunes. Everyone likes show tunes. And some Paul Simon. I'm a real Paul Simon fan. I was coming back from work, and I saw you had a light on in your bedroom, so I went and got my clarinet. Most people like when I play but I guess someone in your building complained. It only takes one person and the police have to come."

"How late was this?" Lula asked.

"It was around midnight," Herbert said.

"What kind of work were you doing at midnight?" Lula asked him.

"Entrepreneurial. I can't go into details. It's sort of secret."

Herbert left and I sent Lula off to get cupcakes.

"Do you really think cupcakes are going to lure Jug into your car?" Connie asked me.

"Can't hurt," I said. "Besides, last time I saw him, I promised him cupcakes."

"How are you going to get into the vineyard?"

"It's got a gated driveway, but it would be easy to walk onto the property. Just have to scoot around some hedges. If it's Jug and his wife and vineyard personnel on-site, it might not be so bad. I might be able to talk Jug into coming with me. If Lou and his henchmen are there it'll be more complicated."

"Do you think it would be better to take Ranger with you?"

"No. I don't want this to turn into a guns-drawn standoff. I need to be sneaky."

"Sneaky is always good," Connie said. "I'm in favor of sneaky."

---

Herbert was in the back seat, directly behind me. He was leaning forward, and he was breathing on my neck. It was high school all over again. We were a half hour out of Trenton, not even to the Jersey Turnpike, and I was already driving with teeth clenched.

"I got two dozen doughnuts," Lula said. "There's a box for Jug, and there's a box for us. Anyone want a doughnut?"

"Yes," I said.

"What kind?" Lula asked.

"Any kind!"

Lula gave me a maple glazed, handed a chocolate covered back to Herbert, and took a blueberry for herself. She surfed on her phone while she ate her doughnut.

"Look here," she said. "Robin Hoodie just uploaded a new video. Last night he cleaned out a drugstore. I guess that makes sense. Homeless people need aspirin and Band-Aids just like anybody else. They look happy to get all that stuff but not as happy as when Robin Hoodie drove in with the taco truck."

"Eugene is going to have his bail bond revoked," I said. "It's not smart to commit another crime when you're out on bail."

"I've been following this case," Herbert said. "It's actually very interesting from a legal point of view. The police have tied Mr. Fleck to the UPS truck hijacking. I believe they have physical evidence linking him to the truck."

"Fingerprints," Lula said.

"From the limited knowledge I've acquired from the press, it seems to me the police can only charge him with that one crime," Herbert said. "I haven't read about any evidence that would connect Mr. Fleck to subsequent Robin Hoodie escapades."

"I never thought about it," Lula said. "You might be right."

"Maybe the police have evidence that they aren't sharing," I said.

Herbert nodded. "Very possible."

"Robin don't seem to be stealing packages off people's porch anymore," Lula said. "I guess that wasn't a real efficient use of his time."

"Hijacking trucks and breaking into stores is also more challenging," Herbert said. "It requires some skills and I imagine it would appeal to someone who enjoyed the game."

"Like he keeps needing to one-up himself," Lula said.

"Yes," Herbert said. "There's also the entertainment aspect. This person might enjoy having an audience. This is a phenomenon we're seeing with the explosion of social media. One can in essence become famous by creating one's own personal reality show."

"So, you think this Robin Hoodie thing is all about a big ego trip," Lula said.

"I was presenting one possibility," Herbert said. "I would like to think Robin Hoodie has the best of intentions. That he cares about the homeless, and he's found a way to help while drawing attention to the problem. I prefer to see him viewed as a hero."

"Eugene doesn't look like much of a hero," Lula said.

"Those are the best kind," Herbert said. "Peter Parker is the perfect example."

"I like him better when he's Spider-Man," Lula said. "Sometimes he's kind of wimpy when he isn't in the suit."

"You've put some serious thought into Robin Hoodie," I said to Herbert.

"I think a lot of serious thoughts. I have a genius IQ," Herbert said. "I haven't actually been tested but I'm sure I'm exceptionally smart. And I'm smart in many directions. I'm musically adept and I'm superior at analyzing situations. Plus, my mechanical and electronic skills are like nothing you've ever seen before. I can even work my Apple products after they've been updated. And I can follow product instruction sheets for kitchen appliances. Once I fixed my Dyson after it became clogged with dirt."

"That's impressive," Lula said. "Can you work your TV?"

"Mostly," Herbert said. "Voice recognition doesn't like me and sometimes I get a blank screen for no reason, but I've been able to crack the code that gets rid of closed captions."

"I wouldn't mind knowing how to do that," Lula said.

"You need to have extremely quick eye-to-hand reflexes," Herbert said.

I got onto the New Jersey Turnpike at exit 7 and headed north. This felt like progress. In less than an hour, I'd be crossing the George Washington Bridge and I'd be in New York. Then I'd take the Cross Bronx Expressway and the Throgs Neck Bridge to Long Island. Once I got to Long Island I hadn't a clue. I was at the mercy of the GPS lady.

I had half a plan for when I got to the vineyard. If I could separate Jug from the herd, I thought I could talk him into coming back to Trenton. We'd get back late, after the court was no longer in session, but I might be able to find someone who could set bail. Then I had to find someone who would write the bond since Vinnie wasn't interested. If I got Bruno alone and couldn't talk him into returning to Trenton, I'd stun gun him. After I stun gunned him I'd have to move to New Zealand because when he came around, he'd put a contract out on me.

---

I'd set out this morning feeling confident that I knew what I was doing. The closer I got to Bruno Jug's lawyer's house, the less confident I felt. This could turn out to be a big wild goose chase. I suspected that Lula and Herbert were having similar feelings because we were approaching the North Fork of Long Island and conversation had stopped. Lula was sitting next to me with her hands clenched in her lap, staring straight ahead. I had no idea what Herbert was doing in the back, but he was quiet, and he was no longer breathing on my neck. For all I knew, he could have fainted or had an aneurism.

"This isn't a big commercial winery," I said. "Connie did some research for us, and I did some more last night. Jug's lawyer, Anthony Bordelli, owns thirty-one acres. He uses twelve acres for his grapes. There are several outbuildings on the property and a large mansion-type house and a smaller guest mansion. We're coming up on his driveway. I saw it on Google. There's a small sign at the start of the driveway and an elaborate iron gate. You can't see the house from the road. He has the property surrounded by a greenbelt of trees and shrubs.

"Here it is," Lula said. "I see the sign. It says 'ABCL Vineyard.' And the gate is open."

"ABCL are the initials for Anthony Bordelli and his wife, Charlotte Loch," I said. I pulled to the side of the two-lane road and parked. "We need a place to launch the drone," I said to Herbert.

"I'm on it," Herbert said. "I've got Google Maps up on my laptop. We're in an area of large houses set on fairly large pieces of land. Bordelli's is one of the larger ones. Difficult to see because they all have these hedges bordering their property. It looks like there's another vineyard backed up to Bordelli's. If you take a left at the next road, we should be able to access it. The driveway doesn't look gated. Looks like they have an outbuilding with a parking lot. Maybe it's a wine store or a restaurant. It's in a good location for the drone. It's well within its one-mile range."

I drove to the intersection, turned left, and almost immediately came to the driveway with a sign advertising wine tasting. I followed the drive to a parking lot and a rustic-looking barn-type building. There were a couple cars in the lot. There was a sign on the barn door that said OPEN. Beyond the barn I could see a vineyard.

I parked at the back end of the lot, away from the other cars. "Set up here," I said to Herbert. "If someone comes asking questions, let me talk. I'll say we're from *Wine Lovers* and we're doing a piece on North Fork vineyards."

"I wouldn't mind looking in the barn," Lula said. "I might buy a bottle of wine or a cheese board or something."

"Don't talk to anybody," I said. "I'll text you when we're ready to leave." I called Connie, told her we were on-site, and asked her to check on the lawyer's location. Was he at his Trenton office?

I hung up with Connie and watched Herbert assemble his drone. When he was done, he gave me an iPad.

"I have an app on the iPad that allows you to see in real time what the drone sees," Herbert said. "I have a screen on my controller that shows me the same thing. I've got about an hour of flight time, and I've got a backup battery so I can recharge and still fly."

Connie texted me that Bordelli was in his office and would most likely be in Trenton for the weekend. He was holding a political fundraiser at his Bucks County house on Saturday.

Herbert launched the bird and I saw it fly away, over the treetops. The drone cleared the trees and flew over an open area with a helipad.

"This is a really nice drone," Herbert said. "It's especially good for our purposes because it has a wide-angle lens. I'm going to take her over the main house and outbuildings at a relatively high altitude so we can get the lay of the land and see if anyone is out on the property."

I'd been able to see some of this on Google Maps, but the drone had more clarity. We didn't see any motion below the drone, so Herbert dropped it down and let it hover above the main house and guesthouse. A black SUV was parked in front of the garage. He moved the drone to the vineyards at the back of the property. There was a large outbuilding and a parking lot with several cars and trucks. Men were working in the rows of grapes.

"I went online and read about the growing season here," Herbert said. "We're at the tail end of grape harvesting. That's probably why the gate was open. They've got workers going in and out. That could be to our advantage."

He took the drone back to the main house and guesthouse, and we watched the screen. After forty minutes he brought the drone back, changed the battery, and sent it off over the trees.

Lula joined us. "It's a real nice store," she said. "I got to taste a bunch of wines and I got a couple bottles. And I got a T-shirt with the name of the winery on it and a ball cap."

Lula currently was sporting a pink Afro, and I couldn't imagine how she would get a ball cap on it. It was soft to the touch, but it was *a lot* of hair.

"We have motion at the main house," Herbert said.

"It looks like Lou," I said.

He crossed the drive court and went into the guesthouse. Minutes later he came out with Jug's wife. They got into the black SUV and drove off.

"She's going shopping," Lula said. "She didn't have a lot of time to pack on account of they hustled her out of the house to get on the helicopter. She's going to Saks. There's gotta be a Saks store on Long Island with all these rich people. She's going to come home with a Gucci bag and some Chanel flats for starters. And she's taking Lou so he can carry her bags."

Herbert and I looked at each other and shrugged. Sounded reasonable.

"If I have any luck at all, that leaves Jug in the guesthouse all alone," I said. "I'm going in."

Herbert took what looked like an AirPod out of his pocket. "Wear this so I can talk to you. I'm going to stay here and keep watch. If you touch the button on the top you can talk to me."

I'd worn a similar device when working with Ranger. He always had the newest and the best technology. I expected Ranger to have a variety of listening devices. I was surprised that Herbert would be carrying this gizmo around in his pocket.

"That's like CIA gear," Lula said.

"Yeah," Herbert said. "I got it online when I got the drone. There were all kinds of accessories you could get. This was part of something they called a Spy Kit. I didn't think much about it when I originally got it, but now I'm thinking I might change my life plan. I might want to be a spy instead of an undertaker. Spies have really cool stuff. It would be easy for me to be a spy. I already have some of the equipment and I've seen all the James Bond movies."

I took the earpiece from Herbert. "I'm going to cut through the greenbelt to get to the guesthouse. I'm sure they have security cameras everywhere, so this is going to have to go fast. Once I give you the signal, you don't want to waste any time picking me up."

"You could take the path," Lula said. "You can't see it on the screen because of the trees. It's like a cart path and it goes from the back of the store into the woods. They have a patio out back where you can sit with a glass of wine. A picnic table and some benches. I'm thinking people sit out there in the summer or on weekends when there's more wine tourists, but there wasn't anybody out there when I looked. I asked about the cart path and the lady handing out samples of wine said it was for the winery next door to bring bottles over. This store is like a co-op. It's got wine from three local wineries."

"Brilliant," I said. "If I can persuade Jug to come with me, I'll bring him on the path. It'll be safer than bringing the car up to the guesthouse and running the risk of being seen and having the gate closed on us."

I walked around the side of the barn and found the cart path cutting into the densely forested greenbelt. The paved path curved slightly and was perhaps a hundred feet long. I walked the path and paused at the tree line. A small grassy field was directly in front of me. It served as backyard to the guesthouse. The path took a right turn and continued on to the large outbuilding at the edge of the vineyard. I could hear the faint insect whine of the drone overhead and some muffled chatter from the men in the vineyard.

Herbert was in my ear. "I don't see you," he said.

I touched the talk button. "I'm at the end of the path through the woods. I'm looking at the guesthouse. I'm going to try the back door. If that doesn't work, I'll go around to the front."

"No activity in the front," Herbert said. "I'll let you know if that changes."

I crossed the field and tried the guesthouse's back door. Locked. I walked around the house and tried the front door. Open. I stepped inside and looked around. I was standing in a small foyer. Living room in front of me. Dining room to the side. I could see a family room through an archway, and I assumed the kitchen was attached.

"Hello?" I called out. "Anybody home?"

Jug appeared in the archway. "What the heck?" he said. "What's going on?"

"Remember me? Stephanie Plum."

"How'd you get in?"

"The door was open."

"Stupid bimbo wife," Jug said. "Doesn't know enough to lock a door."

Mr. Big trotted up to Jug, stopped, and growled at me.

"That's nice," I said. "He remembers me."

"You punted him halfway across my lawn."

"I'm sorry. It was a reflex action. He was trying to kill me."

"What do you want?"

"You didn't get a chance to register for a new court date. I thought this would be a good time to try again."

"This is a lousy time to try again. I'm not even in Trenton."

"Trenton is just a short drive down the road. We can have you back here in time for a late dinner. And then you don't have to worry about me showing up anymore. You have to admit, that would be good, right?"

"I don't know," Jug said. "I'm kind of getting used to you. Are you alone?"

"Lula is with me."

"That's the big fat Black girl with the giant hooters?"

"Yes, but don't call her fat to her face or she'll take you apart piece by piece."

"Hah! She's okay. She liked my ice cream."

"So, what do you say? Are you going to come with me?"

"Maybe. I haven't got anything else to do today. Nobody's here. Everybody went back to Trenton except Lou, and he went shopping with the bimbo."

"We brought cupcakes."

"Seriously?"

"You didn't get to eat any last time, so I brought new ones. I keep my promises."

"I could use a cupcake."

"I'm parked next door by the wine store. We can cut through the woods." I touched the button on my earpiece. "Pack up. We're on our way."

# CHAPTER FOURTEEN

I put Herbert up front with me, and Lula and Jug in back with the cupcakes. By the time we got to the Throgs Neck Bridge, the cupcakes were half gone, and Lula had opened one of her screw-cap wine bottles. They didn't have glasses, so Jug and Lula were chugging out of the bottle between cupcakes.

We hit traffic on the Cross Bronx and progress slowed to a crawl. After an hour we inched our way past fire trucks, cop cars, a tow truck, and a large black cinder that used to be a car. It was almost eight o'clock when I got on the turnpike.

"It's too quiet in the back seat," I said to Herbert. "What are they doing back there?"

"I'm afraid to look," Herbert said.

"Look anyway."

He turned in his seat and flashed his phone light on Lula and Jug. "They're asleep."

"They're okay? They're breathing?"

"I don't know if they're okay, but I think they're breathing."

"Good enough. Unless we hit more traffic, we should be home around nine."

"I'm not going to last until nine," Herbert said. "I'm hungry. I had doughnuts for lunch and nothing since."

I was having the same thought. I was hungry. I was tired of driving. My ass was falling asleep. I had a leg cramp. I needed a potty break. And it wasn't as if I had to get to Trenton by a certain time. Connie hadn't been able to find a judge who would do us a favor and set bail after court hours. That meant I would have to turn Bruno over to the police and he'd be held until Monday. I would do it, but I wouldn't feel good about it. So bottom line was, I might as well stop for coffee and a burger.

"There's a service area just ahead," I told Herbert. "I'll pull in there. We can get something to eat and use the restroom."

Five minutes later, I took the turnoff and cruised into the rest stop. There weren't a lot of cars in the massive lot. Rush hour had come and gone, and day-tripping tourists were locked away in budget hotels.

"We can take turns going into the building," I said to Herbert. "I don't want to leave Lula and Bruno asleep all by themselves in the car. You go in first."

I watched him walk to the building, he disappeared inside, and Morelli called.

"Sorry not to have phoned sooner," he said. "I'm on call and I got tapped to check out a bloodbath on Bendle Street. I'm going to be stuck here for at least another hour. Where are you? There's a lot of background noise."

"I'm at a rest stop on the Jersey Turnpike. I hear the noise too. I don't know what it is."

"What are you doing on the turnpike?"

"I went to Long Island to pick up Jug."

"And?"

"I have him in the back seat with Lula. Is there anything new on Zoran Djordjevic?"

"Nothing good. He's sitting tight somewhere."

"I know the neighborhood was canvassed. Did anything come of that?"

"People remember him moving in. And it sounds like he was friendly at first and then it was almost as if he didn't live there anymore."

"How about the Werly family? Was he friendly with Julie?"

"Not in a way that seemed to deserve further attention. Just the normal wave and hello to her and her family. I have to go. The ME just arrived. I'll talk to you tomorrow. Be careful driving."

The noise from outside was a lot louder. It was the distinctive *wop, wop, wop* of a helicopter. A spotlight swept over my car and scanned the surrounding area. My immediate thought was that police were searching for someone. The helicopter touched down in the lot at some distance from me and I froze. It was a Sikorsky. I was thinking, no way, give me a break, while my brain was racing through my options. I could try to get Lula's gun out of her tote bag and bluff my way into keeping Jug. That would involve climbing into the back seat and searching through her bag. I didn't think I had time for that. Lou and another very large man were out of the helicopter, headed in my direction. Second option was to stomp on the gas and roar out of the lot and onto the road. That would involve abandoning Herbert. This had a lot of appeal, but I couldn't do it. No man left behind.

I stayed at the wheel and lowered my window when Lou approached. "Did you just drop in for a burger and fries?" I asked him.

"Yeah," he said. "We were in the neighborhood." He looked over my shoulder at Lula and Jug in the back seat. "Dead or alive?" he asked.

"Sleeping it off," I told him. "They ate a dozen doughnuts and chugged a bottle of wine. How did you find me?"

"We plant AirTags on him. Every now and then he forgets to take his meds and he wanders away."

"I don't suppose you'll let me keep him."

"The family wouldn't like it. He's on ice for a while."

I popped the door locks and Lou dragged Jug out of the car and stood him up.

Jug half opened his eyes and leaned into Lou. "Hey, Lou, how's it hanging?"

"Do I get a receipt for merchandise returned?" I asked Lou.

"Stop by the office and I'll give you another fruit basket," Lou said.

Lou and the big guy got on either side of Jug and walked him to the helicopter. They went up the stairs, the door closed, and the helicopter lifted off and disappeared into the night.

Lula woke up. "What's going on? Where is everybody? I was dreaming that I was being chased by a helicopter."

"We're at a rest stop," I said. "Herbert got hungry."

"Where's Jug?"

"Lou came and got him."

"Are you kidding me? When did this happen?"

"A couple minutes ago."

"I missed it!"

"There wasn't much to miss," I said. "The helicopter landed in the parking lot, Lou and another guy got out and repossessed Jug, and the helicopter flew away with them."

"That's a bitch," Lula said. "Is this the rest stop with Chick-fil-A?"

Twenty minutes later we were all back in the car with our bags of food. I wolfed down a double cheeseburger followed by a venti caffè mocha. Plus, I had an additional caffè mocha in the driver's-side cupholder. I pulled out of the lot with Lula riding shotgun next to me, eating at a more leisurely pace.

"There's something voodoo going on with Jug," Lula said. "It's not normal the way we keep almost bringing him in and then *whoosh*, he gets snatched away. And this is going on at the same time we got a vampire on the loose and we can't find him. There's stars in misalignment somewhere. It's like when all those spooks got set loose in *Ghostbusters*."

I thought an alternative explanation might be that I sucked as a bounty hunter.

"Call Connie," I said to Lula. "Tell her she can stop trying to get a judge for Jug."

---

I dropped Herbert off at the office and helped him transfer his equipment into his Prius. "Thanks for flying the drone," I said. "It was really helpful."

"This was great," Herbert said. "Usually, I'm looking at a building or a park or something boring. This was like private investigator or CIA stuff. I'm sorry I didn't see the helicopter land. That had to be exciting. I've never seen a helicopter land in person. At least I saw it leave. I was coming out of the building, and I saw it lift off. You probably see stuff like that all the time."

"Not all the time," I said.

"So, call me if you need anything," Herbert said. "They were supposed to hang your television today. I hope they did a good job. I would have supervised, but since I couldn't be there, I asked your building super to make sure everything was okay."

"Television?"

"I hope it's not too big, but I figure big is always better. Except for ears and noses. Mine might be borderline too big, but my mother thinks they're perfect. I guess she should know, right?"

"Right."

"I got you a premium package and it's paid up for a year, so you don't have to worry about anything. You can watch Netflix and Amazon Prime and all that stuff. I watch a lot of shows on BritBox. Maybe sometime we can watch some shows together. I could come over now to get you started if you want."

"Jeez."

"If tonight is bad, I could come over tomorrow."

"I'll call you," I said. "I have to check my schedule. And I might be coming down with something. Maybe COVID."

"Yeah, you look a little feverish. I thought it was just the caffè mochas. I get blotchy if I have too much caffeine."

I got back behind the wheel and looked at myself in the rearview mirror. "Do I look feverish?" I asked Lula.

"You look fried," Lula said. "I think you had too much mocha. Your one eye is twitching."

I put my finger to it to make it stop.

"Maybe I should drive you home," Lula said.

I pulled away from the curb. "You drank half a bottle of wine. *I'm* driving *you* home."

"Okay, but then you have to pick me up tomorrow for whatever it is that we're gonna do, because I won't have my car."

"Not a problem."

"And since we're on the topic . . . what are we gonna do?"

"I don't know. I have to go home and think about it."

"Are we going back to Long Island?"

"No."

"That narrows down our activities to shopping, pedicure, or hunting a vampire."

I idled in front of Lula's apartment. "I'll pick you up at eight o'clock."

"Should I bring garlic?"

"Wouldn't hurt."

I drove home on autopilot and parked, and while I was in the elevator I promised God I would be a better person if he would make sure Herbert wasn't waiting for me in my apartment. I entered my apartment and looked around. No Herbert. Hard to tell if God had anything to do with it, but I'd be on my best behavior for a day or two just in case.

I said hello to Rex, dumped my messenger bag on the dining room table, and stood with my mouth open and my eyes wide, staring at the giant television attached to my living room wall. The remote and some instructional material were on the end table next to the couch. I turned the television on and flipped through a bunch of channels. The picture and sound were fantastic, but nothing jumped out at me that I'd want to see. I shut the television off and went back to the dining room and reviewed everything I had on Zoran. I went onto the internet and researched vampires. Some of them sort of looked like Zoran. Good thing I didn't believe in vampires or else I'd have been pretty freaked out. My eye was twitching again. Stupid caffè mocha. I went into the kitchen and got a banana. Bananas and Pop-Tarts are two of my favorite things because you just peel off the wrapper and eat it. Pop-Tarts have an edge over bananas because they don't turn black if you forget about them. I collected my thoughts while I ate the banana. Either Zoran actually believed he was a vampire or else he enjoyed the pretending. Maybe it was some of both those things. It could be hard to separate reality from lunacy when you were on shrooms and acid.

# CHAPTER FIFTEEN

I picked Lula up at eight o'clock. She'd traded in the pink Afro for a lot of copper-colored curls. She was wearing seven-inch spike-heeled thigh-high boots and a denim spandex dress that skimmed the tops of the boots. I was wearing the same old, same old. To compensate for the clothes, I'd lined my eyes, added an extra sweep of mascara, and gone with cherry-red lipstick instead of a natural gloss.

"I like the boots," I said to her.

"Being that it's Saturday I thought I'd dress down and do denim. I got the garlic in my bag and a bottle of water. They were able to melt the Wicked Witch of the West with some water in *The Wizard of Oz* so I thought it wouldn't hurt to pack some."

"And it'll come in handy if we get thirsty."

"Fuckin' A," Lula said. "What are we doing today?"

"I want to go through Zoran's house."

"Lordy, Lordy," Lula said. "I was afraid it was gonna be something like this."

"I'm sure Zoran isn't there."

"Yeah, but it's gonna have vampire cooties."

"You can do lookout, and I'll go in."

"I guess that would be okay. What about the doughnuts? Connie gets extra Boston cream on Saturdays. And coffee? Did you bring coffee and doughnuts?"

I was embarrassed to tell her that I'd made myself a scrambled egg for breakfast and that I'd had a glass of orange juice. It was so healthy. It felt totally wrong.

"We can stop at the office and pick up a couple doughnuts," I said. "And I could use coffee."

The coffee part was true. I'd made coffee, but it sucked. Connie made better coffee. And truth is, my scrambled egg wasn't all that good either, but honestly, is a scrambled egg ever fantastic? I mean, it's not like pancakes and bacon.

I drove to the office and waited at the curb while Lula ran in and got the doughnuts and coffee.

"I'm good to go," she said, getting into the car and putting two containers of coffee in the drink holders. She buckled herself in and opened the box of doughnuts. "Connie kept a couple for herself and gave us the rest. She had a new FTA for you too. Came in late yesterday. I have it in my tote bag."

"Is it worth anything?" I asked her.

"I don't know. I didn't read it."

I took a doughnut and drove to Exeter Street. I didn't see any cop cars in front of Zoran's house. No one doing surveillance. I parked at the curb, and Lula and I got out and walked around to the back.

"Do your thing," I said to Lula.

Lula took a small hammer and screwdriver out of her bag and *bang!* The door was open.

"Go out front and watch for vampires," I said. "I'm going inside."

The police go through a house and collect evidence. Knives, guns, cell phones, laptops, scribbled notes, items with DNA on them. I had the right to enter with cause, but I didn't have permission to remove anything from the premises. Of course, I could snoop through a computer or phone or files as long as it wasn't obvious that I'd snooped. Unlike the police, I wasn't necessarily looking for evidence. I was looking for something that would support my theory that he was holed up somewhere on Stark Street. The Exeter Street neighbors didn't seem to see him around a lot. His car sat in the driveway and was rarely driven. My gut told me he had a hidey-hole somewhere close to the laundromat. I envisioned him leaving the laundromat, buying drugs, getting high in a bar, and crashing somewhere a few steps away. The fact that he'd attacked a woman in the laundromat was worrisome. It suggested that he was no longer in control of his obsession. That also would suggest that he needed his drugs. And that would keep him on Stark Street.

I entered the house and did the required shout-out announcing myself. I started in the kitchen. It was relatively clean. A spoon and a coffee cup in the sink. A small amount of coffee left in the carafe that went with the coffee maker. Almost nothing in the fridge. A canister of powdered Coffee-Mate, a single bottle of beer, American cheese slices, half a loaf of bread with blue mold. There was a box of cereal in the cupboard. A bag of ground coffee. This guy made me look like Ina Garten. The dining room off the kitchen had a table and six chairs. They screamed secondhand store. Not that this was terrible. Before the fire, most of my furniture had come from dead relatives. Nothing to see in the dining room. The living room was unremarkable. A couch and a club chair. A coffee table, an end table, a floor lamp. A television. Nothing on any of the tables. No family pictures, no coasters, no crumpled Cheetos bags.

I heard the back door open and Lula call out, "Anybody home?"

"I'm in the living room," I said.

Lula came into the living room and looked around. "This looks even worse than your apartment."

"I thought you didn't want to come inside."

"I got lonely out there, and I was wondering what kind of décor a vampire would have."

I spread my arms wide. "This is it."

"Did you search the kitchen? Did he have blood stored in the refrigerator or freezer?"

"No blood. Just some moldy bread."

"Have you been to the bedroom yet?"

"That's next."

"I'm gonna poop my pants if he sleeps in a casket," Lula said. "Especially if it's a nice one. The kind with the silk lining. If I was a vampire, I'd have one of those."

We walked down the short hallway to the bedrooms. Two were empty. No furniture. Very small. The third had a bed that had been slept in. Completely rumpled. Obviously, a restless night. No telling when the bed had last been used.

"This is disappointing," Lula said. "He's just got a sad-ass bed."

There was a bedside table with a lamp. There was a phone charger on the table and a used tissue. Socks on the floor.

Lula looked down at the socks. "Here's something," she said.

"Vampire socks. I've never seen vampire socks before. That's something you don't ordinarily think about. You don't ordinarily think about what kind of socks vampires wear."

Lula took her cell phone out and took a picture of the socks. There was a sweatshirt hanging in the closet. A beat-up pair of sneakers. The usual guy clothes were housed in a couple drawers of a dresser. Sweats, jeans, T-shirts, underwear. Nothing was folded. Hard to tell what was clean and what was laundry.

I moved to the bathroom. There was a grungy bath towel hanging on a hook. Deodorant, a can of shaving cream, and a razor by the sink.

Lula let out a shriek and my heart jumped to my throat.

"Omigod," she said. "Omigod, omigod."

"*What?*" I asked, whipping my head around, looking for a body, a vampire, a guy with a machete.

Lula pointed to the sink. "It's his *toothbrush*! It's in that filthy glass by his razor. He uses that toothbrush on his fangs. He scrubs the blood and flesh slime away with that toothbrush."

I was relieved that there was no guy with a machete, but I was grossed out by the toothbrush. My gag reflex kicked in and my breakfast was threatening to leave my body one way or the other.

"I gotta see what kind of toothpaste he uses," Lula said. "I bet he goes for the extra-whitening kind." She opened his medicine chest, and a dead cockroach fell out. "Whoa," she said. "That's a giant cockroach. That's a record breaker." She took a picture of the cockroach and the toothbrush.

I needed air. I could have walked away from the toothbrush, but the roach finished me off.

"I'm done here," I said to Lula.

"Did we learn anything?"

"Zoran sleeps here at least some of the time, but he doesn't live here. He lives at the laundromat and at the bars on Stark and someplace else. We have to find the someplace else."

We left through the back door and walked to the car. I looked up the street and saw the Werly house.

"Call Connie," I said to Lula. "Ask her to check on Zoran's financials. Has he used his credit card? Has he withdrawn money from a bank account? I'm going to talk to Mrs. Werly."

There was a mix of houses on Exeter Street. Zoran was renting a small bungalow. The house next to him was a Cape Cod. The Werly house was a two-story colonial. All of the lots were the same size. Zoran had a driveway but no garage. Most of the other houses on the street had garages. In spite of its proximity to Stark Street, it was considered a safe neighborhood. The Werly house was on the corner. I rang the bell and a woman about my mom's age answered. She was slim with brown hair going gray.

I showed her the badge I bought on Amazon and told her I was doing a follow-up inquiry on Zoran.

"I don't know very much," she said.

"Have you recently seen him in his yard or going for a walk? Lights on in his house at night?"

"I can't remember the last time I saw him, but sometimes there are lights on at night. I haven't really paid attention to his house."

"What about his truck? Have you seen him driving the truck?"

"Not lately. Sometimes there would be a van parked in the driveway. It would be behind the truck. And it was never there very long. It was tan. It looked old. It had a dent in the back, by the wheel."

"I know about your daughter," I said. "I'm so sorry."

"I still expect her to walk through the door," Mrs. Werly said. "It's just hard to believe she's gone."

"Was she friends with Zoran?"

"Julie was friendly to everyone. She was a special person. Zoran was . . . odd. He had those teeth that looked like fangs. I imagine he must have been teased in school. And he had an odd way about him. He wouldn't look you in the eye. I think he was shy. I think he might have had a crush on Julie, and Julie was always nice to him, but she never saw him socially. She made a point of keeping some distance."

"The police report said there was blood but no body."

Mrs. Werly nodded, blinked back tears. "From the couch to the back door and out into the yard and then it just stopped."

I thanked her for her time, left the house, and walked around the corner. The backyard wasn't fenced but there was a patchy collection of shrubs that gave them some privacy. Zoran or whoever could have zipped the body into a bag, stepped between the shrubs, and dumped the body into the trunk of a car or into the back of his truck.

None of this was helpful in finding Zoran but it might turn out to be helpful in capturing him. I went back to Lula, we got into the car, and I ate another doughnut. I rationalized that it was to settle my stomach, but really, I just wanted a doughnut.

"Was Connie able to find anything on Zoran's financials?" I asked Lula.

"Last night at eleven thirty Zoran got money out of an ATM on Olcott Street, one block away from Stark. He hasn't used his credit card."

"Perfect."

"She also said you needed to look at the new FTA because it could be easy money for you, and it would make Vinnie happy if you brought him in." Lula pulled the file out of her tote. "I'll read the file, and you can drive. It says here that his name is Zachary Zell. People call him Zach. Gives his address as 401 Dorsey Street.

That's not far from here. He's seventy-eight years old and lives with his daughter. She also put up his bond."

"What did he do?"

"Armed robbery."

"Any priors?"

"Nope. Not even a traffic ticket."

"Call Connie back and ask her if there are any other cars in Zoran's history. Ask her about a tan van."

I drove the short distance to Dorsey Street and parked in front of Zach's house. It was a two-story colonial in okay shape. Two Big Wheels were sitting in the small front yard, which also contained a doll without a head, a kid's sneaker, and a big plastic dump truck.

I grabbed the sneaker, stepped onto the front porch, and rang the bell. No one came to the door, but yelling and screaming could be heard from inside. I rang the bell again. Still, no answer. The door was unlocked, so Lula and I walked in. Three dogs rushed at us. Two were small, one was medium size, and all were mixtures of every breed possible. All were overly friendly, jumping on Lula and me, eyes bright, tongues hanging out looking for something to lick. Beyond the dogs was bedlam. Three kids running around, waving their arms and screaming. No one was bleeding. Seemed to be some sort of game. A man who I assumed was Zach was standing in the middle of the room, holding a toddler on his hip and a phone to his ear.

"Yeah," he yelled into the phone. "One of the dogs pooped on the carpet in the family room, and I think Jonathan ate it. His teeth are brown, and he has real bad breath."

I moved into his line of sight and waved at him.

"Gotta go," he said into the phone. "There's some ladies here."

"Are you Zachary Zell?" I asked him.

"Yep," he said. "People call me Zach."

I held the sneaker up. "I found this on the front lawn."

"That's Jonathan's. He don't like wearing shoes. There's another sneaker around here somewhere."

I introduced myself and told him he needed to reschedule his court date.

"I didn't know I missed it," he said.

"It was yesterday," I said.

"It's a little crazy here," he said. "My granddaughter is an ER nurse and works weekends. Her husband is a paramedic and alternates weekends. Needless to say, this is his weekend to work. My daughter is usually with the kids on weekends, but her husband's brother had a heart attack, so my daughter and husband are in Virginia. That leaves me doing day care, and I don't know what the hell I'm doing."

The kids had stopped running and came over to size up Lula and me.

"The gap-toothed one is Ian," Zach said. "He's seven. His sister, Emmy, is five, and the one with oatmeal in his hair and no shoes is Jonathan. He's four. I got baby Sue on my hip."

"I'm hungry," Emmy said.

"I'll get you a snack right away," Zach said, "but I've gotta brush Jonathan's teeth first. Your mama said it's not good to leave dog poop on his teeth."

"I don't want my teeth brushed," Jonathan said.

Zach handed me baby Sue. "I'll be right back. See if you can find something in the kitchen that Emmy wants to eat."

I looked at Lula. "Help," I said.

"Hey, don't look at me," Lula said. "I don't know anything about babies."

Emmy stood with her hands on her hips. "Well?" she said. "Are you going to feed me, or what?"

"Un-ah," Lula said. "You don't want to pull attitude with us. If you want something to eat, you better be nice."

"I'm five," she said. "I don't have to be nice."

"The heck you don't," Lula said. "Look how much bigger I am than you. If I sat on you, I'd squish you like a bug."

"Eeeeeee!" Emmy screamed, and she ran upstairs.

"Jeez Louise," I said to Lula. "Couldn't you just go get her a snack?"

"My mama would whup me upside the head if I talked like that. Course she wasn't home a lot. Most of the time she was working her corner or in jail."

I carried baby Sue into the kitchen and went through the cupboards. I found a bag of cookies and took it back to the living room. Emmy was sitting halfway down the stairs, looking through the balusters. Lula was in front of the television watching cartoons with Ian.

I rattled the bag at Emmy. "I brought you some cookies."

"What kind?"

"It says they're chocolate-on-chocolate sandwich cookies."

Emmy took the bag to the couch and sat next to her brother.

"You aren't supposed to eat those," Ian said. "They're only for Grandpa Zach."

"I don't care," Emmy said. "I'm hungry and she gave them to me."

Ian looked over at me. "She isn't supposed to eat them."

"Okay," I said to Emmy. "Give me the cookies and I'll get something else for you."

"No," she said. "I want these cookies. If you don't let me keep them, I'll scream."

Lula cut her eyes to me. "You want me to sit on her?"

"No! I'll get something else from the kitchen." I handed baby Sue over to Lula. "Don't sit on this one either."

I ran into the kitchen and found a box of Ritz crackers. I returned to the living room and Emmy had shoved half a bag of cookies into her mouth. There was chocolate everywhere.

"I'll swap you the cookies for these Ritz crackers," I said.

Emmy crammed more cookies into her mouth and hugged the almost-empty bag to her chest. "No."

I reached for the bag, and she started screaming.

"She's turning red," Lula said. "And she's looking all swelled up."

"That's because she's not supposed to eat those cookies," Ian said. "She's allergic to chocolate. She's probably going to die now."

"*What?*" Now I was at shriek level.

Jonathan hopped down the stairs, and Zach ambled after him.

"Okay, where were we? Something about my court date?" Zach asked me.

"Emmy ate your cookies," Ian said. "And now she's going to die."

Zach took a close look at Emmy. "How many cookies did she eat?"

"She ate almost the whole bag," Ian said. "You should call Mom."

Zach hauled his phone out of his pocket and dialed. "Sorry to bother you again, honey, but Emmy ate a whole bag of those chocolate cookies. She's red and blotchy and her face is swollen." There was a pause. "Yep," Zach said. "Yep. Got it."

He hung up and slipped his phone back into his pocket. "We're going to the ER. Everybody to the van."

Lula and I helped buckle the kids into their car seats.

"I'm going to ride with Zach," I said to Lula. "Find Jonathan's sneakers, lock up here, and meet me at the medical center ER."

"Then what? Do you have a plan?"

"The immediate plan is to help with the kids and make sure Emmy is going to be okay."

I was used to kids. My sister, Valerie, had a pack of them. One of them thought she was a horse, but to my knowledge none of them ate poop. I took that as a good sign that my gene pool might be more aligned to cake eaters.

It was a short drive to the medical center. Zach stopped at the ER entrance and went inside with Emmy. I got behind the wheel and parked the van in the adjacent lot. By the time I had all the kids unbuckled, Lula was parked next to the van. We got Jonathan into his shoes, and we trundled the kids into the ER reception room.

Zach was at the desk, filling out a form. "Emmy's in the back with her mom," Zach said. "She'll be okay. One time she ate a giant Hershey bar, and her face looked like it had been inflated by an air pump. They emptied her stomach and filled her full of antihistamines, and she was good as ever. Then there was the time she ate half a chocolate birthday cake when no one was looking. She didn't get as swollen from that one because she barfed it all up."

I took a seat, and put baby Sue on my lap and a kid on either side of me. I tapped into Disney+ on my phone and pulled up *PJ Masks*. This made everyone happy. When Zach was done at the admissions desk, I handed baby Sue, Ian, Jonathan, and my phone over to Lula.

"I need to talk to Zach," I said to Lula. "Don't let anyone wander away."

"I'm on it," Lula said.

"You need to reschedule your court date," I said to Zach. "That means I need to take you to the municipal building."

"I guess that would be okay. They're going to keep Emmy here for a couple hours." He looked at his watch. "I'm late getting lunch for everybody. And then after lunch I'm supposed to put baby Sue and Jonathan down for a nap. When they wake up from the nap, I can get Emmy and then we can go to the municipal building."

That would have been great, except it was Saturday and Zach would be held over until Monday and there would be no one to watch the kids.

"You're charged with armed robbery," I said. "I'm curious. What was that about?"

"My daughter's next-door neighbor is a jerk. That's all I have to say."

"You need to say more. What did you steal?"

"It's embarrassing."

"A little embarrassing or a lot embarrassing?"

"Oh hell," he said. "It was a picture. It was Ed and Marie's twenty-fifth wedding anniversary and they had a big renewing-vows party at some fancy garden place in Pennsylvania."

"Ed is the jerk next door?"

"Yeah. They had a photographer, and he took a picture of them cutting the cake. It was a real nice picture, but in the background you can see me taking a leak on a bush."

I had to clap a hand over my mouth to keep from laughing out loud.

"I had a couple beers, and I really had to go, and I didn't think anybody could see," Zach said. "They were all watching the cake-cutting ceremony. It wasn't like I was doing it in public on the sidewalk or something."

I tried to look sympathetic.

"Nobody noticed it when they were looking at pictures to buy.

If you weren't looking close, you would think I was standing there admiring the scenery. Anyway, they bought this picture and had it framed because it was their favorite. I go over and I see the picture on their end table in the living room, and it's me taking a whiz. So, I offered to buy the picture. I figured it was the right thing to do. I should pay for the picture, right? I mean, I can't have a picture of me peeing in their living room. They take a close look at the picture, and they're horrified. Like no one ever peed on a bush before. Marie is hysterical because I ruined her anniversary. Ed is ready to punch me in the nose."

"You were friends with them before this picture incident?"

"Yeah. Best buddies. Go figure."

"What happened next?"

"Ed wouldn't give me the picture. Ed said they were going to leave it there for everyone to see. They were going to have a big party and show everyone the picture."

"So, you went home and got a gun and came back for the picture."

"I was steamed. Who acts like that? I'd be the laughingstock of the neighborhood. Once you knew where to look you could see . . . you know."

"Everything?"

"Not everything, but enough. I got a pretty good fire hose. Anyway, I slapped a twenty on the table, took the picture, and left. Next thing the police are at my door. It's those damn Ring doorbells. They got a video of me with a gun in one hand and the picture in the other."

"Would you have used the gun?"

"Damn right." He slumped a little and gave up a sigh. "No. Who am I kidding? I'm a total pussy. We had a seven-foot snake in the laundry room, and I couldn't shoot it. My daughter shot it."

"Do you still have the picture?"

"Yeah. It's under my bed. I told the police that I burned it and threw the frame away."

"Why don't you just have someone remove you from the picture?"

"I could do that?"

"Yes. I know someone who might do it for you. And maybe Ed will drop the charges if you apologize and fix the picture."

He thought about it for a beat. "Okay, but he's still an A-hole."

"I'll follow you back to your house, and you can give me the picture."

"I'll put it in an envelope, and you have to promise not to look at it."

"Promise. And I'm sorry about the cookies."

"It's my bad," he said. "I shouldn't have them in the house."

Lula and I helped Zach get the kids into the van. I followed him home and waited while he got everyone inside and returned with the photo.

"What are you going to do with that?" Lula asked me.

"I'm going to see if Eugene can fix it. It seemed like he has the ability to Photoshop."

"In the beginning it looks like you're being a good person and doing something to help Zach, but I'm thinking it's more that you see an opportunity to check on Eugene," Lula said.

"I'm thinking you're right."

# CHAPTER SIXTEEN

I cut across town and stopped at Giovichinni's Deli. I got turkey and Swiss on seeded wheat for myself and chicken salad for Connie, and Lula got a Cuban, fries, coleslaw, and a tub of pasta salad.

I pulled a chair up to Connie's desk. "Anything new?" I asked her.

"Local news is all about Jug," Connie said. "Nobody knows where he is. The latest speculation is that he's in South America someplace. Saturday morning news interviewed a woman in Newark who said she saw Jug board a plane for Brazil."

"Hunh," Lula said. "Imagine that."

"Did a helicopter really land at the rest stop and take Jug back to Long Island?" Connie asked me.

I unwrapped my sandwich. "Yep. They had him AirTagged."

"What about the tan van?" I asked Connie. "Were you able to find anything? Mrs. Werly said sometimes a tan van would be parked in Zoran's driveway."

"Nothing," Connie said. "Nothing in Zoran's history or his parents' or his uncle's."

"Could just be some worker's van," Lula said. "A pest control guy."

"You saw that cockroach in his bathroom," I said. "He's not hiring pest control."

"Suppose you marry Morelli?" Connie asked me. "Are you still going to have Ranger tracking you?"

Good question. I thought the answer was yes. I held an odd place in Ranger's life. From the very beginning he'd assumed the role of protector. That role had stayed constant no matter if I was in an intimate relationship with him or with Morelli. I suspected it wouldn't change if I married Morelli. In fact, I suspected very little of Ranger's behavior would change if I married Morelli.

"I'm pretty sure Ranger has stopped dropping bugs into my pockets and purses without my knowledge," I said. "He just has a GPS gizmo attached to my car sometimes. It comes in handy when I run out of gas."

I finished my sandwich and called Eugene. No answer. Lula was still working her way through the pasta salad, so I called Ranger.

"Babe," Ranger said.

"Do you have a minute?"

"Yeah. Maybe two."

"I went through Zoran's house today. I couldn't find any evidence that he's returned since the laundromat killing. And before the killing he wasn't spending a lot of time there. He was sleeping there but he wasn't living there. I think he has a pad on Stark or Freemont. Probably Stark. That's where the blood trail ended. That's where he got his drugs and hung out. How do I find him? Can you access any street cameras on Stark?"

"There aren't any government cameras on Stark. They kept

getting shot up, so they were removed. There might be some businesses with security cameras, but it's not likely. I can have the control room check. For the most part, security on Stark is gang and mob controlled. We don't have any clients on Stark. His drug supply was coming from the alley. We can try setting a camera there. I doubt anyone thinks to sweep the alley. The problem is that it will tell you what you already know. That he's in the hood. It's not going to help you catch him. He'll be gone by the time you get there. The good news is that it might convince the police to put someone undercover on Stark. I'd put a man there for you, but I'm short right now. And it's not really what we do." He paused for a beat. "Is there anything else you need from me?"

We were no longer talking about work. This was foreplay, and he was a master at it. His voice was soft with a hint of a smile.

I smiled back. "A camera would be enough for now."

"Babe," he said. And he hung up.

I tried Eugene again. Still no answer. I called his mother's cell, and she answered immediately.

"Mrs. Fleck," I said. "It's Stephanie Plum."

"How nice to hear from you. Are you looking for Eugene?"

"Yes. I tried calling him, but he isn't answering."

"He never answers," she said. "He turns the ringer off when he needs to concentrate."

"Is he at home?"

"No. I believe he's at the garage."

"Saddle up," I said to Lula. "Eugene's mom thinks he's at the garage."

I took Hamilton to Liberty and parked around the corner from Martino Auto Body. We went to the door leading to the loft and found it unlocked. We climbed the stairs and knocked on the loft door. I knocked a second time and Eugene opened the door.

"Hey," he said. "What's up? Am I in trouble?"

"I have a favor to ask," I said. "I need help with a photo. Can you do Photoshop?"

"Sure. Come on in. I was in the middle of writing software for a game. Can you give me five minutes?"

"Take all the time you need," I said.

Lula went to the couch and opened an app on her phone. I prowled around, looking for hijacked goods. I didn't find anything that might have been hijacked, but I found a stack of pictures of Kevin in action poses. I was paging through them when Eugene came over.

"We use them as references when we're writing games," he said.

"Where's Kevin now?"

"He works in the body shop during the day. It's a trade-off for use of this space."

"Do you work in the body shop too?"

"No. But some mornings I work in the dog wash."

"You have a lot of equipment here."

Eugene looked around as if he was seeing it for the first time. "It doesn't seem like a lot. It always feels like we're missing something we need."

"What exactly is the purpose for all this photo stuff?"

"We have a blog that's seeing good growth. We started by taking selfies with our phones. That was okay, but it was limiting, and the quality wasn't always great. We still do phone selfies but more and more we use the studio equipment."

"And the drone?"

Eugene grinned. "It's a toy."

"What happens to all this when you get convicted and go to jail?"

"I can't imagine that happening. I would love to be Robin Hoodie because he's beloved and he's making a fortune, but I'm not Robin Hoodie. And it's only a matter of time before he gets caught. I'm sure he'll get caught before I get locked up."

"So, the blog that you do isn't the Robin Hoodie blog?"

"No. Not even close. It's a gaming blog. I'll send you a link." He took his phone out of his pocket and texted the link to me.

"You could do both. You could do the gaming blog and the Hoodie blog."

"I suppose that's true."

I gave him Zach's picture. "I need to get rid of the man watering the shrub in the background."

He took the photo out of the envelope and looked at it. "Hah! Too bad you want to get rid of him. This is classic."

"Can you do it?"

"Yeah, no problem. Do you want to wait for it? Or do you want to come back?"

"How long will it take?"

"Not long. Five minutes to a half hour."

"I'll wait."

I joined Lula on the couch, and I used the link Eugene had just sent me to go to his blog. It was nicely done. A mixture of short personal videos and more professional, longer tutorials and snippets of games. I'm not a gamer so the tutorials were lost on me, and after ten minutes of scrolling I was having a hard time staying awake.

Lula leaned in. "What are you looking at?"

"Eugene's blog."

"Robin Hoodie?"

"No. Eugene swears he's not Robin Hoodie. This is his gaming blog."

"Is it any good?"

"It looks nice, but I'm not a gamer, so it's like I'm trying to read a foreign language."

"I never could see him being Robin Hoodie," Lula said. "On my planet, Ranger would be Robin Hoodie."

"I don't think Ranger has time to be Robin Hoodie."

"Just sayin'."

Eugene came over. "This is the photoshopped one," he said, handing the photo to me. "I think it turned out pretty good. I got rid of the leaker, and I did a little work on the woman's face and arms. She should be happy. The original is in the envelope."

I looked at the new photo. "This is amazing," I said. "You would never know it was altered." I slid the new photo into the envelope with the original. "From the beginning you've denied being Robin Hoodie. I'm starting to believe you. Do you have any ideas on the identity of the real Robin Hoodie?"

Eugene shook his head. "No, but he's not a one-man show. He's got a videographer and a studio setup that's better than mine. Sometimes he's got more than one camera angle. That would indicate more than one videographer."

"He's got Merry Men," Lula said.

"And they aren't homeless," Eugene said. "They're good at what they do, and they're making good money."

I tucked the envelope into my messenger bag. "What do I owe you for this?"

"Nothing," he said. "Good luck finding the real Robin Hoodie."

I drove back to Zach's house and gave him the envelope.

"It's so quiet," I said.

"Everyone's taking a nap. Even the dogs. It won't last long. It's almost time for them to get up."

"If I take you in now, you'll be stuck in jail until Monday," I said. "You can't get bonded out until you have an arraignment and a judge sets bail. And judges don't work on the weekend. If you can get Ed to drop the charges on Monday, this will all go away."

"I'll do my best."

I went back to the car and got behind the wheel.

"How'd it go?" Lula asked.

"Zach said he's going to do his best to get the charges dropped."

"If it was me, I'd rather go to jail than babysit those kids."

"I thought you wanted to be an auntie."

"Yeah, but I'm resigning if it turns out you have a poop eater."

"Fair enough."

"Now what?" Lula asked.

"Now we go home. I'm done for the day."

---

A fruit basket and a bottle of wine had been left in front of my door. No note attached. None was necessary. The basket was now sitting on my kitchen counter. The wine was in the fridge.

I was in the kitchen, pawing through the fruit basket, reviewing my possible excuses for not sleeping with Morelli or Ranger tonight. It was Saturday. They were going to want to spend the night with me and I was going to have to beg off.

I bypassed the apples and oranges and found a packet of caramel popcorn. I opened the packet, and a text came in from Morelli. His brother had tickets to a fight at the Garden and had invited him to go along. They were on their way into the city and wouldn't be home until late, so maybe we could get together tomorrow. What the hell! I just got dumped for a New York City prizefight. Okay, so I'd dodged a bullet, and I should have been grateful, but I didn't feel grateful. I felt pissed off that Morelli would rather see two idiots beat the crap out of each other than get me naked.

I ate the caramel popcorn and talked myself into feeling grateful.

Ranger called. "The camera is going up tonight," he said. "Once it's live I'll send you an app so you can access it. My control room will also be monitoring it. Do you need anything else?"

"No. Just the camera."

"Are you sure?"

Loaded question. "I think the camera will be great."

"Babe," Ranger said.

The line went dead.

I was feeling a little pissy again. He could have tried harder. It was like he was relieved not to have to tear himself away from his stupid work. I needed a glass of wine, but there was the possible baby, so I hunted through the basket and found some cookies. I was cracking under the pressure of a potential pregnancy. I was making mountains out of molehills. I was pathetic.

A text message popped up on my phone. *We met once very briefly. The next time we meet will be more enjoyable. I know you've been looking for me. Soon enough.*

I was breathless. I literally couldn't breathe. I put my hand out to the counter to steady myself, and I had a flashback of the woman in the laundromat, bleeding on the floor. I blinked the vision away and sucked in air. That wasn't going to be me. I wasn't going to be this monster's victim. I was going to be vigilant. I was going to put bullets in my gun. First, I would have to buy some. Mental note: Buy bullets. Second mental note: Screw negative thinking. Embrace positive thinking. Shake it off. Be the woman in charge.

So, where do I go from here? I cut my eyes to the refrigerator. The woman in charge should make dinner. I went to the refrigerator and spied a package of ground meat. This was a good beginning.

I called Grandma. "I want to make meatloaf," I said. "I made it once before, but I can't remember the recipe."

"I could come over and help," she said. "Your parents are going to a pancake supper at your dad's lodge. They could drop me off."

"Yes! That would be amazing."

Hooray. I had Grandma coming for dinner. I cleared my laptop and notes from the dining room table and set out placemats and place settings. I didn't have napkins, so I folded some paper towels. I thought it looked pretty good. I used to have candles, but they melted in the fire.

Grandma showed up a half hour later.

"Look at this," she said. "You've got new carpet and new paint and some new furniture. It looks real nice." She stepped into the kitchen and fixed on the fruit basket. "You got another one of those baskets."

"It's from Jug."

"Other men give out candy to get their way with little girls. Jug gives woven fruit baskets."

"This is a good one. No pears and it's got packets of caramel- and chocolate-covered popcorn."

"Did you bring him in?"

"Almost."

"That's better than not nearly," Grandma said, going to the refrigerator and finding the wine. "This is the most important ingredient when you make meatloaf."

"You put wine in meatloaf?"

"No, you drink it."

She poured herself a glass of wine and pulled a bunch of stuff out of the fridge.

"We need a big bowl," Grandma said. "And a big wooden spoon."

"I don't have a big wooden spoon," I told her. "I only have a big plastic spoon."

"Not a problem."

I gave her a bowl and she dumped the meat in it. She added eggs, ketchup, breadcrumbs, a bunch of seasoning, some milk, and some minced onion.

"Do you have parsley?" she asked me.

"No."

"Not a problem."

We got the meatloaf mixed and packed into a loaf pan. Grandma slid it into the oven and topped off her wine. I peeled potatoes, cut them into chunks, and dropped them into a pot of water.

"You've got a lot of potatoes and broccoli," Grandma said. "That's good. You'll have leftovers for tomorrow."

There was a knock on the door, and I froze, terrified that it might be the vampire. No, I told myself. That's ridiculous. He wouldn't come to my apartment and knock on the door. He would slip out of a shadow and take me by surprise. Still, wouldn't hurt to be careful.

I went to the door and looked out through the peephole. It was Herbert. This wasn't as horrible as having a vampire on my doorstep, but it wasn't wonderful either.

"It's Herbert," I said to Grandma.

"Who's Herbert?"

"Herbert Slovinski. I went to school with him. He's sort of attached himself to me."

"I know him," Grandma said. "Everybody knows Herbert. He's a regular at Stiva's. He's studying to be a funeral director. Everyone likes him. He's such a polite young man."

Grandma came to the door, opened it, and looked out at Herbert.

"Mrs. Mazur," Herbert said. "Wow! What a surprise. This is my lucky day. My two favorite people in one spot. This is even better than when we're all at the funeral home because we're all close and personal here. Of course, I have a lot of lucky days because I have an excellent guardian angel. One of the best in the business. I hope I'm not interrupting something here. I try to be sensitive about interrupting things."

"It's not an interruption," Grandma said. "We were just making meatloaf."

"I love meatloaf," Herbert said. "It's one of my favorite things. My mother makes meatloaf every Wednesday. Sometimes on Thursday, but usually on Wednesday. Some people put ketchup on meatloaf, but I like to put mayonnaise on it."

"You're welcome to stay, if you want," Grandma said. "We made extra broccoli and potatoes."

"Sure," Herbert said. "That would be awesome."

"Was there a reason for this visit?" I asked Herbert.

"I wanted to make sure you knew how to work your new television. They can be tricky sometimes. And I brought a list of good shows just in case you wanted to watch something. I have the list in categories depending on your mood. And I brought a bottle of wine. It was my mother's idea."

He handed me the wine and he stepped inside and looked into the kitchen. "Is that a fruit basket? Is that from Jug? Is he back in town already?"

"I think one of his minions dropped it off."

"Too bad. It was a shame that he was snatched away from you, but at least you got a fruit basket."

I put the wine in the fridge, and I set an extra place at the table for Herbert.

"This has turned into a real party," Grandma said to me. "We should set out some snacks."

I didn't know how to roast a chicken or make a meatloaf, but I knew about snacks. I grabbed a box of crackers from the cupboard and pulled a couple different kinds of cheese out of the fridge. I was arranging all this on a plate when the doorbell rang.

"I'll get it," Herbert said. "It might be more fruit."

I heard him unlock the door and open it, and then I heard him screaming. "Eeeeeeee! Eaaaaaa!" The door slammed shut, locks clicked, and Herbert ran into the kitchen, arms waving in the air, eyes bugged out of his head, face contorted. "Eeeeeee!"

"What the Sam Hill?" Grandma said.

Herbert stopped screaming. His face went from red to white and he fainted, spread-eagle, flat on his back on the floor. Grandma soaked a kitchen towel and put it on his forehead.

He opened his eyes and took a couple beats to focus. "I think I might have wet myself."

"Not that I could see," Grandma said.

I went to the door and looked out the peephole and only saw an empty hall. I unlocked the door and stepped out. Definitely empty. I closed the door, relocked it, and went to Herbert.

"There's nothing out there," I said.

"He was there. The killer vampire," Herbert said. "They were talking about him on the local news this morning. He killed a woman in a laundromat, and he sucked all her blood out and then he ran away. People saw him but they couldn't stop him, and now the police can't find him."

"I heard about him too," Grandma said. "Everybody was talking about him when I was at the market yesterday."

"He had crazy eyes," Herbert said, "and his mouth was open, and I could see his fangs. And he was holding a big knife, and his arm was raised like he was going to stab me. I started screaming and his face changed, and he got snarly. His eyes were red with flames in them."

"Flames!" Grandma said. "That's serious."

"I might have imagined it," Herbert said. "I have an advanced imagination."

"What on earth was he doing here?" Grandma asked.

"Maybe he was lost," I said, trying hard not to show panic. "Maybe he was going door-to-door, looking for an empty apartment where he could hang out."

"I hate to think that he's hanging out in your building," Grandma said.

"Probably Herbert scared him off," I said. "I didn't see him in the hall."

Ranger called. "Having a dinner party tonight?"

"Yes, but the vampire decided not to stay."

"Can't blame him with all that screaming."

"Do you have a camera covering the parking lot?"

"Yes. We saw him leave but he disappeared before I could get a man on the scene. Are you okay?"

"Mostly."

"My best to Grandma."

I returned my phone to my pocket. "Ranger says hello," I said to Grandma.

"Was that your fiancé?" Herbert asked me.

"Yes."

"I thought it was Ranger on the phone," Grandma said.

Mental head slap. "It was! Duh. Sorry, brain fog from all the drama." I turned to Herbert. "That was Ranger. He owns Rangeman Security. The hall outside my apartment has video and audio surveillance and Rangeman monitors it."

"My parents have a Ring doorbell," Herbert said. "It's awesome. It shows when people steal your delivery packages. And we keep getting notices about dogs that get lost."

"It needs to give people notices about vampires," Grandma said.

Herbert nodded. "I never believed in vampires before, but I believe in them now."

"There's lots of things we don't know about," Grandma said. "I wouldn't be surprised if aliens from outer space landed here. That vampire could be one of them. Did you get a good look? Did he have pointy ears like Spock? Was his skin sort of greenish?"

"I didn't notice any of that," Herbert said. "I got a little flustered. I must have low blood sugar because usually, I'm a cool cucumber. I'm good in an emergency. Like if there's a building on fire and there's a cat inside that needs rescuing, I just go in and get it."

"No kidding," Grandma said. "You did that?"

"Not yet," Herbert said. "The opportunity hasn't come up."

We helped Herbert get to his feet, and Grandma gave him a glass of wine.

"I'm not much of a drinker," Herbert said. "As an entrepreneur I feel I should always be alert in case new opportunities arise."

"This is a new opportunity to try out some wine," Grandma said. "Did the vampire tell you his name?"

"No," Herbert said. "He didn't say anything, but he hissed at me. He looked surprised to see me at first and then when I started screaming, he got mad. He stuck his tongue out and made this hissing sound like a demon. It was freaky. I don't like to think about it. Holy crap. I'm never going to be able to sleep tonight. Maybe I'll have to sleep here."

"No," I said. "Not gonna happen."

I had to give it to Herbert for his tenacity.

"The news I got was sketchy," Grandma said. "They didn't give out any names of the deceased or the bystanders."

Thank you, Morelli and Jimmy. If my mother knew I'd walked in on a vampire with a fresh kill she'd have been dropping Xanax into her Big Gulp of whiskey. Bad enough that I had to live with it. And now I had Zoran at my door with a knife in his hand. My heart was doing backflips in my chest.

"Do you think we should call the police?" Herbert asked.

"No," I said. "I think we should mash the potatoes."

I figured this was like sex. Every now and then you run into a situation where it's just best to fake it and move on. So, I dredged up some bravado and did my best impression of a kick-ass, cool-as-snot Jersey girl. I've got a raving lunatic vampire stalking me. Big deal. Bring it on. Holy shit. Who wants meatloaf?

We all went into the kitchen and at Grandma's instruction, I took the temperature of the meatloaf.

"It's almost there," Grandma said, looking at the digital thermometer I was holding. "It's hard to read the thermometer with your hand shaking like that."

"It goes with my eye twitch," I said. "It's a phenomenon that happens when your cojones shrink to the size of raisins."

"I thought women didn't have cojones," Herbert said.

"A common misconception," I said. "Our cojones are out of sight, attached to our ovaries."

"I didn't know that," Herbert said. "That makes sense. I have extremely large cojones. My mother always said that my cojones were too big for my britches."

"I wish I didn't hear that," Grandma said.

By the time the meatloaf got to the table Grandma and Herbert were on the second bottle of wine.

"I wish I'd seen the vampire," Grandma said. "I've never seen one up close. I've only seen vampires in movies. He must have been real scary looking."

"Yeah," Herbert said, "but not as scary looking as the knife."

"I'm surprised you could get the door closed and locked," I said to Herbert.

Herbert gave his meatloaf another glob of mayo. "He backed up when I started screaming. He didn't try to get in."

That was because he'd expected me to open the door, I thought. He wanted to kill me. He wasn't interested in Herbert.

I broke out a bag of cookies for dessert, and we moved into the living room to watch a movie. Grandma had tea with her cookies and Herbert finished off the wine.

"That was excellent wine," Herbert said. "I'll have to get myself some next time I'm shopping. It's happiness in a glass. And it hasn't tarnished my mental accluety. I'm still sharp as a tack. Ask me an answer. Anything. I'll know the question. I would go on *Jeopardy!*, but I haven't the time because of my entrenuering. These cookies, on the other hand, are making me dizzy."

He stretched out on the floor in front of the television and instantly fell asleep.

"The little tyke's had a big night," Grandma said. "Between the wine and the vampire, he got all tuckered out."

My parents showed up halfway through the movie and took Grandma home. I was left with Herbert.

"Hey!" I said to Herbert. "Wake up."

No response. I nudged him with my foot to make sure he was alive.

"Stupid cookies," he said.

I threw a blanket over him, watched the end of the movie, and went to bed, locking my bedroom door.

# CHAPTER SEVENTEEN

Music blasted out of my phone into my dark bedroom. I grabbed the phone and tapped it on.

It was Ranger. "I'm coming in."

I looked at the time. Four thirty. Good God. This man never slept. The lock on my bedroom door clicked open and Ranger walked in.

"You have a man sleeping on the floor in your living room," Ranger said.

"That's Herbert. He had too much to drink."

"Do you want me to have him removed?"

"No. He lives with his mother. She'll freak out if you bring him home now. If you haven't noticed, it's four thirty. Normal people are asleep at four thirty. I'd like to be asleep at four thirty."

"Your vampire isn't asleep at four thirty," Ranger said. "We picked him up on camera. He was trying to buy Ecstasy, and the supplier didn't have any. He was told to come back at five thirty, when someone named Tok would be in the alley. I'd grab him for you, but I have no authorization to arrest."

I dragged myself out of bed. "I need coffee."

"Get dressed," Ranger said. "I'll make coffee."

I went with the abbreviated bathroom routine, omitting mascara and lip gloss. I ran a brush through my hair and pulled it into a ponytail. I dressed in my usual uniform and went to the kitchen, where my coffee was waiting in a to-go cup. Herbert was sound asleep and snoring, so I pinned a note to his shirt. It read, *Herbert, go home.*

Ranger was driving a fleet SUV. I took this to mean that in case of a capture he didn't want his personal Porsche Cayenne sullied by vampire DNA.

"About Herbert," Ranger said.

"I went to school with him. He sat behind me in algebra class. Our paths crossed last week, and I can't get rid of him."

"Stalker?"

"More like a harmless nerd who lives with his parents and hasn't any friends. He just shows up and tries to do nice things for me. I came home from work one day and he'd painted my apartment."

"How did he get in?"

"Bribed the super. Then another day he had carpet installed. And a television. It's always all done when I'm not home."

"He has money."

"Apparently. He says he's an entrepreneur. I don't exactly know what that means. Grandma came over for dinner last night and Herbert showed up. Turned out Grandma knew him, so he got invited to stay for meatloaf."

Ranger stopped for a light and looked over at me. "You made meatloaf?"

"Grandma made it . . . but I bought the meat."

That got a smile. "Tell me about Zoran."

I read the text message to him. "It came in at four thirty," I said. "Herbert showed up around five thirty, and maybe ten minutes later, Zoran rang my bell. Herbert answered it, took one look at Zoran with the fangs and a knife in his hand, and started screaming like a little girl. He said Zoran backed off, and he was able to get the door shut and locked. And then he fainted. After that he chugged a bottle of wine and passed out on my living room floor."

"Zoran expected you to answer the door."

"Yes."

"When you move out of this apartment and go offline, life will be dull for the men who monitor my accounts," Ranger said. "I'll have to fit you with a body cam, so they have something bizarre to report on once in a while."

It was dark in the car. I had my coffee. It was quiet. The streets were empty. I was feeling a weird combination of comfy cozy because I was with Ranger, and at the same time a slow drip of adrenaline because we were on the hunt for a crazed killer. Ranger was in his zone. Alert. Outwardly relaxed. Probably had a heart rate of thirty-four. My heart rate was probably closer to a hundred and thirty-four.

"Do we have a plan?" I asked.

"I have a car in place on Freemont, and I'm going to put us on Stark. The plan is to trap Zoran in the alley. The control room will be watching and listening in, plus my man on Freemont has the camera app and I have the app and I sent the app to you, so we should all be able to see what's going down. When I move, you move with me. Stay close. Stay behind me."

Ranger turned onto Stark and parked behind a junker car. The alley was a car length in front of us. We couldn't see into the alley but we could see the alley on our app.

"If you're going to keep working for Vinnie and you're going to have a caseload that includes freaks like Zoran, you need to carry and you need to know some self-defense," Ranger said.

We'd had this discussion before, and it always ended in failure. I hated guns and I was a self-defense disaster. This time might be different. I had more motivation. I was genuinely terrified of Zoran.

"We need to get you certified to carry," Ranger said. "I have two men who are certified firearms instructors. You can work with them, get your skill level up, and they'll complete your paperwork. In the meantime, you can do an illegal carry. There's a loaded SIG Sauer P229 nine in the gun box under your seat. It has a slide with a red dot. It's yours. When we're done here, we'll go back to Rangeman and get you started with one of my instructors."

We sat in silence after that. Impossible to guess what Ranger was thinking. I was thinking about Cheerios. I had the camera app up on my phone. The alley was dark. It looked empty. A couple guys in gang colors entered the alley from our side. They hung close to the street and after a couple minutes a chunky dude in a tracksuit, carrying a small duffel bag, strolled down the sidewalk and joined the two gangbangers. Their voices were low, and they were speaking Spanish.

Ranger grew up one block off Calle Ocho in Miami. He speaks fluent Spanish, and he can salsa dance. I can't do either of those things.

"They're negotiating," Ranger said. "The gangbangers are unhappy with the price."

"Do you think that's Tok in the tracksuit?"

"They aren't using names."

A kid came out of a building two doors down. Baggy jeans, gray hoodie. From his build and height, I'd say he was in his early teens. He entered the alley and walked toward the guy in the tracksuit. The gangbangers turned their back to the kid and went to their phones.

"I need some Ecstasy and meth," the kid said to the tracksuit. "It's for Fang."

The kid took a bag from Tracksuit and turned to leave, and a black SUV pulled up to the alley. A guy got out and fired off a bunch of shots, and the kid and Tracksuit went down. The gangbangers grabbed the duffel bag and ran for the SUV. They got in and the car sped off. Ranger was on his feet, talking into his earpiece, calling for backup and medical. I was right behind him. We ran to the kid, who was moaning and crying. Blood was seeping through his jeans. He was shot in the leg. Tracksuit wasn't moving. The two Rangeman guys from the Freemont Street car went to Tracksuit, determined that he was dead, and moved to Ranger and the kid.

"Shot in the leg," Ranger said. "Scoop him up and take him to the medical center."

Ranger stood, and we turned toward Stark Street. A shadowy figure was at the end of the alley. He was slim with brown hair slicked back, and he had a large knife in his hand.

I felt a chill rip through me. "Zoran," I said. More question than statement. It was very dark and it was hard to see his face, but his mouth was wide open and I saw the fangs.

"We meet again," he said. "Your destiny brings you to me. It's preordained. You'll be mine in the very near future. I'll feast on your blood and we'll be immortally joined. We'll experience the rapture together."

"When we're done here, remind me to sharpen my wooden vampire stake," Ranger whispered in my ear.

Zoran whirled around and took off running. Ranger ran after him, and I ran after Ranger. Zoran crossed the street, ran into a building, and slammed the door shut and locked it. Ranger kicked the door open, and we heard Zoran on the stairs above us. By the time we got upstairs there was no sign of Zoran. There were three doors on the second floor. All were shut. We heard a woman scream behind one of the doors and Ranger kicked the door open.

"He go out the window," the woman said.

We ran to the window and saw Zoran on the fire escape. He dropped to the ground and disappeared in the dark alley that ran the length of the first three blocks of Stark.

"He's pretty agile for a drugged-up lunatic," I said to Ranger.

"Vampires have superpowers when they're on meth," Ranger said.

We exited the building in time to see a fire truck pull onto Stark. A cop car was behind it. A second Rangeman fleet SUV was angle parked by Ranger's SUV. Ranger's second in command, Tank, was standing beside it. Tank's partner was standing guard at the body. Ranger and I walked over to Tank.

"Looks like the guy in the alley sold his last bag," Tank said.

"Yeah. Drug deal gone wrong," Ranger said. "A kid who was running an errand for Zoran got shot. Jules and McKinney took him to the medical center. I want to talk to him. Tell whoever gets assigned to this case that I'll be in touch later this morning."

"You got it," Tank said. He nodded and smiled at me. "Nice to see you."

"Nice to see you too," I said. And I meant it. Tank was in Special Forces with Ranger. He had Ranger's back then and he still has it now. His name is only half-appropriate. He's a total tank on the outside. On the inside, he's a marshmallow.

We got into Ranger's SUV and drove off before we were pinned in by emergency vehicles. Ranger called McKinney and told him to watch the kid until we got there.

"We can canvass the alley behind Stark when it gets light," Ranger said. "Too dangerous to do it in the dark." He glanced over at me. "You look a little pale. Are you okay?"

"I didn't have time for makeup. I also didn't have time for food."

"I can't help with the makeup, but I've got food. There's a compartment in the console that's filled with protein bars."

I picked one out that advertised peanut butter and chocolate chips.

"Does Ella cater the cars?" I asked him.

"Her husband is in charge of cars," Ranger said. "After we talk to the runner, we can go back to Rangeman, where there's a larger selection of breakfast foods."

"I should check in at the office after the medical center."

"It's Sunday, babe. There is no office."

---

Everyone was still in the ER when we got to the medical center. Jules was in the waiting room and McKinney was bedside with the runner.

"They're working on him now," Jules said. "They said it wasn't necessary to take him to the operating room. They just shot him full of a local and gave him a tranq. His name is Clay Wong. He's sixteen. Street kid."

We found seats in the waiting room and forty-five minutes later, Ranger was able to go back to talk to Clay. Jules and I passed the time with hangman and twenty questions. Ranger reappeared, went to the desk, filled out some forms, and finally came back to Jules and me.

"He's getting discharged," Ranger said to Jules. "He has some scripts that need to get filled. After that he's going to Rangeman. McKinney will bring him out in a couple minutes." Ranger looked down at the pad with the hangman scribbles. "You don't ever want to play games with her," he said to Jules. "She's vicious."

"Tell me about it," Jules said.

Ranger wrapped an arm around my shoulders and steered me out of the building, to the SUV.

"Why is Clay going to Rangeman?" I asked him.

"He's a runaway. Living on the street. No money for antibiotics. No place to recover from a gunshot wound. Says he's clean. Just can't go home. I'll let him stay in one of the dorm rooms until we sort it out."

"What did he say about Zoran?"

"Not much. Zoran saw him sleeping in a doorway and said he'd pay him to get drugs for him."

"That was it?"

"Yes."

"That's a bummer. Why do you suppose Zoran didn't get his own drugs?"

"Maybe he didn't want to get shot."

"Does that happen a lot?"

"Often enough," Ranger said.

---

Rangeman occupies an entire building on a quiet side street in downtown Trenton. It's seven stories, with the top floor devoted to Ranger's apartment. The fifth floor contains the control room, offices, and a pleasant lounge with tables and chairs and a twenty-four-hour buffet. The ground floor has a small lobby and more offices. Ella and her husband have an apartment on the second floor, the third floor is a state-of-the-art gym, and floors four and six are dorm rooms and miscellaneous-use rooms. There's an ultra-secure garage and a shooting range belowground.

Ranger pulled into the Rangeman garage and parked in a space reserved for fleet cars.

"I rushed you out of your apartment this morning," Ranger said. "You have a firearms session with Skip now, but you can go upstairs and have a shower and get clean clothes and breakfast, if you want. Or you can grab something on the fifth floor and go straight to the gun range."

"I'll get something on the fifth floor," I said. "Wouldn't want to keep Skip waiting."

We took the elevator to the fifth floor and Ranger texted Skip that I was in the building. I went to the buffet. The food is constantly being refreshed and changed. It's organic or natural and healthy. Fresh fruit, fresh vegetables, sandwiches, hot selections, snacks. No doughnuts. Ever. There are some huge, muscle-bound Rangemen, but there are no fat Rangemen.

I grabbed an orange juice and a bagel with cream cheese. Ranger got coffee. I suspected he would go upstairs to his apartment once I got settled with Skip. Ella would have Ranger's breakfast waiting. A fresh fruit plate, salmon with capers or caviar, toast points. Sometimes breakfast would be a vegetable frittata.

Skip walked in and suggested we take a table off by itself, in a corner.

"We'll talk about guns before we go downstairs to shoot," he said. "If it's okay with you, we'll pretend you're a beginner."

"Great," I said. "I *am* a beginner. The truth is, I hate guns."

"You don't have to love them," Skip said. "You just have to know how to use them successfully and safely."

Already, I liked him.

"You eat and I'll talk," he said. "Do you have your gun with you?"

I pulled it out of my bag.

"Nice choice," he said.

"Ranger gave it to me."

"Ranger knows what he's doing . . . always."

After an hour, I knew why the gun was perfect for me, right down to the red dot. I could take it apart and put it back together. I could insert a clip. I could hold it without fear of accidentally shooting myself.

I followed Skip downstairs to the shooting range. I'd been there before, and the results weren't impressive. It turned out that I had a good eye and could hit a target, but I had a horrible attitude and couldn't get comfortable carrying a gun. Especially if it was loaded. I decided to improve my attitude this time around.

When we broke for lunch I felt like the lame-brained kid who finally aced a math test. I found Ranger at his desk, in his office.

"Congratulations," Ranger said. "I just talked to Skip, and he said you qualified. Ramon is up next for self-defense."

"No! No self-defense. Last time I tried self-defense, I cracked a toenail and ruined my pedicure doing kickboxing. My toenail has never been the same."

"Babe, it's just a toenail."

"It's not *just* a toenail. Toenails are important. They're part of the pretty package. It goes with getting a good haircut and highlights and having a signature lipstick."

"I missed that memo," Ranger said.

"A girl has to have priorities."

"Toenails over self-defense?"

"Any day of the week."

"How about lunch. Is that a priority?"

"Yes. What's on the menu today?"

"Ella made some hand pies. Chicken curry and steak and potatoes. And the usual salads and sandwiches. I need to finish reviewing a floor plan. Grab a bottle of water and a steak pie for me. We can eat here while I work and then we can check out the alley behind Stark."

I filled a tray and brought it back to Ranger's office. Egg salad sandwich, mac and cheese, and a water for me. Ranger's water and steak pie.

The day of the week didn't matter for Ranger, Morelli, or me. We were always on call. The job didn't stop at five o'clock Friday. That would change for me if I had a baby. I might continue to work, but not in the field as a bounty hunter. Or, maybe not at all. I grew up with a full-time mom. Grandma was just down the street. There was always someone close by to put a Band-Aid on my bloody knee. It was a good childhood. With the exception of Morelli. He was the forbidden fruit of my childhood. He was the scourge of the neighborhood. He was the bad-boy heartthrob of my high school. And now I was engaged to him. And the thing is, he turned out to be a really good guy. Go figure.

Ranger finished his lunch and signed off on the floor plan. "Thanks for waiting. I'm still playing catch-up."

"Not a problem," I said. "Do you think Zoran will move away from Stark Street after this morning?"

"If he was sane and clean, yes, he'd move. Since he's neither sane nor clean, no. He's going to stay close to his drug supplier."

"His drug supplier just got dead."

Ranger stood and came out from behind his desk. "Even before they carted Tok's body out of the alley, someone was waiting in the shadows to take his place."

I followed Ranger to the garage and watched while he took another fleet SUV.

"You aren't driving one of your personal cars," I said, getting in next to him.

"The fleet SUVs are recognized as Rangeman vehicles and most of the gang members on Stark know not to touch them."

Ranger pulled out of the garage and drove the short distance to Stark. We cruised three blocks on Stark, and Ranger turned onto a cross street and parked. We got out of the car and walked back to Stark.

I was wearing my new gun in its new holster, and I was concealing it with my hoodie. Ranger was in black Rangeman fatigues, and his holstered gun was concealed by a black windbreaker. He also was carrying an ankle gun, a knife, self-defense spray, cuffs, and a collapsible baton. I had a few extras in my bag, too. Lip gloss, hairbrush, self-defense spray, cuffs, and another bagel from the Rangeman buffet.

It was Sunday, early afternoon, and people were out enjoying the nice weather. Hookers strutted their stuff on the corners, gangbangers slouched against graffiti-covered buildings, druggies were curled in doorways and sprawled on sidewalks. A steady stream of cars rolled down the street, looking to buy whatever was for sale. No one bothered us. Ranger had the tight-ass walk of a kid with street cred, and the rest of him said he wasn't a kid and he wasn't someone you'd want to mess with.

We walked three blocks, taking the temperature of the street, cataloging details, keeping a watch for Zoran. We walked past Lucky Linda's and the bar with the mop guy. We crossed the alley where Tok had been shot. No yellow crime scene tape. Some bloodstains waiting for rain to wash everything clean. We went to the end of the first block, crossed the street, and walked back toward our SUV.

"This feels pointless," I said to Ranger.

"It's not pointless," he said. "You notice things that you miss when you're in a car. You see what's inside an open door, drug transactions, faces looking out windows, places where people hang and places that they avoid. When we get to the end of the third block we'll walk the alley."

"This is what you did when you were a bounty hunter?"

"Yes. I see detail. I'm good at tracking. I always took point when I was in the military."

"Do you miss being a bounty hunter?" I asked him.

"Sometimes. I miss the hunt. I don't miss the takedown."

"That's surprising. I've watched you do a lot of captures, and you're good at it. You're the best."

"I have skills."

"And the job that you have now?"

Ranger smiled. "It's a mixed bag. I hate being trapped in my office, but I like designing security systems. I like the idea that I can keep people and businesses safe."

"You wear a lot of different hats. You design systems. You ride patrol. You put on a suit and talk to future clients. You have a lot of people working for you."

"I never wanted to own a business. I liked the independence I had as a bounty hunter. As a favor, I agreed to help a friend with a startup security agency. The agency grew faster than expected, and I had less and less time to hunt down felons. And then due to a series of unlikely events, I ended up owning the company. My original intention was to make it successful enough to sell, but it turned out that I like providing security. I like the variety of the job. I like the people who work with me. I like the technology we use. I don't like being a salesman. I need to hire a sales specialist." He wrapped an arm around me and hugged me to him. "Would you like the job?"

"No! I'd be horrible at it."

We were at the end of the third block. We went around the corner and picked up the alley that intersected Stark Street and Mallow Street. Ranger moved his jacket so that his gun was exposed and accessible. This part of the alley was a dumping ground for garbage and the worst of the homeless. Broken-down tents, human waste, needles, and hollow-eyed junkies. Ranger spoke to a couple men. He asked them if they knew Fang. They said no or didn't reply at all.

The second block was better. It was littered with garbage and a couple junker cars, but there was only one tent, with an older woman and a dog inside. Ranger asked the woman if she knew Fang and whether she'd seen anyone come off the fire escape this morning. She said she'd seen Fang on the street, but not lately. Ranger gave her twenty dollars and thanked her for her help. He stepped back and looked up at a three-story tenement.

"We chased Zoran into this building," Ranger said. "He came down this fire escape and turned toward the first block."

Twenty years ago, a fire had raged through the first block of Stark. The entire block had been razed, and new buildings replaced the old tenements. The new buildings didn't have external fire escapes. They had a single-door rear exit. There were six buildings. They all had small businesses on the ground floor and apartments above. No garages. No back entrances to cellars.

Ranger tried all the doors. All were locked. The other side of the alley was commercial. Cinder block single-story buildings. A warehouse. An auto body shop.

"I was sure Zoran was hiding out here," I said to Ranger. "Now I'm not as convinced. He found a way to get to my apartment building, so it isn't as if he's tethered to Stark Street. I was assuming he didn't have transportation because his truck was parked in his driveway, but there are other possibilities. He could steal a car, or someone might be hiding him. Hell, for all I know it could be another vampire with a car."

"Or it might be that our search area was too small, or our search was incomplete," Ranger said. "We walked the street and the alley. We didn't go door-to-door."

"You think he's here on Stark."

"I think he's in the area."

"Where do we go from here?"

"We wait for him to make another drug buy."

We walked back to the car, and Morelli called just as I was about to get in next to Ranger.

"What time do you want me to pick you up?" Morelli asked.

I drew a total blank. "Where are we going?"

"Your aunt Stella's birthday party. She's eighty, right?"

"Omigod. I completely forgot. I've been so wrapped up in work that I never thought to check my calendar."

"According to the text you sent me a couple weeks ago, it's at Valerie's house," Morelli said. "Buffet dinner at six o'clock."

"Okey dokey. Pick me up at five thirty."

I got into the SUV and checked my text messages. One from Grandma. *Did you remember to get Stella a present? She likes lavender soap.*

"I have to go home," I said to Ranger. "I'm supposed to be at my aunt Stella's birthday party at six o'clock, and I need to stop someplace and get her a present."

"Babe," Ranger said.

# CHAPTER EIGHTEEN

Morelli rang my bell and opened my door at precisely five thirty. I was showered. My hair was washed, dried, and round-brushed. I was wearing my only dress-up outfit: the navy skirt and jacket. I was putting the bow on Aunt Stella's present.

"Wow," Morelli said, walking into the living room. "You've been busy."

"Not me. Herbert Slovinski."

"We went to high school with him," Morelli said. "He was a year behind me. He played clarinet."

"You were friends?"

"No. The band was lined up on the side of the field before halftime and I ran for a pass and plowed into him. Knocked him on his ass. Clarinet ended up in the trombone section."

"I'd forgotten. That was the game with New Brunswick. We lost."

"Yeah. We lost a lot," he said. "The band wasn't very good either."

"The majorettes were good."

Morelli grinned. "You were hot in your little costume. You couldn't twirl a baton for crap, but you could really strut out in a parade."

"My one talent," I said. "Strutting."

"You have other talents. I'd tell you about them, but we'd end up late for the party." He looked around the room. "What's your connection to Herbert? As I remember him, he was too weird to even be a geek. He had a couple other weird friends, and they used to play D & D at lunchtime. I think he took his mother to the prom."

"I ran into him at the Luger viewing, and I can't get rid of him. He keeps trying to do nice things for me. Like paint my apartment, and get carpet installed, and buy me a television. He always does it when I'm not home. He bribes the super to let him in."

"Honey, that's creepy."

"I thought so in the beginning, but it's not like he's a predator. I think he's just needy. Grandma was here for dinner yesterday, and Herbert popped in. Turned out Grandma knew him, so he got invited for dinner."

"You made dinner?"

"I helped."

Another grin from Morelli. The men in my life thought it was amusing that I might attempt to make dinner. I had to admit that the amusement was justified.

I handed my phone to Morelli. "Read the text message. It came in yesterday. It's from Zoran."

He read the message and handed the phone back to me. "I talked to Jimmy about Julie Werly. He said it was an odd case.

There was a blood trail that started in the living room, led through the house and into the yard. He said it wasn't a lot of blood. Just steady drips. And then it stopped in the yard. He thought the body had been loaded onto something or into something and dragged across the yard and through the hedge to the sidewalk. It all ended there. It was assumed the killer had a truck or a car parked on the side street, loaded the body into it, and took off. There are a lot of open questions. What was the motive? Why was the body removed? What was the murder weapon?"

"Why was it determined that Julie was killed?"

"The blood, the imprint on the grass, and that something heavy had been dragged through the hedge. It's six months and she hasn't surfaced."

"Julie is one of four women who were associated with Zoran and went missing. One was his wife. The other two were hookers."

"We've had his house under electronic surveillance, and he hasn't returned," Morelli said. "We've also been watching the uncle and the parents. He hasn't shown up at either doorstep."

"You've been watching the wrong doorstep. He rang my bell when Grandma and Herbert were in my kitchen. Herbert answered the door and almost messed himself. He said Zoran had a knife raised, like he was going to kill someone, and his mouth was open, and he could see his fangs. And then Zoran hissed at Herbert, and Herbert said he thought Zoran's eyes were red with flames in them."

"And?"

"And then Herbert started screaming and Zoran sort of backed up, and Herbert slammed the door shut and locked it. Then Herbert ran into the kitchen and fainted. Crash. Onto the floor."

"This happened yesterday?"

"Yep."

"When were you planning on telling me this?"

"I was waiting for the right moment."

"I'm afraid to even ask you about Bruno Jug."

"Not a problem there," I said. "He's a big sweetie pie. He gives me fruit baskets."

---

My sister, Valerie, lives in a large colonial in Hamilton Township. She has four kids, and she's married to a sweet but clueless lawyer named Albert Kloughn.

Valerie was always the perfect little girl, and I was always the kid who tried to fly off the garage roof and broke her arm. We aren't sure how we fit into our parents' perception now. We're just trying to get through the days as best we can. Valerie very nicely volunteered her house for Stella's party, and I suspected she was already regretting it. Stella is actually my *great*-aunt on my father's side and she's a couple cans short of a case. She lives in an assisted-living community with her husband, Marty. It's suspected that Marty might have Alzheimer's, but for as long as anyone has known Marty, he hasn't been able to find his keys or figure out how to exit a parking lot. So, it's difficult to diagnose exactly what's wrong with Marty. The thing is, now that they're in their eighties, surely there has to be *something* wrong with them other than just being annoying.

The driveway was filled with cars, and cars were lined up in front of the house. Morelli parked behind the last car in line and looked at me.

"Do we really want to do this?" he asked.

"No," I said. "We'll say happy birthday, give her the present, grab a couple pigs in a blanket, and leave. It's a big party. No one will notice we're gone."

He leaned over and sniffed at me. "You smell like s'mores."

"It's smoke damage from the fire."

"I like it."

"Me too. It makes me want to go camping."

"We could go camping on our honeymoon," Morelli said. "We could get a pop-up tent and sleep under the stars."

"Not nearly," I said. "I'm not a tenter. I'm more a motorhomer. The bigger the better. Something with state-of-the-art plumbing and a comfy bed. It should also be bug-and-snake-free."

"Maybe you're more a hotel-resort type," Morelli said.

I was thinking with our schedules we were more of a "no honeymoon at all" type.

We let ourselves in and I took stock of the room. Lots of people I didn't know. Lots of old people. Valerie's kid, Mary Alice, galloped past me, toward the kitchen.

"Looks like she still thinks she's a horse," Morelli said.

"Not always," I said. "Sometimes she's a reindeer."

I followed Mary Alice and found Valerie in the kitchen.

"Hiding?" I asked her.

"There's no place to hide in this house. These people are everywhere. Someone is upstairs taking a nap in my bed."

"Where did they all come from? Are we related to any of these people?"

"I didn't make up the guest list but I'm sure we're related to some of them. The rest came in a bus from the senior living complex."

I set my purse and Stella's present on the kitchen counter. "That explains a lot. Are Grandma and Grandpa Plum here?"

"No. They're in Florida," Valerie said. "They said they're saving their airplane allowance for when there's a hurricane. Otherwise, they're not coming back to Jersey."

"I guess they really like Florida."

"They divide their time between the casino and the track. And Grandma Plum said they sunbathe naked in their backyard."

"Gross!"

"I don't know," Valerie said. "It's kind of sweet that they still get naked together at their age."

"The last time I saw them was two years ago, just before they moved. They didn't look that good fully clothed. I don't want to think about them naked."

Grandma Mazur came into the kitchen with two shopping bags. "I got the rolls from the bakery and the deli platters from Giovichinni. Your mother is right behind me with the cake." She set the bags on the kitchen table. "Who let all those old people in? The living room is full of them."

"They came from senior living," Valerie said, unpacking the rolls.

"Those old people will go through this food like a swarm of locusts," Grandma said. "They'll be filling their pockets with pickles and ham sandwiches."

My mother came with the cake and my father followed her. My father was in his church suit, wearing his church shoes.

"If I make it to eighty, just give me a can of beer and set me in front of the TV," my father said.

"Last I saw, Aunt Stella was on the couch with Ginny and Bernard Crosdale," Valerie said. "Uncle Marty is wandering around somewhere. Someone should check on him. Make sure he doesn't get out of the house and walk into traffic."

My father gave a grunt and went off to look for Marty.

I emptied the bags of rolls into a bowl, unwrapped the deli platters, and added them to the casseroles that were already on the dining room table. There was a lot of yelling coming from the backyard. I went to the door and looked out at a bunch of little kids who had Marty tied up and were throwing Nerf balls at him.

"I found Marty," I said to Valerie.

"As long as he's in the backyard and the gate is closed," she said. "Do we need to put more wine out?"

I glanced over at Morelli. He was off to the side, talking on his phone. The expression on his face wasn't good. It was his cop face. Focused. Unreadable. Serious.

I took a couple bottles of red wine from the case on the floor and put them on the table with the food. Morelli ended the call and motioned for me to come to him.

"You're wearing your cop face," I said.

"I have a cop face?"

"Yeah. It's almost the same as your poker face. What's up?"

"That was Jimmy on the phone. It looks like there might have been another vampire murder. This one was in your neighborhood. The woman was just found. Jimmy said it looked like she'd been dead for a while. Probably was killed early last night."

That sucked the air out of me. "That's terrible. Do you think Zoran didn't get to kill me, so he found a substitute?"

"It's possible. It's also possible that you would have been his second kill of the night. Jimmy made his best guess at time of death. The ME will be more precise. It's also possible that this wasn't Zoran's kill."

"But Jimmy thought it might have been Zoran?"

"She had bite marks on her neck similar to the woman in the laundromat."

A wave of nausea curled through my stomach. The laundromat horror was still fresh in my mind. I couldn't shake it.

"I told Jimmy I'd meet him at the scene," Morelli said.

"I'll go with you."

"That's not necessary."

"The alternative is to stay at this party."

Morelli looked into the living room. There was music playing. "Stayin' Alive" by the Bee Gees. The old folks were trying to dance to it.

Morelli grinned and did the classic "Stayin' Alive" move, channeling his inner Travolta.

"If you want to give up being a cop, you could have a career with Chippendales," I said to him.

"Get your purse," he said. "Jimmy's waiting."

---

The crime scene was about a quarter mile from my apartment building. It was a residential area of single-family houses with yards that were large enough for swing sets and grills. There were lots of mature trees and shrubs. The cop cars, an EMT truck, and a clump of gawkers were clustered around a wooded area between two houses. Morelli angle parked next to a cop car.

He'd said it wasn't necessary for me to tag along, but from my point of view, it was necessary. This wasn't something I could walk away from. Even if the memory of the laundromat made me sick, I had to keep working to find the killer. He had to be stopped. It was necessary for me to know that I was doing my best to help stop him.

Jimmy was standing a short distance from the body. He waved when he saw us.

"What have you got?" Morelli asked him.

"She's wearing shorts, a T-shirt, and running shoes. She was probably out getting exercise. No ID on her. She has a gash on the back of her head. He might have come at her from behind and knocked her down. There's some blood on the road by the curb. Then it looks like he dragged her into the wooded area. It's a utility easement. A dog found her. He kept pulling on his leash and barking. The owner finally came to investigate and stumbled onto the woman. He was pretty shook up. He's with the paramedic."

"Is there a weapon?"

"No. There are bite marks on her neck. Similar to what we saw in the laundromat. Actually, fang punctures."

I gagged and Morelli turned to look at me. I waved him away.

"I'm good," I said.

"The interesting part is that the fang punctures weren't enough to cause death," Jimmy said. "Her throat was slit. Again, like the laundromat murder."

Morelli walked over and looked down at the woman. I kept my distance. Searching for clues by examining the newly dead wasn't now, and never would be, part of my skill set. The ME and a forensic photographer arrived and went to the body. Everyone stood around, talking, gesturing. The ME and the photographer went to work. Jimmy stayed by the body. Morelli came back to me.

"I'm having a problem with my serial killer hypothesis," I said to him. "There are four women who had ties to Zoran and disappeared. One left drops of blood. Three just disappeared. Now there are two women dead who were bitten, had their neck slashed, and were not made to disappear. I'm comfortable saying Zoran killed these last two women. I don't know if I'm comfortable tying him to the four disappearances."

"You don't have to be sure with a hypothesis," Morelli said. "A hypothesis is an idea that needs further investigation. I've watched you bumble your way through your bail bonds job with no skills and a partner who wears five-inch stiletto heels to work and is the worst shot in the entire state. I have no idea how you do it, but you manage to track people down and drag their sorry asses back to jail. I think you do it on luck, grit, and instinct. So, if your gut tells you that Zoran is responsible for two murders, maybe more, I'll go with your gut."

Wow. That was unexpected. I felt like I had a tennis ball in my throat and there were tears collecting behind my eyes. I choked it all back because Morelli had just told me I was a hard-ass, and I didn't want to ruin the moment.

"Oh jeez," he said. "You aren't going to cry, are you?"

"No."

He grinned, wrapped an arm around me, and kissed me on the top of my head. "You're such a cupcake."

"Thanks," I said. "Are we done here?"

"Yeah. I'll get together with Jimmy tomorrow. Do you want to go back to the party?"

"No!"

"I'm starving," Morelli said, "I need food. And beer. Not necessarily in that order."

"I'm in the mood for a Pino's pizza burger."

"Not only do you have gut instincts, but you can read minds," Morelli said. "Do you know what else I'm thinking?"

"I have a pretty good idea. We can discuss it at Pino's."

---

Pino's was packed but we scored a booth. The candle was fake, and the menu was stained with spaghetti sauce. I would have been disappointed if it was any different. I knew the two guys behind the bar, and I knew three of the waitresses. They were all related to Pino. The original Pino had gone to the big pizzeria in the sky ten years ago, and now Pino's was owned and managed by Little Pino and his extended family. I have a hard time imagining my life without Pino's. I might eventually learn how to roast a chicken, but there's no hope that I would ever be able to replicate a Pino's pizza.

Morelli ordered beer and I asked for a Coke.

"What's with the Coke?" Morelli asked. "No wine? No exotic drink with a jalapeño in it?"

"I'm trying to clean up my life."

"That sounds serious."

"It's occurred to me that you've reached a level of maturity that I envy. You have a respected job that provides you with a stable income. You own a house, and it doesn't get firebombed. You can scramble an egg and grill a burger. You have your own washer and dryer. You have a dog."

"You have a hamster," Morelli said.

"I love Rex, but he doesn't rush out of his soup can to say hello when I walk into my apartment. I chose to have a hamster because I didn't think I could manage the responsibility of having a larger pet. You have friends and family and a routine. You play poker with guys you've known all your life. You helped your brother put a swing set together. You decided you wanted to get married, and you acted on it. You got rid of your billiard table and bought dining room furniture."

Morelli studied his half-empty glass of beer for a beat before looking across the table at me. "You're trying to tell me something."

"I feel like I need some time to think. I've got some things going on in my life right now that I have to straighten out."

"Can I help?"

"I have to do this myself."

"Are we breaking up?"

"No! I just want a couple days to get a grip on myself."

"Okay. What about sex?"

"No sex."

"Damn. I was hoping the straightening out didn't mean no sex."

"But dinner is fine," I said. "We can have dinner."

"That's better than nothing. Can we still fool around?"

"Yes. A little."

We ordered burgers, fries, onion rings, and slaw.

"I don't feel good about you staying in your apartment," Morelli said. "What happens if Zoran shows up on your doorstep again? What happens if he comes after you in the parking lot?"

I pulled the SIG Sauer out of my purse and laid it on the table.

"Whoa," Morelli said. "When you said you were getting a grip on yourself, you were serious. This is a nice gun. I assume Ranger gave it to you. Can you shoot it?"

I took my certificate out of my purse and handed it to Morelli. "I can shoot it, and I'm certified to carry."

"I'd like to say this makes me feel better, but I've got a knot in my stomach."

I caught motion in my peripheral vision. It was Herbert.

"This is so cool!" he said. "I came in to get a grilled cheese and here you are. I get a grilled cheese here a lot. Especially when I'm involved in one of my entrepreneurial projects. Usually, I come in late at night, but my mom is at a prayer supper tonight, so I'm on my own. I could have gone to the prayer supper too, but you have to listen to a lot of praying and sermoning before they let you eat. If it goes on too long, I get low blood sugar. And I think Jesus is a good guy and everything, and you can't go wrong believing in God, but there's a time and place for everything. Am I right?" He looked at Morelli. "Hey, I know you. You ran into me at the football game. Boy, that was something. I hope you didn't hurt yourself. I was okay. You haven't changed much except you're older."

Morelli gave me a sidewise glance.

"I heard you're a cop now," Herbert said to Morelli. "That's great. And Stephanie said you guys are engaged. Congrats on that. Gee, here I am talking just like we were in high school again, and you might not even remember me. Herbert Slovinski. I played the clarinet in the band."

"I remember," Morelli said. "What are you doing now?"

"I'm an entrepreneur," Herbert said. "I was seriously thinking about being an undertaker but I'm not so sure anymore. I could also be a spy or a truck driver. Okay, probably not a spy. I say I'd like to be a spy, but that's just fun talking." He looked down at my gun, lying on the table. "Holy cow, whose gun is that?"

"It's mine," I said, scooping the gun up and returning it to my purse.

"Is it real?"

"Yes."

"I guess you need a gun in your line of work. Dog the Bounty Hunter carries a gun. He's awesome. I don't have a gun. That's another reason why I can't be a spy. All the best spies carry guns. Bautista had a whole suitcase full of guns and knives and stuff."

"Who?"

"Dave Bautista. He won the WWE Championship twice, and the World Heavyweight Championship four times. And he made a movie where he was an undercover spy guy. He totally kicked ass. I could never be a spy like Bautista. He could do everything. He could even ice-skate. He's even more awesome than Dog."

Gina Pino brought a bag to Herbert. "Here's your grilled cheese, and I gave you extra pickles. Make sure you eat it while it's warm."

"I'm going to eat it right away," Herbert said. "And if it cools off, I'll microwave it. It's never the same when you microwave it but it's still good."

"You take care of yourself, honey," she said to Herbert.

"You're welcome to sit with us, if you want," I said to Herbert.

"Gee, that's nice of you, but I have to get someplace. I'm doing research on a new entrepreneurial project tonight."

Morelli waited until Herbert was out the door before leaning in toward me. "There's something wrong with him."

"I know, but he sort of grows on you."

"I can't believe you didn't know Bautista," Morelli said. "He's a legend. I have a Bautista action figure from WrestleMania. Anthony gave it to me for my birthday. And Bautista was Drax in *Guardians of the Galaxy*. Drax!"

So here's the difference between men and women, I thought. Morelli remembers Bautista as Drax and I remember Chris Pratt dancing to "Come and Get Your Love." Drax isn't hot. Chris Pratt is smokin'. Enough said.

# CHAPTER NINETEEN

I woke up Monday morning feeling fantastic. Everything had gone great with Morelli and now I had a little breathing room. No more stupid fibs. I looked at myself in my bathroom mirror and definitely saw a glow. No way to know the origin of the glow. Could have been from the seventeen-layer carrot cake drizzled with caramel sauce that I had for dessert at Pino's. Or it could have been from the feeling of security I had waking up with my loaded gun on my night table next to the bed. Or I could be pregnant. Truth is that this morning it didn't matter. A glow is a glow. I took a closer look and thought the glow was aided by the fact that I hadn't washed my face before bed last night and I still had remnants of blush and Dior luminizer on my cheeks. Thank goodness the fire hadn't touched the bathroom and my makeup stash had survived.

Lula and Connie were already in the office when I walked in.

I bypassed the doughnuts and went for a second cup of coffee. On the way back from the coffee machine I weakened and grabbed a doughnut.

"What's new?" Lula asked. "Did you have a good weekend?"

I didn't know where to begin. "I guess it was good," I said. "I got another fruit basket from Jug."

"That's nice," Lula said. "He's keeping in touch. Did he stick you with more pears?"

"No. It was a good basket. And then Grandma came over for dinner. And Herbert showed up. And then Zoran showed up."

"Hold on," Lula said. "*What?*"

"Yeah, Herbert opened the door and Zoran had a knife and he hissed at Herbert. And then Herbert started screaming and Zoran backed off and Herbert slammed the door shut and locked it. And then he fainted."

"Holy shit," Lula said.

Connie made the sign of the cross.

I decided to skip over the gangbangers and the shooting.

"Then on Sunday I spent some time with Ranger canvassing Stark Street, but nothing came of it," I said. "And later, I went to Aunt Stella's birthday party with Morelli."

"Is she the one who put her cat in the oven?" Lula asked.

"Yes," I said, "but she didn't turn the oven on, so the cat was okay."

"I remember that because it was like 'Hansel and Gretel,'" Lula said. "Anything else go down?"

"A woman was killed about a quarter mile from my apartment. Looked like she was jogging, and someone came from behind and bashed her head in, and then dragged her into a wooded area, and bit her in the neck and then cut her jugular," I said. "We're thinking it might have been Zoran."

Lula threw up in Connie's wastebasket, and I ran to the bathroom and got some wet paper towels.

"Sorry," Lula said, "but it was like the laundromat all over again."

"I went to the crime scene with Morelli, but I didn't look at the victim. I kept a distance."

"So, that was a good weekend?" Lula asked.

"It ended good. Afterward, I went to Pino's with Morelli and told him I needed some time to think, and it was all right with him."

"He's a good guy," Lula said.

"Do you know who Bautista is?" I asked them.

"WWE," Connie said. "And he was in that movie with the kid who wanted to be a spy."

"*My Spy*," Lula said. "I love that movie. The kid was great. She had awesome hair. Her hair was the best part of the movie."

"She had hair like you," Connie said.

"Yeah," Lula said. "We got perfect hair."

Lula went to the bathroom to freshen up and I ran my FTA list by Connie.

"I have Zachary Zell outstanding," I said. "He's going to try to get the charges dropped. And then I have Bruno Jug, who promised to come in when the time was right. And Zoran."

"The time might be right for Jug," Connie said. "His lawyer was all over the local news yesterday. It turns out that the girl wasn't fourteen years old. She was nineteen. And she wasn't date raped with a drug. She was a hooker who decided to squeeze Jug for some money. Apparently, Jug had previously interacted with her, and she'd been getting more than fruit baskets for services given. So, the scandal has changed from raping a young girl to having a hooker make house calls. Or in this case it was warehouse calls."

I looked at Lula. "Do you want to go for a ride? Now that the scandal has been downgraded to something worthy of a big yawn, I'm thinking Jug might have returned to Trenton."

"As long as you don't talk about vampires."

I grabbed a doughnut out of the box on Connie's desk, wrapped it in a paper napkin, and stuffed it into my hoodie pocket.

I drove to the produce warehouse first. I thought the chances of him being there were slim, but it was only fifteen minutes from the bail bonds office, and it was on the way to Jug's house.

"We don't have cupcakes to tempt Bruno," Lula said.

"He already got his cupcakes. This trip he's going to have to be satisfied with sitting next to you."

"I guess that's a big treat right there," Lula said. "Not every man gets to sit next to Lula."

I turned onto State Street and slowed when I got to Jug Produce. The TV satellite truck wasn't there but a handful of photographers were camped out across the street from the front entrance. I drove around the block to the warehouse gate and found a couple photographers there too.

"I don't know what this country's coming to when the big news of the day is Bruno Jug with a ho," Lula said. "That's as interesting as finding Colonel Sanders eating fried chicken. You'd think these photographers could find someone better to harass."

I'd had my share of unflattering press moments, and I thought this could easily be added to that list, so I parked one street over and called Jug. No answer on his cell phone. I called the office and asked for Jug.

"Mr. Jug won't be in his office today," a woman said. "Can I take a message?"

"Tell him Stephanie called," I said, and hung up.

"Do you think that's true?" Lula said. "Jug could be in there, hiding under his desk, eating ice cream."

"I think he's hiding in his house, eating oatmeal with the bimbo."

"We aren't going to his house, are we? Last time we did that, Annie Oakley shot a hole in your back window."

"That was different. We're friends now."

"We aren't friends with Annie Oakley. And what about his killer dog?"

"The killer dog weighs five pounds. I think we can deal with the killer dog."

I left State Street and drove to Jug's pleasant, family-friendly neighborhood. I cruised down Merrymaster and idled in front of Jug's house. No photographers. No Volvo in the driveway. No Annie Oakley standing guard on the front porch.

"What do you think?" I asked Lula.

"I think those photographers who were hanging around Jug Produce already got shot at here and decided a crap-ass picture of Jug wasn't worth a trip to the burbs."

I pulled into Jug's driveway and parked. I had my gun in my messenger bag and cuffs in my back pocket, but I didn't expect to use either of them. A week ago, everyone was worried about Bruno Jug. Now he was the least of my problems. I rang the doorbell. No answer, but the dog was barking on the other side of the door. I rang the bell again and knocked. Nothing. I tried the door. Unlocked.

"I don't care that the door's unlocked," Lula said. "I'm not going in there. That dog'll tear us to shreds."

I took the doughnut out of my pocket and unwrapped it. I opened the door and threw the doughnut at the dog.

"Problem solved," I said, stepping inside.

"Hello!" I yelled. "Anybody home? It's Stephanie and Lula."

"I hear you," Jug said, coming out of the kitchen. "You don't need to yell." He was in his pajamas, and he had a big spoon in his hand. "I need someone to make oatmeal. I have to start my day with oatmeal."

"Where's the Mrs.?" Lula asked.

"She left. Cleaned out her closet, took her stupid electric car, and left. She said she was going to sue me for divorce because I played hide the salami with a hooker."

"Well, you shouldn't have done that," Lula said. "You took sacred marriage vows."

"My marriage vows didn't say anything about banging hookers," Jug said.

"I guess that might make a difference then," Lula said.

"Now that you're back, we thought we could take you downtown to get rescheduled," I said.

"Sure, but I have to have my oatmeal first, and I don't know how to make it."

"Honey, everybody knows how to make oatmeal. You follow the directions on the box," Lula said.

"I can't find the box."

"Did you think to look in the cupboard?" Lula asked him. She opened a cupboard and found the oatmeal. "Get dressed, and I'll make your oatmeal."

"I always eat breakfast in my pajamas."

"Not today you don't," Lula said. "Get dressed."

Jug shuffled off to the bedroom, and Lula measured out oatmeal. "This is easy," she said. "He eats instant. You just microwave it."

The microwave dinged done, and Jug shuffled back to the kitchen. He was wearing a button-down shirt, pajama bottoms, and slippers.

"What the hell is this?" Lula said to him. "You aren't dressed."

"I heard it ding. I like to eat it when it's hot," he said.

Lula gave him the bowl of oatmeal and a spoon. "What else?" she asked him.

"I put some milk in it. And brown sugar. And I need coffee. And Mr. Big always goes out to poop when I eat my oatmeal."

"Just shoot me," Lula said.

"You find the brown sugar, and I'll take the dog," I said to Lula.

There was a canister on the counter that said DOG BISCUITS. I took a handful of dog biscuits and bribed Mr. Big to go outside. I stood on the front porch and watched while Mr. Big walked around the front yard in circles. Nothing was happening poop-wise. I walked into the yard and pointed my finger at Mr. Big and very sternly told him to poop. "Poop!" Mr. Big continued to walk in circles and finally hunched and pooped. I gave him the last dog biscuit and told him he was a good boy, and he ran into the house.

Jug was back in the bedroom, hopefully putting pants on, when I returned to the kitchen.

"He's got one of those fancy coffee makers that I couldn't figure out, so we have to stop at Starbucks," Lula said. "This guy doesn't know how to do anything. Hard to tell if it's because he's always been waited on or if he's not so smart anymore."

Jug joined us, fully dressed. "Did he poop?" he asked me.

"Yes," I said. "Has he had breakfast?"

"Yes. He eats first and then I eat. Otherwise, he sits and barks at me while I eat." Jug took a dog leash from the counter and hooked it to Mr. Big's collar. "We're ready to go get rescheduled."

"That's great," I said, "but Mr. Big has to stay home."

"He can't stay home," Jug said. "There's no one here, and he gets anxiety if he's left alone."

"We won't be gone long. We'll put the television on for him."

"He's not a big television watcher," Bruno said. "He's starting to get cataracts."

"Okay, I'll leave Lula here with him and you can come with me."

"No way," Lula said. "I'm not a dog person."

"I thought you wanted a dog and you were going to name her Chardonnay," I said.

"That's like Herbert wanting to be a spy," Lula said. "It's a fantasy. It don't really happen."

"I have a fantasy that I'm headmaster at a fancy private school for girls, and I have to discipline them," Jug said.

"Yeah, you and every other man on the planet," Lula said. "When I was a ho I charged extra for that one."

"That's it!" I said. "Get in the car. Everyone get in the car. Get the dog in the car."

I drove to Starbucks and sent Lula in for coffee. She returned with coffee for everyone and a cookie for Mr. Big.

"This won't take long, will it?" Jug asked. "Lou is coming at ten with some papers to get signed, and I have a massage scheduled for ten thirty."

"Not a problem," I said. "We'll check you in with the desk sergeant and call Connie."

I parked in the public lot across the street from the municipal building, and we all walked to the entrance.

"They aren't going to let Mr. Big into the building," I said. "He's going to have to stay here with Lula."

Jug tried to hand Lula the leash, and Mr. Big growled and snapped at Lula.

"What the hell," Lula said. "I got a cookie for this excuse for a dog."

I took the leash from Jug, and Big snapped at me.

"No!" I said to Big. "Not acceptable behavior." I held the leash at arm's length, so he couldn't reach me. "Go!" I said to Lula. "You know the drill. The court is in session. Check him in and make sure he gets taken straight to the court. Don't let them put him in a holding cell. I'll call Connie."

Lula and Jug disappeared into the building, and I walked Mr. Big to a patch of grass. I called Connie and told her that Lula was walking Jug through the system and someone was going to have to come down to write the bail bond.

"I'm not allowed to write a bond for him," Connie said. "I told you that a couple days ago."

"It was the only way I could get him here. The choice was to forfeit the bond money that Vinnie already invested or bring him in and write a new bond."

"You delivered him to the desk sergeant, right?"

"Yes. Lula delivered him."

"Then we get our bail bond money back," Connie said. "No problem on our end. Jug has to find a new bail bond agent."

"Okay, give me a contact."

"There are two other bail bond agencies in the area. I'm texting their numbers to you. There's a good chance that they won't write the bond because the amount is going to be too high."

Maybe it wasn't too late. Maybe I could get Lula to whisk Jug out of the building and we could turn him loose.

I called Lula. "Where are you? Have you turned Jug in yet?"

"Yeah. We're waiting for someone to take us to court."

Crap!

"Call me as soon as the bond is set." I looked down at Mr. Big. "This isn't good. This really isn't good."

I took Mr. Big for a walk, and when I got back to the municipal building it was coming up to ten o'clock. I found a bench in the shade, and Mr. Big chilled out while I called Lou.

"Hey," I said. "It's Stephanie."

"You snatched Bruno, didn't you? I'm at his house and nobody's home, including the dog."

"I didn't snatch him. He wanted to get rescheduled. He didn't get cuffed or anything. We even made him oatmeal."

"Yeah, him and the oatmeal. Did he eat in his pajamas?"

"More or less. Here's the thing: He might not make his massage appointment at ten thirty. We're waiting for the judge to set his bail bond."

"What do you want me to do?"

"Nothing. Just sayin'."

"Keep him away from the press and call me when he's done. I'll come get him."

"Great. Good plan."

I hung up.

Lula called. "We're done," she said. "Where's Connie?"

"Connie isn't coming."

"Say what?"

"What's the bond?"

"Same as last time."

"Oh boy."

"What do you mean by *oh boy*?"

"That's a lot of money."

"Yeah, I don't know why they set the bail bond so high. They know he never gets convicted of anything," Lula said. "Is Vinnie coming?"

"There's a hitch."

"Another one? You're full of hitches these days."

"Is that Jug yelling in the background?"

"He isn't exactly yelling. More like talking loud. He's explaining that he can't get locked up because he has a massage appointment."

"Tell him the appointment got canceled and we're trying to get his bond straightened out."

Ten minutes later, Lula met me outside.

"How'd that go?" I asked her.

"It could have been worse. He's kind of a celebrity. All the cops know him. Some of them wanted a selfie with him."

"No one wants to bond him out. He's in a big feud with Harry and Harry won't let Vinny write a bond for Jug. I called the other two bail bond agencies, and they aren't interested. The bond is too high."

"Why doesn't Jug pay his own bond?" Lula asked.

"Good question."

I called Lou.

"Is he ready to get picked up?" Lou asked.

"No. We have a problem. No one will write a bail bond for him."

Silence. "You're kidding me, right?" Lou finally said.

"Apparently Harry the Hammer and Lou aren't talking. Something about a big dis at the Christmas party. So now Harry won't let us bail Jug out. I called two more agencies, and no one will take it. The bond is too high."

"This is not good."

"Why doesn't Bruno bail himself out? He must have millions."

"The company has millions," Lou said. "How much money are we talking about?"

"It's the same as last time."

"I don't know how much Bruno has that's liquid. I'll get Bordelli working on it. You should work on it too or you could end up in a bad place."

"The landfill?"

"No. We don't use that anymore. We dump offshore."

I hung up.

"I need to talk to Harry," I said to Lula. "I'm going back to the office."

"Nobody talks to Harry," Lula said. "I've never even seen him."

---

"I have good news," Connie said when Lula and I walked into the office. "The charges have been dropped on Zachary Zell."

"Do I get my capture fee?" I asked her.

"Ordinarily, you wouldn't. But I'm putting it through because you engineered the dropping. That means you have two payments coming to you. Zell and Jug. Jug is a big one. Do you want me to direct deposit them for you?"

"Yes. It would be nice if I live to spend them. I wasn't able to get a bond posted for Jug, and it was suggested that I might be taking a one-way ocean voyage in the near future if I don't get Jug out of jail."

Connie stopped smiling. "Seriously?"

"Hard to tell," I said. "I need to talk to Harry."

"Nobody talks to Harry," Connie said.

"That's going to change. Where do I find him?"

Connie suddenly realized that I had a dog. Mr. Big was leashed and calmly sitting on my foot.

"What's with the dog?" Connie asked.

"It's Mr. Big," I said. "It's Jug's dog. He has anxiety if he's left alone."

"Yes, but why do you have him?"

"I keep asking myself that same question," I said. "Where can I find Harry?"

"He has an office on Beryl Street, off State. It's a block away from Rangeman," Connie said. "You'll have a hard time seeing him there. You'll have a better chance catching him at lunch. Most days he walks two blocks to Moachie's Grille, and he takes the booth in the back. Sometimes he eats alone and sometimes he's got business partners. Don't approach him if he has business partners. Change tops with Lula and stuff your bra so you've got some cleavage. The word is that Harry doesn't fool around but he likes to look."

I cut my eyes to Lula. She was wearing a magenta tank top that had some shiny magenta threads running through it. It was stretched to maximum capacity over her enormous boobs, and she had about a quarter mile of cleavage showing in the low scoop neck. "It's not going to fit me," I said.

"It's all spandex," Lula said. "It'll shrink up when I take it off. The bigger problem is that I'm going to have to wear your T-shirt, and I don't have a T-shirt personality. Plus, it's going to ruin my ensemble."

"Take one for the team," I said, turning my back to the front window and stripping down to my bra.

Lula took my T-shirt and handed me her tank top. "That lacy bra you're wearing is pretty," Lula said, "but it's for little boobies. I need a major suspension system to hold my girls up."

I pulled Lula's tank top over my head and tucked it into my jeans. She was right about the spandex. The top molded to my body.

"Better," Connie said, looking at me.

"It'll be even better if she stuffs half a roll of toilet paper into her teeny-tiny bra," Lula said.

I went into the bathroom and transformed my B-cup breasts into bulging D cups.

"Now we're talking," Lula said when I came out of the bathroom. "Now your girls are saying, *Hey, Harry, feast your eyes on these titties*."

"Do you really think this is necessary?" I asked Connie.

"Hell yeah, it's necessary," Lula said. "Now you got the power of the tit. Men get confused when they look at big titties. It's a scientific fact that it scrambles their brain. I read it somewhere. You could get a man to agree to almost anything if you show him big titties."

I looked at Connie and grimaced, and Connie shrugged.

"I've said it before, and I'll say it again. You can't dispute science," Lula said.

I shrugged into my hoodie, leaving it unzipped, and settled my messenger bag on my shoulder. "I'm on my way."

"You taking the dog with you?" Lula asked.

"Yes."

"I'm not holding the dog."

"Then you can drive, and I'll hold the dog."

We got into Lula's Firebird, and Big started howling when the sound system ramped up.

"What the heck is wrong with the dog?" Lula asked.

"I think it's your sound system," I said.

"What?" she yelled at me.

"Sound system," I yelled back. "Shut it off."

Lula shut the sound off and Big stopped howling.

"Dogs have sensitive ears," I said.

"I can't drive without my tunes. I won't be able to concentrate."

"Maybe you could play your tunes not so loud," I said.

"What's the point to that?" Lula asked.

"Then maybe you could drive faster."

## CHAPTER TWENTY

Moachie's Grille was in the middle of the block on Kepler Street. Lula parked across from the Grille and I got out with Big and walked him up and down the street, looking in the Grille's window. There was a bar with red leather stools on one side of the room, tables with white tablecloths and red napkins in the middle of the room, and four booths across the back wall. None of the booths were occupied. It was early for lunch. I went back to the car, and Big and I sat and waited for Harry to arrive.

"How are you going to know it's Harry?" Lula asked.

"I've seen pictures, and I saw him at Vinnie's wedding. He's around five foot ten, overweight but not obese, brown hair that's thinning. He looks like a banker. Respectable."

The Grille started to fill up a little before noon. Harry showed up at 12:10. He fit my memory, but with less hair. He was wearing a tan suit. White shirt with the neck unbuttoned. No tie. Not smiling. Walked with purpose. Probably he was hungry. I gave him some time to get settled and order.

"Do you want me to go in with you?" Lula asked.

"No. Wait here. I'm going in with Mr. Big."

"Oh boy. Are you going to tell him to k-i-l-l?"

"No. That's not part of the game plan."

I had Big on a leash, but I picked him up and tucked him under my arm when I got to the Grille's door. I walked in and took a moment to look around. Half of the tables were in use. Harry was in a booth at the back. None of the other booths were occupied. I nodded to the bartender and took a couple steps.

"Excuse me," the bartender said. "You can't bring the dog in here."

"He's a very small dog," I said. "No one will notice."

"It's rules," the bartender said.

"I'm going back to see Harry. Pretend you don't see me."

"What the hell," he said. "Go on back. We've got rats in the kitchen that are bigger than that dog."

I walked past the tables to Harry's booth, making sure my bulging boobs weren't being hidden by my sweatshirt. I stopped when I got to the booth and smiled at Harry. Big looked at him and gave a low growl.

"Hi," I said. "Remember me?"

"No," Harry said, "but I won't forget you a second time."

I slid onto the bench seat across from him and kept a tight grip on Big. "Stephanie Plum," I said. "I work for you."

"Bail bond enforcer," he said. "Vincent Plum Bail Bonds."

"We met at Vinnie's wedding."

His eyes were laser focused on my breasts. "Nice dog you've got there."

"He belongs to Bruno Jug."

That got his attention off my chest. "What are you doing with Jug's dog?"

"I'm stuck with him. Jug was FTA and when I brought him in this morning it turned out that no one would write a bond for him. So, Jug is in jail, and I've got the dog."

"That's a lucky dog. Is he going to get to sleep with you tonight?" This was said with a smile. Friendly banter from the middle-aged almost bald guy to the chick with big bulging boobs.

"I don't want the dog. I want Jug out of jail, so he can reclaim his dog and I can get on with my life."

The waiter brought Harry a dirty martini, three olives.

Harry extracted the toothpick with the olives from the martini and offered me an olive. I declined, so he ate one and put the rest back in his martini.

"Do you want something?" he asked me. "A drink? Lunch?"

"I want you to let Vinnie write a bail bond for Jug."

"Not gonna happen. Jug should rot in jail."

"I heard this vendetta started over the dog."

"He brings the dog everywhere with him. The dog goes into the crapper with him. The dog goes to meetings. One day I had enough of the dog. The nasty little bugger pissed on my pants leg. So, I told Jug what he could do with his dog and that ended a business relationship that was never good from the start."

"He chewed a piece off my jeans and ran into his house with it. Then Jug's wife came out and shot a hole in the back window of my SUV."

Harry looked like he loved this news. Eyebrows went up in elated surprise.

"The new wife? The bimbo?"

"Yes. She packed up and left over the hooker mess. That's why I have the dog."

Harry sipped his martini and went back to staring at my breasts. "Are you sure you don't want an olive?"

"Let's look at this from a different point of view," I said to Harry. "Jug is sitting in jail because no one will bail him out. So, you come along, and he's such a pathetic loser that you throw him some crumbs. And forever and ever Jug knows that he had to beg you to get him out of jail."

"Jug is begging me?"

"In a manner of speaking. I'm begging you for Jug."

"So, it's like a pity fuck," Harry said.

"Exactly!"

"I like it. I'll do it if I can touch your boob."

"No."

"One finger. One touch."

"No!"

I was regretting the toilet paper. I debated pulling it out and handing it over to Harry. He could touch it all he wanted.

"This conversation would be considered sexual harassment," I told him.

He took another hit of his martini. "Yeah," he said. "I'm good at it. I practice every chance I get."

"Does it ever get you anywhere?"

"Sometimes." He gave a bark of laughter. "Almost never, but I do it anyway. I have to keep up my reputation."

"About Jug. It would be great if you could call Vinny and tell him he can write that bail bond."

"Sure. Will do."

"Now."

"Like, right this instant?"

"You're a busy man. You could forget."

"I think you don't trust me."

"Not even a little."

"Okay," Harry said, "but I want Jug to write a thank-you note to me."

"It's a deal. And I'll get him to send you a fruit basket."

"I don't want the one with the pears."

"I'll make a note."

Harry drained his martini, ate the last two olives, and called Vinny. He hung up with Vinny and the bartender brought him a second martini with three more olives.

"Do you just eat olives for lunch?" I asked him.

"Funny," Harry said. "I got a piece of fish coming. It takes two martinis for me to be able to gag it down. I'm supposed to eat healthy. I'm on Lipitor."

I slid out of the booth and Big followed me. "It's been a pleasure," I said to Harry.

"It could have been better," he said.

We exchanged smiles and I left. He wasn't such a bad guy. For someone named Harry the Hammer, he was kind of a softy.

---

"Congrats," Lula said when Big and I got into the Firebird. "Connie just called. She's on her way downtown to bond out Jug. She said we should meet her there with the dog."

I called Lou and gave him the good news. He said he'd meet us in the parking lot.

"You're on a roll," Lula said. "Everything's working out for you. Lou doesn't want to kill you anymore and you haven't seen the vampire since last night."

Lula's idea of good news tied my intestines in a knot. I could have used a break from thinking about Zoran.

"I don't know who I am in this T-shirt," Lula said. "It's a

pretty T-shirt as far as T-shirts go, but I feel all cramped in it. And there's no sparkle. A day without sparkle is like a day without a doughnut, if you see what I'm sayin'."

"We can switch back when we get to the office. Did Connie have anything else to say?"

"She said to remind you that Eugene has to appear in court on Friday and you promised to take him."

Unh! Mental head slap. I'd forgotten about Eugene. I was supposed to put some thought into flushing out the real Robin Hoodie.

I called Morelli. "I'm on my way to the municipal building to help bond out Jug. Do you have time to talk to me?"

"Is this good talk or scary talk?"

"It's talk about Robin Hoodie."

"That's crazy talk. I was just leaving my desk. I thought I'd take Bob for a walk on my lunch break. You can ride along, if you want."

"Does that include lunch?"

"If you don't mind leftovers."

"I love leftovers. I'll meet you in the lobby area by the front door on the court side."

"They won't let you in the building if you're carrying," Morelli said.

"I'll meet you outside by the municipal lot."

"I can't decide if I'm relieved that you're finally carrying or if it scares the hell out of me."

I hung up and admitted to myself that I had the same mix of emotions as Morelli.

"It'd be a shame for Eugene to have to go to jail if he isn't Robin Hoodie," Lula said. "And his mama would be real upset."

She looked over at Mr. Big, curled up in my lap. "Mr. Big likes you. You're like the dog whisperer."

No doubt the doughnut and all the dog biscuits helped the relationship.

Lula drove past the courthouse entrance and parked in the municipal lot. I called Connie and told her we were outside.

"I'm finishing up," Connie said. "They have to return Jug's personal items and then we can leave. We'll be out in five or ten minutes."

A black Audi drove into the lot and parked next to us. Lou was behind the wheel. I got out and handed Mr. Big over to him.

"Connie should be bringing Jug out soon," I said to Lou. "I talked to Harry and it went okay, but I'm going to be needing a fruit basket."

"You want the one with the pears?"

"Yes," I said. "Definitely."

"If you stop by the warehouse, I'll have it at the front desk," Lou said.

"Thanks. I'll pick it up tomorrow morning."

"How did you manage to do this?" Lou asked. "There's been real bad blood between Bruno and Harry." His eyes went to my bulging breasts. "Never mind, I got it figured out. That's a nice sparkly shirt you've got on."

I pulled the toilet paper out of my bra and handed it to Lou. "You might need this in case Mr. Big has an accident."

"Ha!" Lou said. "Ha ha! You're okay."

Connie and Jug walked out of the building and crossed the street to the lot.

"I don't have to plan on taking an ocean voyage now, right?" I said to Lou.

"Right," Lou said. "Unless you want to take the bimbo's place. I'm going to need to find a new companion for Bruno. The deal could include a first-class cruise on Carnival."

"I'll pass on that."

"Smart," Lou said.

"Thanks for taking care of Mr. Big," Jug said to me. "I owe you." He turned to Lou. "I had a Big Mac for lunch when I was in jail. We should stop on the way home and get one for Mr. Big."

"All's well that ends well," Connie said. "I'm going back to the office."

"I'm having lunch with Morelli," I told Lula. "I need to talk to him about Robin Hoodie. I'll meet you at the office after lunch."

I walked out of the municipal lot just as Morelli was leaving the gated cop lot.

"This was good timing," Morelli said. "Bob will be happy to see you. I'm happy to see you too. Especially in that top."

"It's new. Do you like it?"

"Yeah. I'd spend more time looking at it, but I'm afraid I'd run up on the curb."

Imagine if he'd seen me with the toilet paper.

"Eugene Fleck has a court appearance on Friday. He claims he's not Robin Hoodie, and I believe him. Mostly."

"Only mostly?"

"Almost completely. Are there any other persons of interest?"

"There were the usual suspects in the beginning. There are a bunch of porch pirates operating in Trenton. We run them down when we have time. Sometimes we recognize a repeat offender from a Ring camera. We didn't pick up Eugene on any of the Rings. When he hijacked the UPS truck it took it to another level, and we found his fingerprints on the steering wheel, gearshift, door handle.

The only other prints belonged to the UPS driver, and there were some on the inside of the back door from UPS loaders."

"What about all the other Hoodie events?"

"Lots of prints. None belonging to Eugene and the others were meaningless. Stores and food trucks have lots of random prints. We've looked at hours of video and it's inconclusive. Hoodie has the same build and is about the same height as Eugene. He could easily be Eugene."

"I'm surprised that no one in the homeless community has turned him in."

"He wears a mask. He goes in at night when it's dark. He's deep in his hoodie. He wears gloves. And everyone loves him. No one wants him to stop."

"I'm sure the food trucks want him to stop."

"That's the genius of it. They're all begging to be the next hit. You get on the Hoodie blog and you're an instant smash success. People are lined up to buy your hot dogs, tacos, sneakers, Band-Aids. No one will press charges. They write off the initial hit and more than make up for it when the post goes viral."

"Wow."

"Yeah. 'Wow' about sums it up. So far, we have one case against Eugene: the UPS truck. Even if he confessed to being Robin Hoodie, we wouldn't have any more. We'd have to talk one of his victims into charging him, and they aren't going to do it because it would ruin their business."

"Suppose you set a trap. Get your own food truck and beg Hoodie to hijack it. Put a GPS tracker on it."

"We haven't got a budget for that kind of sting operation. It's not like Hoodie is selling drugs."

"Isn't it an embarrassment to Trenton PD that Hoodie keeps operating?"

"Most of the guys are enjoying it. And if you're a cop with a wife or a girlfriend, you better not touch Hoodie or there'll be hell to pay at home. Women love this guy. He's a hero."

"He isn't a hero," I said. "He's letting an innocent man get sent to jail. That's horrible."

"You're assuming that Eugene isn't Hoodie. How do you explain the fingerprints?"

"I can't," I said.

# CHAPTER TWENTY-ONE

Bob did his usual happy dance when he saw us. He got some hugs and a bunch of *good boy*s, and Morelli hooked him up to a leash. Sometimes Morelli takes Bob to the park to run, but mostly Bob gets walked around a couple blocks. Today was a "couple blocks" day.

"Are there any new developments on Zoran?" I asked Morelli.

"Toxicology came back from the woman in the laundromat. She had GHB in her system. And Ecstasy. She was probably drugged before being attacked. And the big thing is that we might have DNA from last night. The victim had a couple strands of hair and some skin cells under her nails. The blow to her head didn't kill her. At some point, she must have put up a fight."

"Did you find a match?"

"Not yet."

"Are you going into Zoran's house?"

"Jimmy's working on it. We have your statement putting

Zoran at the crime, so the search warrant should go through. Right now it's sitting on a desk, waiting its turn."

"It would be easier and faster if someone prowled through his garbage *outside* the house and found his hairbrush or whatever," I said.

"There was no garbage outside his house," Morelli said. "We looked."

"Yes, but there might be later today."

"I didn't hear you say that."

Bob did everything he had to do, and we returned to Morelli's house. We went into the kitchen and stared into his refrigerator.

"Omigod," I said. "Is that your mom's lasagna?"

"Yeah, looks like it. She comes over and leaves stuff when I'm at work."

Morelli had his mom, and I had Herbert.

"Your mom makes the world's best lasagna," I said. "I'm voting on lasagna for lunch."

We pulled the lasagna out along with extra red sauce and grated cheese. We plated it, nuked it, and took it to Morelli's kitchen table. His mom had also brought salad greens, but we left them for another day.

"How's it going with the sorting your life out?" Morelli asked me.

I forked in some lasagna. "Honestly, I haven't had time to think about it. It would help if you guys could get Zoran off the street."

"We're working on it."

A half hour later I was back at the office. I was still in the sparkly tank top, but Lula had stopped off at her apartment and exchanged my T-shirt for a silky poison-green shirt with a low V-neck.

"You can keep the tank top," Lula said, handing me my T-shirt.

"You finally got a gun with bullets in it, now you need to get some glam in your wardrobe."

"Thanks. This will be my first step toward more glam."

"We were watching the new Hoodie video when you walked in," Lula said. "It's a good one. Hoodie hijacked a soft-serve truck. Ice cream sundaes for everyone. And then there was a short video of him breakdancing. It wasn't terrible but it wasn't good, either. And it had to be hard on account of he had one of those whole-head rubber masks on."

I moved behind Connie, and she ran the videos for me. The ice cream truck was wild. Everyone was laughing and eating ridiculous amounts of ice cream. It was easy to see why people liked Hoodie. He made happiness. The breakdancing came next.

"Whoa," I said. "This is awful! This is the equivalent of Herbert playing the clarinet."

"He's got a good move coming up," Lula said. "He sticks a Michael Jackson thing in here."

"Why would he do this?" I asked.

"He's entertaining," Lula said. "He does these odd bits every now and then. Breaks up the monotony of watching homeless folks."

"And he keeps his income stream up," Connie said. "People keep tuning in, so he keeps getting paid. I heard he uses the money to compensate people for their losses. Like when all those UPS packages didn't get delivered."

"That's a lot of money," I said. "I saw the video. There were a lot of packages."

"It's rumored that he's made over a million dollars from his YouTube channel," Connie said.

"So what's up for the rest of the day?" Lula asked. "Now what?"

"I want to go back to Zoran's house."

"Boy," Lula said. "You know how to ruin a perfectly good day."

"I'm on a mission."

"Does this mission have a name?" Lula asked.

"Take Down Zoran."

"This mission might be above your pay grade," Lula said. "It's not like you're Buffy."

I hiked my messenger bag higher on my shoulder. "Are you coming with me or what?"

"Let's do it," Lula said.

---

We bypassed the front door to Zoran's house and went straight to the back door. Lula had already broken the lock the last time we were here, so it was easy entry. I walked in and yelled, "Bond enforcement."

I opened a couple kitchen drawers, found a garbage bag, pulled on some disposable gloves, and started collecting garbage. I cleaned out the fridge and emptied trash. I went to the bedroom and added a sock that was on the floor. I went to the bathroom and added the toothbrush, a comb, his razor, and the roach just for fun.

I did a walk-through to see if there was something I missed the first time around.

"There's nothing to see here," Lula said. "There's no grocery notes or laptops. There's hardly any junk in his junk drawer. And the only thing in his freezer are some breakfast sausages in a baggie."

I hadn't checked the freezer. I went to the kitchen and looked in the freezer.

"These aren't sausages," I said to Lula. "They're fingers with freezer frost. I must have missed it last time I was here."

"No way!"

I added the baggie with the fingers to the big garbage bag.

"Our work is done here," I said to Lula.

I left the garbage bag in the trash can behind the house, pulled my gloves off, stuffed them into my messenger bag, and called Morelli.

"Come and get it," I said. "I cleaned out the freezer, so you don't want to wait too long to pick up the trash."

There was a moment of silence on the other end of the phone where I assumed he was trying to get a grip. "It isn't a head, is it?" he finally said. "I hate when it's a head."

"It's not a head."

Lula and I went back to my SUV and buckled in.

"Are we going shopping now?" Lula asked.

"No," I said, "I'm going to drop you off at the office, and then I'm going to my parents' house. I feel like I need a dose of normal."

"Normal is relative," Lula said. "Seems like these days finding fingers in the freezer is our new normal."

That was the gruesome truth.

I left Lula at the office and drove the short distance to my parents' house. I turned onto Green Street and felt a sense of calm settle in. My family was a little dysfunctional, but at least they didn't have fangs, and the only body parts in their freezer belonged to cows and chickens. The calm disappeared when I saw that a Prius was parked in my spot at the curb. I parked behind the Prius and debated going in. I told myself that Herbert wasn't the only one who owned a Prius. The car could belong to one of Grandma's lady friends. With that in mind I trudged to the front door and let myself in.

My father was asleep in his chair in front of the TV. I could hear clanking sounds coming from the kitchen and the house smelled like cookies. Grandma was at the dining room table with Herbert.

"What's going on?" I asked Grandma.

"I ran into Herbert at Giovichinni's, and he gave me a ride home," Grandma said. "He has a Prius."

"I like to be on the cutting edge with my purchases," Herbert said. "Hybrid is the way to go, and the new Prius has improved acceleration and improved interior design features."

"He's a clever one," Grandma said. "And he knows all about computers. He's coaching me on improving my blog and videos."

"You make videos?" I asked Grandma.

"I just started. I got the idea from Robin Hoodie. Everybody's doing it."

"What kind of videos are you making?" I asked Grandma.

"Originally, I was thinking of breakdancing like Robin Hoodie, but once I got down on the floor, I had a hard time getting back up. Then Herbert and I got this idea to do a blog on funeral parlor viewings."

"Omigod."

"Yeah, that's what I said too," Grandma said. "It's a winner idea. If it takes off, I could make a million dollars. Herbert and I would do it together. And it would all be shot on-site so we wouldn't need a studio setup."

"It's a good idea because we both have extensive knowledge of funeral operations," Herbert said. "There's almost nothing we don't know about viewing dead people. I even went down to the embalming room once. I was looking for the men's room and I ended up in the embalming room. There was a fat man on the table and stuff was draining out of him. I guess we aren't supposed to say *fat* anymore. Some people find it offensive. I personally think it's okay. I mean, it's a description, right? Saying someone is big is different from saying someone is fat. How are you supposed to describe someone fat if you can't say *fat*?"

"It could be someone with extra stuff under their flesh," Grandma said, "but that's a lot of words. I've been down to the embalming room, but I never saw anyone on the table. That must have been something."

"He was undressed," Herbert said. "If I was an undertaker, I would embalm people with their clothes on."

"See, now, that's something people would want to know," Grandma said.

My mother stepped out of the kitchen. "We're having pot roast and there's homemade cookies for dessert. Who's staying for dinner?"

"I am," I said.

"Am I invited?" Herbert asked. "I love pot roast. My mom never makes it because my dad had polyps on his last colonoscopy, and they told him to lay off the beef. They cut all the polyps off and my dad is fine, so I don't know what the deal is with the beef. You eat beef, and you grow new polyps, and they cut them off."

"It's the green vegan people who start bad beef rumors like that," Grandma said. "If it was up to them, there'd be no more cows."

"I like cows," Herbert said. "I like the light brown ones the best. They have pretty faces. I wouldn't get too close to one though. I got close to a cow once at a petting zoo and it stepped on my foot."

"Of course you can stay for dinner," my mom said. "There's always extra helpings with a pot roast."

Oh boy. Herbert, Grandma, and my dad together at the dinner table. If it wasn't for a possible pregnancy I'd start drinking now.

Grandma and Herbert went back to making plans for their viewing project and I went into the kitchen to help my mom.

"There's something wrong with this Herbert person," my mom whispered to me. "I can't put my finger on it. He's nice enough, but odd."

"I agree," I said, "but people say that about Grandma too."

"Not the same," my mom said. "Not everyone thinks she's nice."

I peeled potatoes and set the table, pushing Grandma and Herbert down to one end. My mom was in her groove in the kitchen and I was in the way, so I went into the living room to watch TV with my dad.

"What's going on in the dining room?" he asked. "I hear people mumbling."

"It's Grandma and Herbert."

"Who's Herbert?"

"That's a good question," I said. "I went to school with him, and Grandma knows him from the funeral home. She ran into him at Giovichinni's today, and he gave her a ride home, and here he is. Mom invited him to stay for dinner."

"Oh jeez."

"What are you watching?"

"I don't know. I just woke up. It looks like news."

At six o'clock we were all at the table, and Morelli walked in.

"I don't want to disturb anything," he said. "I saw Stephanie's car parked here, and I need to talk to her."

"We sat down just this second," Grandma said. "We got pot roast and mashed potatoes. I'll get a place setting for you."

"Thanks, but I need to get home to Bob," Morelli said.

Grandma was already on her feet. "You can eat and run, and you can take some pot roast for Bob."

"Who's Bob?" Herbert asked.

"Morelli's dog," I said.

"I don't have a dog," Herbert said. "I have a cat. Her name is Miss Fluff. She's very fluffy. She sleeps with me. Not in a strange way. Like a cat. She could be a show cat but her one eye looks off to the side and she has an overbite. They're picky about things like that at cat shows."

Grandma put a plate and some silverware next to me, and Morelli sat down. "Really?" he said to me.

Food was getting passed around. Grandma offered Herbert a glass of red wine and I suggested that might not be a good idea.

"Herbert gave Grandma a ride home from Giovichinni's," I said to Morelli. "Grandma is a big fan of the Robin Hoodie videos and she decided to make some videos like Robin Hoodie."

Morelli cut his eyes to Grandma. "You're going to steal packages off porches?"

"No. That's old news," Grandma said. "Herbert and I are going to make videos about viewings."

Morelli looked confused.

"Funeral home viewings," I said to Morelli. "Like at Stiva's."

"We could show what dead people look like before and after makeup," Grandma said. "And we could interview the grieving mourners, but we'd do it in a way that would be fun."

My father froze with his fork raised, and a piece of pot roast fell out of his mouth.

My mom raised her Big Gulp glass of whiskey. "Dilly dilly."

Morelli was working hard not to laugh out loud.

"You're going to get a hernia if you keep holding it in like that," I told him.

"This is excellent pot roast," Herbert said. "You must use a good cut of beef to get this flavor."

"Rump roast," Grandma said. "We always use rump roast."

"Gravy," my father said. "I need more gravy. Who's holding up the gravy?"

By the time we got to the cookies, Grandma and Herbert had moved on to alien encounters and Grandma's theory that Zoran wasn't a vampire but could possibly be an alien.

Morelli looked at his watch at that point and said he needed to check in with his partner and feed Bob dinner. My mom gave Morelli some cookies and a nice portion of pot roast for Bob, and I walked Morelli out to his car.

"You wanted to talk to me," I said.

"That was quite the bag of goodies you left for me. I especially liked the fingers."

"They almost got passed up. Lula thought they were sausages."

"I imagine they're trophies," Morelli said. "Three of them. All from different women."

"I identified four potential victims that were before the laundromat killing. Zoran's wife. They only recovered part of her. Two hookers that disappeared and were never found. And Julie Werly. If he got a finger from the laundromat and the jogger, he wouldn't have been able to put it in his freezer without you picking him up on video."

"The jogger was missing a finger," Morelli said. "It looks like he didn't have time to get one from the laundromat victim."

"Ugh."

"Yeah. This guy is a real psycho."

"Were you able to identify victims from the three fingers?"

"Not yet. We have to wait for DNA results. We have the state police and the FBI involved and they're rushing the testing and tracing."

"I'm hoping the missing finger belongs to Werly. It might mean that she's still alive."

"I haven't been to church in a while, but I'd be willing to drop in and say a prayer for that one," Morelli said. He leaned in and kissed me. "Would you like to take Bob for another walk? Maybe stay and watch a movie?"

"I don't know about the movie but walking Bob would be nice."

Morelli's phone buzzed, and he stared down at the ground.

"Are you going to answer it?" I asked him.

"I'm deciding," he said. "I'm still on call. Two guys are out with the flu, and Riley is out with a gunshot wound."

"Who shot Riley?"

"He shot himself. He was playing quick draw and shot himself in the leg." He put the phone to his ear. "Yeah." He listened for a couple minutes and disconnected. "I have to go. Can you feed Bob for me? I don't know what time I'll be home."

"Sure."

I went back into the house, told everyone I was Bob-sitting, and drove to Morelli's. I fed Bob some pot roast and some of his Bob food. I hooked him up to the leash, took him to the front door, and hesitated. It was dark outside. I experienced a small ripple of fear in the pit of my stomach, and I tamped it down. Just be alert, I told myself. Be careful. I closed the door, got my gun from my messenger bag, hooked the holster onto the waist of my jeans, and holstered the gun. The gun felt uncomfortable at my waist, and my biggest fear was that I'd do a Riley and shoot myself in the leg.

"Okay," I said to Bob. "Now we're ready to walk. I'm sure you're more used to the gun than I am. Morelli wears one all the time."

Lights were on in all the houses. Dinner was done and kids were doing homework and watching television. The air was crisp with a hint of autumn. I was glad I was wearing my sweatshirt. Bob was prancing along, enjoying himself. I got to the end of the block and was about to cross the street when Bob stopped and stood stiff-legged, nose up. He growled low in his throat, and a chill ripped through me. I pushed my sweatshirt to one side, exposing the gun. I did a quick look around. I didn't see anything unusual. Bob turned, and I turned with him. I had a tight grip on his leash with one hand and the other hand was on the SIG Sauer. Bob gave a loud bark and lunged on his leash, and I saw Zoran standing in the sidewalk about twenty feet away. He had the knife in his hand, and he was staring at me, mouth open, showing his fangs. It was the first time I'd actually seen the knife. It looked like something Rambo would use. Large and deadly with a hefty handle. I snatched the SIG out of the holster and aimed, and Zoran disappeared behind a parked car. I heard footfalls running down the street and then there was quiet again.

I looked down at Bob. My hero. He was breathing heavily, and I was in the same state, sucking in air. It took a couple beats for the rush of adrenaline to settle and my brain to go from fight-or-flight to *what the heck just happened!* It felt like a nightmare. Imagined. Too horrible and bizarre to be real.

"Good boy," I said to Bob. "I didn't hear him coming up behind me."

We walked back to Morelli's house, both of us on high alert. I had the gun in my hand and didn't holster it until I was at Morelli's door and had to open the door with a key. I left Bob on his leash and went to the kitchen. I wrote a note to Morelli telling him Bob was spending the night with me. I grabbed my messenger bag, and Bob and I went back to my apartment. I felt safer in my own space. Morelli had too many windows and doors. I had one door, and once I locked everything from the inside the only one who could get in was Ranger. I had no idea how he managed it. When I asked him, he said it was magic. I was inclined to believe him.

My apartment is on the back side of the building. My living room windows look out at the parking lot. Not especially scenic but it's quieter than the street side. It's an older building with exterior fire escapes that are now used as little balconies holding potted plants and small grills. My fire escape balcony holds nothing. I always mean to buy plants but never get around to it. At Christmas I string colored lights on the railing, but that's as far as my decorating goes.

I looked out my living room window and scanned the parking lot. It felt benign. Bob had immediately found his place on my couch and looked comfy. I thought that was a good sign. As long as Bob was comfy and not growling, I could relax a little. I put a bowl of water on the floor in the kitchen for Bob, and I gave Rex a slice of apple and a peanut.

I brought my laptop to the couch, put my gun on the little table next to the couch, and sat alongside Bob while I checked my email. I closed the laptop and thought about Zoran. How long had he been following me? I thought he must have picked me up at the office and followed me to my parents' and then to Morelli's house. If Morelli hadn't been called in to work, I would have gone for a walk with him and Bob and then gone home. I would have been alone getting out of my car and walking into my building, and things might have taken an ugly turn. My gun would have been in my messenger bag. I might not have heard Zoran come up behind me. And I might have ended up being another woman who was missing a finger.

Ranger called. "Just checking in, babe. I heard you brought Bruno Jug in."

"It was a little complicated, but everything worked out."

"And I heard there was another Zoran victim."

"Morelli and I were at the birthday party and Jimmy called. I got to tag along to the crime scene. I couldn't bring myself to look at the body, but I got all the details from Morelli. She was a jogger. Hit from behind and dragged into a wooded area. Bite marks on her neck and her throat slashed. And her finger cut off. Zoran keeps trophies. I went through his house again and found three fingers in his freezer. All from different women. I gave them to Morelli to get tested. Also, toxicology came back on the laundromat lady. She had a multi-drug cocktail in her system."

"He drugged his victim and that made the kill easier," Ranger said. "My control room tells me you have an overnight guest."

"Morelli got called in to work, and I said I would babysit Bob."

I wanted to tell Ranger about Zoran stalking me and confronting me when I was walking Bob, but it would set off a chain of events that I preferred not to have happen. He would want me to move back to Rangeman. And there was a part of me that would love to move back. It was by far the safest place for me to stay. Rangeman was impenetrable. Problem is, it would be difficult to explain this move to Morelli.

"What are your plans for tomorrow?" Ranger asked.

"I'm taking a fruit basket to Harry the Hammer."

"Babe," Ranger said. And he hung up.

I remoted the television on and scanned Prime. I settled on a documentary about Antarctica. That was followed by a documentary about Argentina.

I fell asleep halfway through Argentina, and I woke up to Bob growling. Crap! Now what! I shut the television off, grabbed my gun, and sat very still, listening. Truth is, it would have been hard to hear anything over the pounding of my heart. I could have had

# CHAPTER TWENTY-TWO

Bob woke me up at seven o'clock. The sun was shining. It was a glorious day, and Bob had to tinkle. I got dressed, strapped my gun on, shrugged into my sweatshirt, and laced up my sneakers. I stepped out the back door to my building and spotted a Rangeman SUV parked next to my car. This wasn't a big surprise. It was Ranger in protective mode. Bob and I went over to say hello.

Hal was behind the wheel and Ramon was riding shotgun. Hal reached out the window to scratch Bob's head and hand me an AirTag.

"Ranger wants you to wear this," Hal said.

I dropped the AirTag into my sweatshirt pocket. "Have you been here all night?"

"No. We came on duty at six o'clock. Junior and Shank were here last night."

"There's a Rangeman named Shank?"

"Don't ask," Hal said.

"Tell Ranger it's all good here. I'm going to walk Bob and then run a few errands. A security escort isn't necessary."

"I'll pass it on," Hal said.

Bob and I did two blocks and when we got back to my apartment building the Rangeman car was gone. I didn't have any dog food, so I made scrambled eggs and toast for Bob and me. Bob is lactose intolerant so there was no butter on his toast. We had just finished eating when Morelli showed up.

"You're usually at work by now," I said.

"I just got off work," Morelli said. "I'm on my way home. I thought I'd stop in and get Bob."

"How did you know Bob was here?"

"My doorbell cam. I saw you and Bob leave my house and not return."

"Of course."

Morelli looked at the empty bowl on the floor next to Bob's water bowl. "Bob ate breakfast?"

"Scrambled eggs and dry toast."

Morelli grabbed me and kissed me. "Thanks for taking care of Bob."

"Is that why you kissed me?"

"No. I kissed you because it's my second-favorite thing to do."

"And your first favorite?"

"Watching the Giants."

I punched him in the shoulder, and he hugged me closer and kissed me again. His beard was way past five o'clock shadow and looked very sexy. If this kept up, I was going to have beard rash, and it would be totally worth it.

"Before I forget," Morelli said. "We got lucky with the fingers. Three hits. Elena Stockard Djordjevic, Rosa Sanchez, Marianne Markoni. No Julie Werly."

"So, she might be alive."

"We have nothing to prove that she's dead."

Bob was pushing against Morelli trying to get his attention. Morelli bent down and hugged Bob and scratched his ear. He straightened and looked into my living room.

"You have furniture and carpet, and it looks like fresh paint. When did all this happen?"

"Herbert."

"You told me about Herbert doing nice things, but I didn't get the whole picture."

"The whole picture is hard to explain. Mostly because I can't explain it to myself. It's a little disturbing."

"Whoa," Morelli said, eyeballing my window. He crossed the room and ran his finger along the glass. "There's a story here."

"After I was firebombed three times, Ranger decided to install bulletproof glass."

"And?"

"And Zoran tried to break in last night, and I tried to shoot him, but the bullet got stuck in the glass."

Morelli looked down at the floor. I couldn't tell if he was trying not to laugh or trying not to grind his teeth. He picked his head up and crooked his finger at me in one of those *come here* motions. I walked over and he hung his arm across my shoulders.

"Is it too late to cancel the engagement?" he asked me.

I knew he wasn't serious about canceling the engagement. He was making a statement about my job.

"Maybe," I said.

"Your life is . . ." He shook his head. "I have no words."

"If you had words, would they be good words?"

"They'd be words of desperation. I'm crazy in love with you, and you're a train wreck waiting to happen."

"Remember when we were kids, and we played choo-choo and I was the tunnel, and you were the train?"

"Yeah."

"Well, I always wanted to be the train. I don't think I'm a train wreck waiting to happen. I think I'm finally getting to be the train."

"Cupcake, you're one hell of a train."

"Thanks."

"In all honesty, I'd rather you went back to being the tunnel," Morelli said.

"I'm thinking about it. There were some good parts to being the tunnel."

"And I have some new variations on being the train."

"If I decide to be the train, do you want to cancel the engagement?" I asked him.

"Actually, it was dinner with your family that had me on the fence about the engagement."

I punched him in the arm again.

"And the birthday party was the clincher."

"You got to do your *Saturday Night Fever* thing."

"Yeah, I look hot when I do that. Travolta looks like a pussy compared to me."

"This is true," I said.

Morelli looked back at the bullet in the window. "Are you safe here?"

"Yes. I have seven locks on my door and bulletproof glass on my windows, and Ranger monitors the hall."

"Ranger monitors your hall?"

"You have a Ring doorbell, and I have Ranger."

"Fair enough. I have to go. I need sleep. I'll call you later."

---

By the time I got to the office the healthy breakfast was a distant memory and I needed a doughnut.

"How was your normal night at your parents' house?" Lula asked. "Do you have your sanity put back together?"

I almost burst out laughing. "My normal night with my family was completely normal, and my sanity is in good shape." I took a doughnut from the box on Connie's desk. "What's happening here? Anything new?"

"I think we had a no-show at court yesterday, but it hasn't come through yet," Connie said. "No new videos from Hoodie."

"I have a couple errands to run this morning," I said. "I have to pick up a fruit basket from Jug Produce and deliver it to Harry. I need the address for his office on Beryl Street."

Connie wrote the address on a scrap of paper and handed it to me.

"I need to include a note with the basket," I said. "Do we have any note cards?"

"I have some in the back," Connie said. "There are several different kinds. They should be on the first rack by the coffee machine."

I picked out a couple cards and got coffee. "I'm ready to roll," I said to Lula.

"Me too," Lula said. "I want to see Harry's office. I have to see if it's as good as Jug's." She looked at me and shook her head. "Harry's going to be real disappointed when he sees you in that T-shirt."

Lula was wearing a red spandex dress that barely covered her hooha. The top of the dress had a low V-neck, and her giant nipples were straining against the spandex. I didn't think Harry would notice what I was wearing if I was standing next to Lula. I disappeared when I stood next to Lula.

We went to Jug Produce first. The fruit basket was waiting at the desk as promised, but I needed to get the card written out and signed. The woman at the reception desk made a phone call and told us we could go on up.

Jug was at his desk, and Mr. Big was curled up in a blue velvet dog bed placed on a corner of the desk.

"Boy, this dog has the life," Lula said.

"You bet your sweet aunt Mary," Jug said.

I gave Big some ear scratches and handed Jug a blank card. "I thought it would be nice if you sent a thank-you note to Harry for writing your bail bond."

Jug took the card, wrote his thank-you, and handed the card back to me.

> *Dear Asshole,*
> *Thanks for nothing.*
> *Bruno*

"Short but sweet," I said.

"No point getting too nasty," Jug said. "I try to be classy and show some restraint."

"It looks like you're back at work," Lula said to Jug.

"Yeah, my babysitters let me go out of the house, but I'm stuck here at the office. They don't want me talking to the press. They think I'll say something stupid."

"What do you think?" Lula asked. "Would you say something stupid to the press?"

"Probably," Jug said.

We left Bruno's office, picked up the fruit basket, and went back to my Trailblazer. I took a fresh blank card out of my messenger bag and wrote:

*Dear Harry,*
*Thanks for bailing me out.*
*Bruno*

I tucked the card into the fruit basket and drove to Harry's office on Beryl Street. Lula and I went in with the fruit basket and stopped at the reception desk.

"We're here to give this fruit basket to Harry," I said to the woman behind the desk.

"He's in a meeting," she said, "but I'll be happy to give him the basket when he gets out."

"Are you sure he's in a meeting?" Lula said. "Because I'm pretty sure he wouldn't be happy to have missed me."

The woman looked at Lula. "You could be right. Seventh floor. I'll tell his assistant you're on your way up."

The assistant was waiting for us when we exited the elevator. He looked at Lula and grinned. "You have a fruit basket?"

"Yeah, and it's a big one," Lula said, nodding in my direction.

I had my arms wrapped around the basket, holding it against my chest.

"Harry likes big ones," the assistant said. "Follow me."

We were ushered into Harry's inner sanctum office, and Harry looked up when we entered.

"These ladies have a fruit basket for you," the assistant said.

I went to place the basket on Harry's desk and a pear slipped out from the cellophane wrapping and rolled on the floor. Lula bent to pick it up and gave Harry a full moon with her red thong buried deep inside her vast lunar canyon.

Harry stood at his desk to get a better view.

Lula stood, tugged her skirt down, and handed the pear to Harry. "Looks like you've got a lot of pears in this basket," Lula said.

"Do you want some?" Harry asked.

"No thanks," Lula said. "I don't eat pears."

"We're good now," I said to Harry. "The thank-you note is in the fruit basket."

Harry took the note out and read it. "This doesn't look like Harry's writing."

"He dictated it to me," I said. "And I might have paraphrased. He was very sincere about his message."

"Who's your friend here?"

"I'm Lula," Lula said. "I work for you."

"Lucky me," Harry said. "Can I touch your tit?"

"No, but you could take a look at it if you want," Lula said. "I got prizewinning titties. Everybody says so. And my nipples are world-record nipples."

Lula pulled one of the girls out of the V-neck and Harry almost fell on the floor. His face got red, and he started to sweat.

"Wow," Harry said. "Holy crap. Can I see the other one?"

"No," Lula said, stuffing her boob back into her dress. "You only get to see one. Anyways they're both the same."

"We have to go now," I said. "Things to do. Felons to catch. Sorry about the pears."

"Do you want some?" Harry asked me.

"No!" I said. "But thanks for the offer."

I hurried out of Harry's office and Lula followed.

"That went well," Lula said. "And he has a real nice office. It's not Oval Office caliber, but it's still pretty nice."

We got into my SUV, and I sat there for a moment, thinking about my next move.

"We're missing something with Zoran," I said. "He can find me, but I can't find him."

"That's on account of he already knows where you are. Everybody knows where you are. You're at the office or your apartment or your parents' house. He isn't in any of the places where he should be—like his house, his laundromat, or his parents' house."

"He has transportation. He's out buying drugs. He's stalking me."

"So, it's simple. We know where Zoran's going to be," Lula said. "He's going to be wherever you are."

That was like getting hit by a lightning bolt. I don't have to find Zoran. I can let him come to me. I can set a trap with me as the bait. I just have to make sure he doesn't get too close. He likes to come out at night, so I have today to find a location where he'll be trapped and I'll be protected. I'll do some scouting around and then I'll bring Ranger in. And since I have some time, it wouldn't hurt to enlarge the search area. Ranger and I only searched Stark and Freemont.

"You got that look like something's going on in your head," Lula said.

"I want to take a look at the area between the laundromat and Zoran's house. We've never covered those streets."

"That sounds reasonable," Lula said. "We should be looking for abandoned haunted houses and loose manhole covers. No telling where his hidey-hole is located."

If he had Julie Werly, which was a big *if*, it would have to be someplace quiet. Like a cellar. His house didn't have a cellar. It was built on a slab.

I drove to Exeter Street and slowly cruised around, dividing the neighborhood into four-block grids. I was looking for houses that seemed empty or unkempt and larger houses that might have cellars. I designated two houses that had possibilities. One was directly behind Zoran's house and the other was across the street from the Werly house.

The whole time we were doing this I was checking my rearview mirror to see if I was being followed. Cars would come and go, but I didn't see anything that looked like a tail.

I parked in front of Zoran's house.

"Uh-oh, are we going in here again?" Lula asked. "If we're going in here, I'm not looking in the freezer. I'm not looking nowhere."

"I'm not going in. I want to walk around these two blocks and get a better look at the yards and houses. There are two houses that interest me."

"You're just looking from the outside, right?"

"Right."

We walked the two blocks, and we returned to the car. It was almost noon, with bright sun overhead and a couple puffy clouds in the sky. Not vampire-stalking conditions. I had the AirTag in my pocket and my gun on my hip. I didn't feel at risk, but I wasn't going to push my luck either. I thought the two houses warranted investigation. And I thought it best if someone else did the investigating.

"I'm going to get Morelli to take a look at those two houses," I said to Lula.

I called Morelli and he didn't pick up. Probably sleeping with his ringer turned off. I called Ranger and got the control room. I was told he was on a conference call, and they asked if I needed them to break in. I told them it wasn't an emergency, but I'd like him to call me when he was done.

"I need a soda," Lula said. "And a sandwich. They had good-looking sandwiches at the deli on the corner."

We drove down Freemont, parked on the street, and went into the deli. It was part bakery, part deli, and part grocery, with a fresh-fruit section advertising Jug Produce.

"Bruno is everywhere," Lula said. "He's franchising fruit and next he'll have his ice cream all over the place. That's the way it is when you're a tycoon."

We walked past the fruit to the deli counter. We grabbed a couple premade sandwiches, got a couple bags of chips and a couple sodas. Lula went to the ladies' room, and I took our food outside to eat. It was a beautiful day with a cloudless blue sky and a little chill in the air. I sat on the wooden bench that had been placed in front of the deli and set the bag of food and the sodas next to me. I tried calling Morelli again. Still no answer. I put my phone down and unwrapped a sandwich, and a tan van drove by and continued down the street. It was an old panel van with a large dent over the left rear wheel. Sometimes it's better to be lucky than to be good. The van met Mrs. Werly's description. Old tan van with a dent in the back. I grabbed my messenger bag and followed the van. It cruised down the second block of Freemont and crossed the road, and I lost it. There'd been traffic on the cross street and when the street cleared, there was no van.

Halfway down the third block of Freemont, I spotted the rear end of the van. It was parked behind a three-story tenement-type apartment building. Only the back bumper was visible.

I went to my jeans pocket to get my phone and there was no phone. Mental head slap. I'd been so fixated on following the van that I'd left my phone on the bench. Not a problem. I was wearing my smartwatch, I had Ranger's AirTag in my sweatshirt pocket, and my gun was on my hip.

I stood there for a couple minutes listening, looking for activity. I didn't pick up anything coming from the back of the tenement, so I crept down the driveway. It was the same van that I saw drive by the deli. Tan. Dented. No windows in the back doors or on the sides of the van. I moved up to the driver's-side door and looked in the window. There was a brown paper grocery bag, a grungy sweatshirt, and a ball cap on the passenger seat.

The back door to the building was cracked open. It was just steps away from the van. I went to the door and looked in. Small entrance hallway with stairs leading up to a landing and more stairs, and stairs leading down to a short hall with two doors. I'd seen enough. I needed to get help. I took a step back to leave, a basement door opened, and Zoran walked out into the hall. We locked eyes for a beat, and he charged up the stairs at me. I had a gun, but my first instinct wasn't to use it. My instinct was to run. I stumbled going over the threshold, and he caught me at the van.

He grabbed the back of my sweatshirt and yanked me off my feet. I screamed for help and tried to kick him. We rolled around on the ground with me scratching and clawing at him. He managed to get me facedown with his knee on my back and *zzzzt*. Everything went black.

---

A split second before I went scramble brain, I'd seen the stun gun in Zoran's hand. I'd been stun gunned before, so I knew the drill. You come back slowly. Muscle contractions stop. Eyes open. Blurry. Tingling in fingers. Arms wake up. This time it was different. I'd been out for a while. I was foggy. Not tingly. Fingers and toes were working. I was on my back. Popcorn ceiling. Who has a popcorn ceiling? Popcorn ceilings went out thirty years ago. Popcorn ceilings dampened sound, but they contained asbestos. My building had popcorn ceilings in the basement laundry room. Probably illegal.

The fog was starting to lift. My eyes were focusing better. I tried to sit up and got slightly nauseated. I stayed down for a couple minutes, waiting for the nausea to pass. I tried sitting up again. No nausea. I looked around the room. The size of a small bedroom. Dimly lit by an overhead bulb. No windows. Two doors. A cot against a wall. A small table and a metal folding chair. A trash can. A large screw eye embedded in a concrete floor. Chain attached. The other end of the chain was attached to a thick metal bracelet that was latched onto my ankle. More nausea. This time the nausea wasn't drug induced. This time the origin of the nausea was raw, cold terror.

I no longer had my gun. I felt for the AirTag. Gone. I got onto all fours and then onto my feet. I took a moment to steady myself. I heard something whimper, and my heart skipped several beats. Something was huddled in a dark corner next to what looked like an under-the-counter refrigerator. There was movement. It was a woman. She was crouched in the corner, but I could see that she was very thin. Large, frightened eyes.

"Julie Werly?" I asked.

"Yes!"

"I came to rescue you."

The instant I said it, I realized how ridiculous it sounded. I'd totally messed up. I'd allowed myself to get kidnapped, and now I was chained to the floor in some dungeon with a popcorn ceiling. I made a sound that was halfway between a bark of laughter and a sob, and tears were collecting behind my eyes. I'd found Julie Werly, and she was alive. I was happy and scared and pissed off that I hadn't been able to come in like Batgirl and rescue her. Get it together, I told myself. This isn't the time to fall apart.

I looked down and realized a second chain was attached to the screw eye, and the chain went to Julie Werly. The chains were long. Long enough to reach one of the doors, which I assumed was a bathroom. I tugged on the chain. It was too strong to break. Solidly cemented into the floor.

"Are you okay?" I asked Julie. I could see that she was alive. I could also see that she wasn't okay.

She made soft whimpering sounds and I realized she was crying, trying not to make a lot of noise, trying to choke back the sobs.

"I'm sorry," she said, wiping tears away. "He gets angry if he hears me crying, so I try not to cry, but I'm getting worn down. I miss my mom and my dad and my students. I'm afraid I'll never see them again." She sucked in another sob and bit into her lower lip.

"It's going to be okay," I said. "I'm not alone. I work with professionals who are good at finding people and rescuing them. I'm sure they're tracking me. Pretty soon this nightmare will end and you'll be back home with your parents."

"Have you spoken to them?" she asked. "Are they all right?"

"They're good," I told her. "They haven't given up hope that you'll be found and that you're okay."

"I think I'm okay," she said. "I'm surviving. I think he keeps me alive for my blood. He doesn't talk to me or hit me. I don't think I've been sexually violated. He brings me food. Sometimes the food is drugged, and I fall asleep, and when I wake up, I have a small Band-Aid over a needle puncture. I'm always tired and I know I'm getting weaker. I imagine he brought you in here to replace me. There was a woman here before me. Her name was Rosa. She was very sick, and one day I woke up and she was gone, and I've been alone ever since."

"Do you know where we are?"

"No. This is where I woke up." She put her hand to her neck. "I had bite marks on my neck."

"Do you know how he got you here?"

"Not exactly. I was at home, watching television. Zoran came to the door with pizza, and I let him in. He was always a little odd, but he was always polite. I felt sorry for him. He didn't seem to have any friends."

"So, you ate the pizza and passed out?"

"Yes."

I walked to the door that was open and looked in. Bathroom. My chain didn't reach to the door that was closed.

"What's in there?" I asked Julie.

"It's a small all-purpose room. There's a kitchenette of sorts, a couch, and a television. Sometimes when he brings food, I can look through the door and see the other room. I think lately he's been living there. I hear the television."

"What happens when he brings the food?"

"He tells me to get into the corner by the little fridge. If I move from the corner, he takes the food away and I don't have anything to eat until the next day. If I stay in the corner, he sets the food tray on the table and leaves. He usually feeds me twice a day, I think. The light stays on all the time, and I haven't got a watch or anything, so I don't really know if it's day or night."

The door opened and Zoran walked in. "Now that you're awake and have met your roommate, I suspect you know the process. You go to the corner by the fridge while I set your food on the table. If you move from the corner, I take the food away. I carry a Taser, so I have the ability to cause pain if needed. I also have a very nice SIG Sauer which I've recently acquired and have clipped to my belt."

I went to the corner and crouched next to Julie. Zoran put the food on the table and stood still for a moment. Something was scratching in the other room. Zoran turned on his heel and went to investigate the scratching. I heard the apartment door open, and Zoran swear. There were some pitter-patter sounds, and Mr. Big ran into the dungeon room and rushed over to me. He was excited. Jumping up and down. I swear he was smiling.

Zoran followed Mr. Big. "Do you know this dog?" he asked me.

"No," I said, "but he seems to like me."

Zoran took one of the fast-food burgers off the table and unwrapped it. He moved into the doorway and held the burger out for Big to see. "Come and get it," Zoran said to Big.

Big ran to get the burger and I yelled out his name.

"Mr. Big!"

Big stopped and turned and looked at me. I pointed to Zoran and yelled, "Kill!"

Big jumped at Zoran and sank his spiky little teeth into Zoran's leg. Zoran staggered back and batted Mr. Big away. Mr. Big attacked again, this time getting Zoran in the crotch. I ran to the table, grabbed the chair, and hit Zoran full force, in the back. He turned, and I smashed him in the face with the chair. Big unlatched himself from Zoran's privates, and Zoran went down to his knees, stunned, blood pouring out of his nose. I grabbed the gun out of the holster and shot Zoran in the leg, and then, just to be safe, I shot him in the other leg. Zoran was on his back and screaming, and I was frozen, not sure what to do next. I had no phone. I was chained to the floor. I should have looked in his pocket for a key to my ankle bracelet, but I didn't want to get that close to him. And then Ranger ran in, followed by Lula, Lou, and Bruno.

The burger was lying on the floor. "Don't let Mr. Big eat the burger," I said. "It might contain drugs."

"Holy cow," Lula said. "Holy moly. Holy hell."

"Is there anyone else we should worry about?" Ranger asked me.

"No," I said. "Just Zoran. I yelled 'kill' and Mr. Big attacked

Zoran, and I hit Zoran in the face with the chair, and then I shot him. Twice."

Zoran was moaning and making weird hissing sounds.

Tank and another Rangeman came into the room. Tank looked at me, still holding the gun, and then he looked at Zoran, bleeding from his face and both legs.

"Did you shoot him in the face?" Tank asked.

"No," I said. "I hit him in the face with the chair."

Tank smiled. "Nice."

Tank's partner ran to get the med kit, and Tank started triage on Zoran.

Ranger was talking to his control room, telling them that there were multiple victims needing medical assistance, and asking them to get Morelli on the phone. Bruno and Lou were looking on from the kitchen area. Bruno was holding Mr. Big. Lula was with Julie. I dragged my chain into the bathroom, splashed cold water on my face, and dried off with a paper towel. I looked at myself in the mirror. My face was pale, and I could have used some lip gloss, but other than that, I looked almost okay.

Ranger was waiting by the door when I came out. "Babe," he said. "Feel better?"

"Yeah."

He tucked a strand of hair behind my ear and wrapped his arms around me, holding me close. "I had some bad moments on this one. This one really scared me," he said.

I nodded against him. "Me too."

"Can you walk me through it?"

I gave him the short version that ended with getting stunned and drugged. "Where are we?"

"Third block of Freemont," Ranger said. "Probably the three-story tenement you entered. It's used by druggies. Half-empty.

We're in the basement. I imagine this was the manager's apartment. Maybe Zoran is the manager."

"How did you find me?"

"Lula called. She saw your phone and food on the bench and couldn't find you, and she went into panic mode. Control room said she was screaming on the phone, so they broke into my conference call. When I got to the deli she was with Bruno and Lou. They came to get lunch and check on the Jug Produce display. I guess it's new."

"Zoran took my AirTag."

"He didn't take it. It must have fallen out of your pocket when he was moving you. I was able to track it to the van behind the building. It was lying on the ground. The dog found it. We were organizing a search when Bruno realized the dog was missing. Bruno and Lou walked around to the street to look for the dog, and Tank and I went to the back door to get into the building. The door was locked but the whole door is rotting away. I'm sure that's how the dog got in. There was a gap on the bottom of the door that he was able to squeeze through. We kicked the door open, and we were standing in the back hallway when we heard gunshots coming from the basement."

Now that the doors were open, I could hear street sounds. Sirens. People talking. Paramedics came in. A couple of cops walked in with them. One of Ranger's men came with a key for the ankle iron and went to work setting me free.

"I called Morelli," Ranger said. "He's on his way."

Tank came over. "Do you want me to have the cars moved so the first responders can get closer?" he asked Ranger.

"Yes. Everyone can be dismissed back to standard."

"What cars?" I asked him.

"I have half of Rangeman on the street. I didn't know what

I was going to find here or how extensive the search was going to be."

A couple of paramedics and Lula had Julie Werly on her feet. Bruno and Lou were still in the little kitchenette, taking it all in. And Morelli's partner, Jimmy, was standing in the hall, talking to a uniform.

"Fill Jimmy in," I said to Ranger. "I need to talk to Bruno and Lou."

I walked over and gave Mr. Big some ear scratches. "This is the hero of the day," I said to Bruno and Lou. "He distracted Zoran so I could take him down."

"So, you hit the vampire in the face with the chair and then you shot him . . . twice," Lou said.

"Yes."

"Let me know if you ever need a job. I could find a place for you."

"I'll keep that in mind."

"Or you could marry me," Bruno said. "The divorce will go through any day now."

"Gee, thanks," I said, "but I'm engaged."

## CHAPTER TWENTY-THREE

I woke up to a nice quiet apartment. No vampire stalking me. No dog to walk. Just me and Rex. The sun was shining and everything was right in my world. I went to the bathroom and found out I wasn't pregnant. There was a pang of disappointment, but honestly, it was okay. I'd have plenty of chances to get pregnant after I was married. Or not. That would be okay, too. What mattered right now was that I was alive, and Julie was alive, and it was a brand-new day.

I took my time with a shower. Used the big round brush drying my hair. Made myself toast and eggs and coffee. And I didn't even eat standing at the sink. I took everything into the dining room and sat like a real person.

It was close to ten o'clock when I finally strolled into the office.

"You're looking like you got a big glow," Lula said. "Is it because you're preggers?"

"No," I said. "It's because I'm alive."

"Yeah," Lula said. "I can relate to that."

"I did some research on the building where Julie Werly was being held captive," Connie said. "Zoran was property manager of sorts, using the name Bill Smith. He wasn't getting paid. He was just allowed to live in the building for doing maintenance, which was probably zero. The van belonged to the original owner of the building. Dobey Szajack. Died a year ago and left everything to his nephew in Romania. Not sure if the nephew even knows of his inheritance."

I checked out the doughnut box on Connie's desk. It was all Boston cream. My favorite.

"It's in honor of your being alive," Lula said. "Connie cleaned them out of Boston creams."

I took one, got coffee, and came back to Connie's desk. "I don't have any FTAs, so I thought I would take some time off."

"Sorry to bust that bubble," Connie said. "We have to go downtown to write a bond for someone."

Lula was practically vibrating. "Wait until you hear this!" she said. "This is crazy."

"What?" I said.

"You don't listen to the news, do you?" Connie said.

"Not usually. Did I miss something?"

"And you don't go online to see what's happening in Trenton, or in this case, the whole world."

"No."

"Tell her! Tell her!" Lula said to Connie.

Connie typed something into her computer. "Here," she said. "Come around and look at this."

I walked behind Connie and looked at her monitor screen. The headline read *Robin Hoodie Caught in the Act.*

"They caught Eugene in the act?" I asked Connie.

"Look at the photo," Lula said.

"It looks like Eugene in his hoodie, being cuffed next to a truck selling fried dough."

"Look closer," Lula said. "Does that look like Eugene?"

Connie enlarged the picture and zeroed in on the face.

"Omigod," I said. "It's definitely not Eugene."

Lula and Connie burst out laughing.

"Who is it?" Connie asked me.

I could barely say the name. "Herbert?"

"Yes! We have to go downtown to bond him out."

I was flat-out gobsmacked. "Herbert is Robin Hoodie? I can't believe it."

"Believe it," Connie said. "He's national news. He's already been interviewed by the CBS affiliate. I thought Grandma would have called you by now."

"My phone was turned off. I wanted to sleep in and have a sane morning," I said.

"So much for sane," Connie said. "Lula's right. This is crazy."

"And it was real sneaky the way they caught him," Lula said. "Someone suggested to the police that they get a food truck set up with surveillance and everything and they lure Robin Hoodie into hijacking it. And it worked on the first day. Brilliant, right? Trenton PD is looking real smart on this one."

"Jeez," I said. "Go figure."

"I waited until you got here to bond him out," Connie said. "I thought you'd want to go with me. He's probably in a bad way. It's not like he's a career criminal. They got him at ten o'clock last night and he spent the night in a cell. That's always terrifying for first-timers."

Connie closed the office, and we all piled into her car. I was in the back seat, and I was feeling guilty that I was the one who suggested the food truck and got Herbert arrested. Herbert, the entrepreneur, who had an unexplained source of income. I guess there were signs, but I missed them. I did not see this coming. Herbert was an even worse candidate for Robin Hoodie than Eugene.

"Wasn't Herbert the one who gave you the carpet and television?" Lula asked me. "I bet they were hijacked, along with the paint for your apartment. Everything he gave you is probably hot. Here you are an officer of the law, sort of, and you're living with an apartment filled with stolen stuff."

"I'm going to pretend I didn't hear you," I said to Lula.

"Yeah," Lula said. "I'm never gonna say it again, but it's kind of funny, right? Ironic."

She was right. It was kind of funny. It was ironic. It got me back to smiling again. I hoped Herbert was okay. This was his first offense. He'd compensated people for their losses and, according to Morelli, everyone, including the police wives, loved Robin Hoodie to the point where no one was any longer pressing charges. With luck, he'd get a slap on the wrist.

---

Herbert was a little disheveled when they brought him out to us. His hair wasn't neatly parted on the side. He was rakishly bedheaded, probably from sleeping in his hoodie. He had a five o'clock shadow that took me by surprise. I had never thought of Herbert as being someone who needed to shave. He was dressed in Robin Hoodie black, and he looked very different without his glasses and 1950s clothes. He didn't look like a geek. He looked like a guy.

"Gee," he said when he saw us. "This is really great of you to come get me out of jail. I hope it wasn't too much trouble. Like, I didn't disrupt your day or anything, did I? I apologize if I did, but boy, I'm glad to see you. Jail wasn't as bad as I thought it would be, but I'll be happy to go home. I hope my mom remembered to feed Miss Fluff, and she probably was lonely last night because she always sleeps with me. Miss Fluff, not my mom. It would be weird to sleep with my mom. My dad does it and that's okay."

We were all smiling. The package was different, but it was still Herbert.

"Have you talked to my mom?" Herbert asked. "Does she know I was in jail?"

"She posted your bail bond money," Connie said.

I took Herbert by the arm. "A word in private?" I asked, leading him to a quiet corner away from Connie and Lula. "Call me crazy, but I think there are some missing parts to the Robin Hoodie story."

"What sort of parts?" he asked.

"The Eugene parts. Eugene denied being Robin Hoodie but he never hired a lawyer to help prove his innocence. Instead, he did what he could to avoid going to court. It was as if he just wanted to prolong the process. And I wasn't seeing any of the actual fear of a first-time offender. You don't by any chance known Eugene, do you?"

"You aren't going to tell anyone, right?"

"Right," I said. "This is just between you and me."

"I met Eugene a couple of years ago and our interests intersected. We were both Robin Hood freaks. And we got caught up in the concept of redistribution of consumer goods. Like Robin Hood. Taking from the rich and giving to the poor. Eugene thought it was an interesting concept but he wasn't willing to actually take from the rich. So it sort of ended there. He went on to do his gaming blog. And I went on to do my entrepreneurial activities which included being Robin Hoodie. Honestly, I didn't mean it to be this whole big deal. It just mushroomed, and all of a sudden I needed help. So I got Eugene to do my internet stuff. It was removed from the taking from the rich, you know? It was just electronics."

"If he wasn't involved in the taking from the rich, how did his fingerprints get on the UPS truck?"

"I drove the truck through a bunch of muck to get to the homeless camp and it got to be a mess," Herbert said.

"I'm thinking that you had a crew by then. You had a videographer and someone flying a drone."

"Yes, but I don't want to get them involved," Herbert said.

"Okay, so tell me about the fingerprints."

"I didn't want to give the truck back to UPS in bad condition, so Eugene met me at his friend's father's garage, and Eugene took the truck through the car wash. We never thought about his fingerprints. The rest of us were wearing gloves."

"So you let him get accused of being Robin Hoodie."

"It was his idea. If he told the police about the car wash, it would end the adventure. No more drawing attention to the homeless, and no more fun videos. So we kept it going for a while longer. Eugene knew I wouldn't let him go to prison. In the meantime, he was sort of enjoying it. He really liked when he was rescued out of your car by all the homeless guys. Anyway, it finally became obvious that our time was running out, so I hijacked the food truck with the cops in it."

"You knew they were cops?"

"It wasn't much of a secret," Herbert said.

I brought Herbert back to Connie and Lula. "We're good," I said. "We're ready to leave."

"I don't know how any of this works," Herbert said. "What do I do now?"

"Now we take you home, and you give up being Robin Hoodie," I said.

"I imagine you're going to be upset to have to stop being Robin Hoodie," Lula said.

"It's okay," Herbert said. "It was a lot of work, and I was having a hard time finding new things to give away. And I have a lot of irons in the fire. That's the way it is with us entrepreneurs. I have an exciting project going with Edna. We've already made some reels."

"Who's Edna?" Lula asked.

"Grandma," I said.

"And I just got a phone call from a big publisher in New York, and they want me to write a book. And they said they'd give me two million dollars for an exclusive. I wouldn't have time to be Robin Hoodie anyway if I'm going to write a book," Herbert said.

We walked him down the hall to the front door of the municipal building, and when we stepped outside a cheer went up. There were easily two hundred women waiting to catch a glimpse of Robin Hoodie. The police had stretched crime scene tape to keep the women at a distance.

"Oh gosh," Herbert said. "Are they expecting someone important?"

The women started chanting, "*Robin, Robin, Robin.*"

"They're here to see you," Lula said. "You're famous. It's like you're a rock star."

"A rock star?" Herbert said. "Really? Me? Do I look okay? Is my hair okay? I didn't have a comb."

"You look great," I told him.

"Yeah," Lula said. "You look like Robin Hoodie."

The women were throwing bouquets of flowers and panties at Herbert. They kept chanting "*Robin, Robin*," and they were taking pictures with their cell phones. A clump of professional photographers stood to one side and a satellite TV news truck was parked behind the women.

"What should I do?" Herbert asked. "Should I pick up the panties?"

"No, dude," Lula said. "Just wave and smile and back up. We need to take you out the back door or we'll get trampled."

---

We dropped Herbert off at his parents' house and returned to the office.

"Now that we have Robin Hoodie put to rest, I'm going to take my time off," I said to Lula and Connie.

"What are you going to do?" Lula asked. "Shopping?"

"Shopping is part of it. I'm also getting married."

"Get the hell out," Lula said. "Shut the hell up."

"It's going to be a very small private ceremony," I said. "Just you two and family. We're going to have it at Valerie's house on Saturday."

"I need a doughnut," Lula said. "Good thing there are doughnuts left. I gotta calm down. I might hyperventilate."

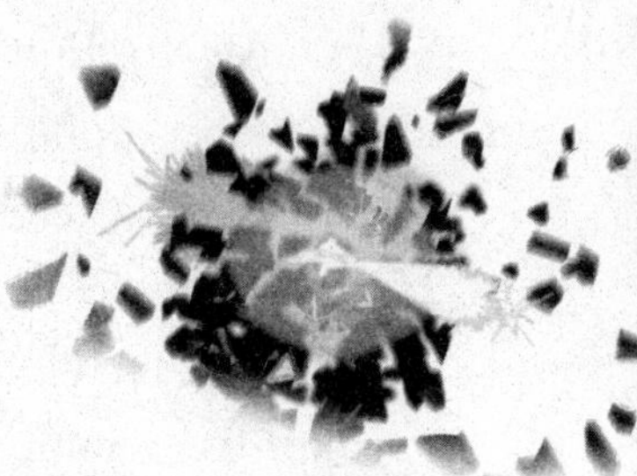

# CHAPTER TWENTY-FOUR

It was Sunday. I'd been married for twenty-four hours, and it was roast chicken day at my parents' house. Mashed potatoes, gravy, green beans, cranberry sauce, and stuffing. And I'd asked for pineapple-upside-down cake for dessert. Dinner is always at six o'clock. It used to be that if you were five minutes late getting to the table, everything was ruined. The chicken was dry. The stuffing was cold. Lately, my mom was much more mellow and flexible with timing. I attributed this change to the bottle of Jack Daniel's she kept in the cupboard. Nevertheless, I tried to be on time for dinner, and I did my best today, but I was almost ten minutes late.

I parked at the curb and ran for the front door. I hurried into the dining room and took my place at the table.

"Sorry," I said. "Time got away from me."

"I was afraid you were in a car crash," Grandma said. "We were getting ready to call the hospitals."

Grandma didn't mean it. It had become a family joke. It was her place to say it. My mom didn't look worried, and my father was busy working his way through a mountain of roast chicken and mashed potatoes. I put my napkin on my lap and Grandma passed the platter of chicken to me. I two-handed the platter and Grandma looked at my left hand.

"That's such a pretty wedding band," she said. "And it was a beautiful ceremony. At first, I was disappointed that there wasn't going to be a big wedding, but this was better. Next time I get married I'm going to just have cake and champagne like you."

"And I didn't have to wear my church shoes," my father said. "Best wedding ceremony ever."

"Where's the groom?" Grandma asked. "We gotta do one more toast to the two of you."

"He's on his way," I said. "He got hung up at work."

The front door opened and closed. Bob galloped into the dining room and stole a piece of white meat off the chicken platter. Morelli followed. He kissed me on the top of my head and took his seat next to me.

I was pretty sure I'd made the right decision. It had been difficult. I went with the safe choice. I knew everything there was to know about Morelli . . . and I loved what I knew. I loved what I knew about Ranger, but I didn't know everything. Ranger was the man of mystery, and he would always be the man of mystery. There was a bond between us, and it would continue. When I'd told him I was going to marry Morelli, he hadn't looked surprised. "Babe," he'd said. "You made the smart choice." He'd kissed me with a touch of tongue, smiled, and slipped a new AirTag into my sweatshirt pocket. "A box of doughnuts says you don't make it two months."

**Not the end.**